UNMASKED BY THE MARQUESS

UNMASKED BY THE MARQUESS

A Regency Impostors Novel

CAT SEBASTIAN

AVONIMPULSE
An Imprint of HarperCollinsPublishers

UNMASKED BY THE MARQUESS. Copyright © 2018 by Cat Sebastian. All rights reserved. Printed in the United States of America. No part of this book may be used or reproduced in any manner whatsoever without written permission except in the case of brief quotations embodied in critical articles and reviews. For information, address HarperCollins Publishers, 195 Broadway, New York, NY 10007.

Digital Edition APRIL 2018 ISBN: 978-0-06-282065-5

Print Edition ISBN: 978-0-06-282160-7

Cover art by Christine Ruhnke

Cover photographs © hotdamstock (couple); © romancenovelcovers (man's shirt); © ArtOfPhotos / Shutterstock (man's hair); © Anna Baburkina / Shutterstock (bed); © Marahwan / Shutterstock (blanket)

Avon Impulse and the Avon Impulse logo are registered trademarks of HarperCollins Publishers in the United States of America.

Avon and HarperCollins are registered trademarks of HarperCollins Publishers in the United States of America and other countries.

FIRST EDITION

18 19 20 21 22   HDC   10 9 8 7 6 5 4 3 2 1

Nil penna sed usus

Acknowledgments

This book would have remained buried on my hard drive without the enthusiasm of my agent, Deidre Knight, and my editor, Elle Keck. Many, many thanks Jordan Hawk and Anna Zabo for their insight and feedback, which helped shape Charity's character. Margrethe Martin and Ruby Lang read early drafts of this story and I'm grateful for their time and support.

Chapter One

Alistair ran his finger once more along the neatly penned column of sums his secretary had left on his desk. This was what respectability looked like: a ledger filled with black ink, maintained by a servant whose wages had been paid on time.

He would never tire of seeing the numbers do what he wanted them to do, what they *ought* to do out of sheer decency and moral fortitude. Here it was, plain numerical proof that the marquessate had—finally—more money coming in than it had going out. Not long ago this very library was besieged by a steady stream of his late father's creditors and mistresses and assorted other disgraceful hangers-on, all demanding a piece of the badly picked-over pie. But now Alistair de Lacey, eighth Marquess of Pembroke, could add financial solvency to the list of qualities that made him the model of propriety.

This pleasant train of thought was interrupted by the sound of an apologetic cough coming from the doorway.

"Hopkins?" Alistair asked, looking up.

"A person has called, my lord." The butler fairly radiated distress. "I took the liberty of showing her into the morning room."

Her? It couldn't be any of his aunts, because those formidable ladies would have barged right into the library. Alistair felt his heart sink. "Dare I ask?"

"Mrs. Allenby, my lord," Hopkins intoned, as if every syllable pained him to utter.

Well might he look pained. Mrs. Allenby, indeed. She was the most notorious of his late father's mistresses and if there was one thing Alistair had learned in the years since his father's death, it was that the arrival of any of these doxies inevitably presaged an entry in red ink in the ledger that sat before him.

And now she was sitting in the morning room? The same morning room his mother had once used to receive callers? Good Lord, no. Not that he could think of a more suitable place for that woman to be brought.

"Send her up here, if you will, Hopkins."

A moment later, a woman mortifyingly close to his own age swept into the library. "Heavens, Pembroke, but you're shut up in a veritable tomb," she said, as if it could possibly be any of her business. "You'll ruin your eyes trying to read in the dark." And then she actually had the presumption to draw back one of the curtains, letting a broad shaft of sunlight into the room.

Alistair was momentarily blinded by the unexpected brightness. Motes of dust danced in the light, making him uncomfortably aware that his servants were not doing an adequate job with the cleaning, and also that perhaps the room had been a trifle dark after all.

"Do take a seat," he offered, but only after she had already dropped gracefully into one of the chairs near the fire.

The years had been reprehensibly kind to Portia Allenby, and Alistair felt suddenly conscious that the same could not be said for himself. She had no gray in her jet-black hair and no need for spectacles. The subdued half mourning she had adopted after his father's death made her look less like a harlot who had been acquired by the late marquess on a drunken spree across the continent some eighteen years ago, and more like a decent widow.

"I'll not waste your time, Pembroke. I'm here about Amelia."

"Amelia," Alistair repeated slowly, as if trying that word out for the first time.

"My eldest daughter," she clarified, patiently playing along with Alistair's feigned ignorance. *Your sister*, she didn't need to add.

"And which one is she?" Alistair drummed his fingers on the desk. "The ginger one with the freckles?" All the Allenby girls were ginger-haired and freckled, having had the great misfortune to take after the late marquess rather than their beautiful mother.

Mrs. Allenby ignored his rudeness. "She's eighteen. I'd like for her to make a proper come out."

So she wanted money. No surprise there. "My dear lady," he said frostily, "you cannot possibly need for money. My father saw to it that you and your children were amply provided for." In fact, his father had spent the last months of his life seeing to little else, selling and mortgaging everything not nailed down in order to keep this woman and the children he had sired on her in suitably grand style.

"You're quite right, Pembroke, I don't need a farthing." She smoothed the dove-gray silk of her gown across her lap, whether out of self-consciousness or in order to emphasize how well-lined her coffers were, Alistair could not guess. "What I hoped was that you could arrange for Amelia to be invited to a dinner or two." She smiled, as if Alistair ought to be relieved to hear this request. "Even a tea or a luncheon would go a long way."

Alistair was momentarily speechless. He removed his spectacles and carefully polished them on his handkerchief before tucking them into his pocket. "Surely I have mistaken you. I have no doubt that among your numerous acquaintances you could find someone willing to invite your daughter to festivities of any kind." The woman ran a monthly salon, for God's sake. She was firmly, infuriatingly located right on the fringes of decent society. Every poet and radical, not to mention every gently born person with a penchant for libertinism, visited her drawing room. Alistair had to positively go out of his way to avoid her.

"You're quite right," she replied blithely, as if insensible to the insult. "The problem is that she's had too many of those invitations. She's in a fair way to becoming a bluestocking, not to put too fine a point on it. I hope that a few evenings spent in, ah, more exalted company will give her mind a different turn."

Had she just suggested that her own associates were too serious-minded for a young girl? It was almost laughable. But not as laughable as the idea that Alistair ought to lend his countenance to the debut of any daughter of the notorious Mrs. Allenby, regardless of whose by-blow the child was. "My dear lady, you cannot expect—"

"Goodness, Pembroke. I'm not asking for her to be presented at court, or for vouchers to Almack's. I was hoping you could prevail on one of Ned's sisters to invite her to dinner." If she were aware of what it did to Alistair to hear his father referred to thusly, she did not show it. "The old Duke of Devonshire acknowledged his mistress's child, you know. It can't reflect poorly on you or your aunts to throw my children a few crumbs."

So now, after bringing his father to the brink of disgrace and ruin, she was an expert on what would or would not reflect poorly on a man, was she? The mind simply boggled.

"Of course I wouldn't expect to attend with her," she continued.

He reared back in his chair. "Good God, I should think not."

Only then did she evidently grasp that she was not about to prevail. "I only meant that I would engage a suitable chaperone. But I see that I've bothered you for no reason." She rose to her feet with an audible swish of costly silks. "I wish you well, Pembroke."

Alistair was only warming to the topic, though. "If I were to acknowledge all my father's bastards I'd have to start a charitable foundation. There would be opera dancers and housemaids lined up down the street."

At this she turned back to face him. "You do your father an injustice. He was not a man of temperate desires, but he and I shared a life together from the moment we met until he died."

"I feel certain both your husband and my mother were touched to discover that the two of you had such an aptitude for domestic felicity, despite all appearances to the contrary." Mr. Allenby had been discarded as surely as Alistair's mother had been.

Was that pity that crossed the woman's face? "As I said, I'm truly sorry to have bothered you today." She sighed. "Gilbert is a regular visitor at my house. I mention that not to provoke you but only to suggest that if you're determined not to acknowledge the connection, you ought to bring your brother under bridle."

She dropped a small curtsy that didn't seem even slightly ironic, and left Alistair alone in his library. He felt uncomfortable, vaguely guilty, but he knew perfectly well that he had behaved properly. His father had devoted his life to squandering money and tarnishing his name by any means available to him: cards, horses, women, bad investments. And he had left the mess to be cleaned up by his son. Alistair, at least, would leave the family name and finances intact for future generations.

He paced to the windows and began pulling back the rest of the curtains. It annoyed him to admit that Mrs. Allenby had been right about anything, but the room really was too dark. He had been working too hard, too long, but even now with all the curtains opened, the room was still gloomy. The late winter sun had sunk behind the row of houses on the opposite side of Grosvenor Square, casting only a thin, pallid light into the room. He went to the hearth to poke the fire back to life.

His plan had been to double check the books and then

go out for a ride, but the hour for that had come and gone. He could dress and take an early dinner at his club, perhaps. Even though the Season had not quite started, there were enough people in town to make the outing worthwhile. It was never a bad idea for Alistair to show his face and remind the world that this Marquess of Pembroke, at least, did not spend his evenings in orgies of dissipation.

As he tried not to think of the debauchery these walls had contained, there came another apologetic cough from the doorway.

"Another caller, my lord," Hopkins said. "A young gentleman."

Alistair suppressed a groan. This was the outside of enough. "Send him up." He inwardly prayed that the caller wasn't an associate of Gilbert's, some shabby wastrel Alistair's younger brother had lost money to at the gambling tables. He glanced at the card Hopkins had given him. Robert Selby. The fact that the name rang no bells for him did nothing to put his mind at ease.

But the man Hopkins ushered into the library didn't seem like the sort of fellow who frequented gambling hells. He looked to be hardly twenty, with sandy hair that hung a trifle too long to be à la mode and clothes that were respectably, but not fashionably, cut.

"I'm ever so grateful, my lord." The young man took a half step closer, but seemed to check his progress when he noticed Alistair's expression. "I know what an imposition it must be. But the matter is so dashed awkward I hardly wanted to put it to you in a letter."

It got worse and worse. Matters too awkward to be put in letters inevitably veered toward begging or blackmail. Alistair folded his arms and leaned against the chimneypiece. "Go on," he ordered.

"It's my sister, you see. Your father was her godfather."

Alistair jerked to attention. "My father was your sister's godfather?" He was incredulous. There could hardly have been any creature on this planet less suited to be an infant's godparent than the late Lord Pembroke. "He went to church?" Really, the image of his father leaning over the baptismal font and promising to be mindful of the baby's soul was something Alistair would make a point of recalling the next time his spirits were low.

"I daresay he did, my lord," Selby continued brightly, as if he had no idea of the late marquess's character. "I was too young to remember the event, I'm afraid."

"And what can you possibly require of me, Mr. Selby?" Alistair did not even entertain the possibility that Selby was here for the pleasure of his company. "Not an hour ago I refused to help a person with a far greater claim on the estate than you have."

The fellow had the grace to blush, at least. "My sister and I have no claim on you at all. It's only that I'm in quite a fix and I don't know who else to turn to. She's of an age where I need to find her a husband, but . . ." His voice trailed off, and he regarded Alistair levelly, as if deciding whether he could be confided in. Presumptuous. "Well, frankly, she's too pretty and too trusting to take to Bath or Brighton. She'd marry someone totally unsuitable. I had thought to bring her to London, where she would have a chance to meet worthier people."

Alistair retrieved his spectacles from his coat pocket and carefully put them on. This Selby fellow didn't seem delusional, but he was speaking like a madman. "That's a terrible plan."

"Well, now I know that, my lord." He smiled broadly, exposing too many teeth and creating an excess of crinkles around his eyes. Alistair suddenly wished that there was enough light to get a better look at this lad. "We've been here a few weeks and it's all too clear that the connections I made at Cambridge aren't enough to help Louisa. She needs better than that." He shot Alistair another grin, as if they were in on the same joke.

Alistair opened his mouth to coolly explain that he could not help Mr. Selby's sister, no matter how good her looks or how bad her circumstances. But he found that he couldn't quite give voice to any of his usual crisp denials. "Have you no relations?"

"None that suit the purpose, my lord," Selby said frankly. This Mr. Selby had charming manners, even when he met with disappointment. Alistair would give him that much—it would have been a relief to see Gilbert develop such pleasant ways instead of his usual fits of sullenness. "Our parents died some years ago," Selby continued. "We brought an elderly aunt with us, but we grew up in quite a remote part of Northumberland, and if we have any relations in London, we've never heard of them."

Northumberland? Now, what the devil could Alistair's

father have been doing in Northumberland? Quite possibly he had gotten drunk at a hunt party in Melton Mowbray and simply lost his way home, leaving a string of debauched housemaids and misbegotten children in his wake.

That made something else occur to Alistair. "There's no suggestion that your sister is my father's natural child?"

"My—good heavens, no." Selby seemed astonished, possibly offended by the slight to his mother's honor. "Certainly not."

Thank God for that, at least. Alistair leaned back against the smooth stone of the chimneypiece, regarding his visitor from behind half-closed lids. Even though there was nothing about Selby that seemed overtly grasping, here he was, grasping nonetheless. There was no reason for this man, charming manners and winning smile, to be in Alistair's library unless it was to demand something.

"If you want my advice, take her to Bath." He pushed away from the wall and stepped towards his visitor. Selby was a few inches shorter than Alistair and much slighter of build. Alistair didn't need to use his size to intimidate—that was what rank and power were for—but this wasn't about intimidation. It was about proximity. He wanted a closer look at this man, so he would take it.

Selby had tawny skin spotted with freckles, as if he were accustomed to spending a good deal of time outside. His lips were a brownish pink, and quirked up in a questioning sort of smile, as if he knew what exactly Alistair was about.

Perhaps he did. Interesting, because Alistair hardly knew himself.

Alistair dropped his voice. "Better yet, go home. London is a dangerous place for a girl without connections." He dropped his voice lower still, and leaned in so he was speaking almost directly into Selby's ear. "Or for a young man without scruples." The fellow smelled like lemon drops, as if he had a packet of sweets tucked into one of his pockets.

For a moment they stood there, inches apart. Selby was ultimately the one to step back. "I knew it was a long shot, but I had to try." He flashed Alistair another winning smile, more dangerous for being at close range, before bowing handsomely and showing himself out.

Alistair was left alone in a room that had grown darker still.

"What did he say?" Louisa asked as soon as Charity returned to the shabby-genteel house they had hired for the Season.

"It's a nonstarter, Lou," she replied, flinging herself onto a settee. She propped her boots up onto the table before her. One of the many, many advantages of posing as a man was the freedom afforded by men's clothing.

"He turned you away, then?" Louisa asked, looking up from the tea she was pouring them.

"Oh, worse than that. He asked if his father had gotten your mother with child, then advised me that if I allowed you to stay in London, you'd end up prostituting yourself."

Louisa colored, and Charity realized she had spoken too freely. Louisa had, after all, been raised a lady. "Oh, he didn't say that last thing quite outright, but he dropped a strong hint." She hooked an arm behind her head and settled comfortably back in her seat. "Besides, what does it matter if he thinks we're beneath reproach? He's never even heard of us before today. His opinion doesn't matter a jot."

"Maybe he's right, though, and I shouldn't stay in London." Instead of looking at Charity, she was nervously lining up the teacups so their cracks and chips were out of sight.

"Nonsense. As soon as these nobs get a look at you, you'll take off like a rocket."

Louisa regarded her dubiously. But it really was absurd, how very pretty Robbie's little sister had turned out to be. Her hair fell in perfect flaxen ringlets and her skin was flawless. Other than her blond hair she looked nothing like Robbie, thank God, because that would have been too hard for Charity to live with.

Charity shook her head in a futile attempt to dismiss that unwanted thought, and then blew an errant strand of hair off her forehead. "I only have to figure out how to make them notice you in the first place, and if that prig of a marquess isn't willing to help, then we'll find another way."

"Was he really that bad?"

Charity put her hand over her heart, as if taking an oath. "I tell you, if he had a quizzing glass he would have examined me under it. He seemed so dreadfully bored and put upon, I nearly felt bad for him. But then I remembered all his money and got quite over it."

That made Louisa laugh, and Charity was glad of it, because it wouldn't do for the girl to worry. Charity was worried enough for both of them. Going to Pembroke had been a last resort; he was such a loose connection of the family, but he was the best Charity could come up with. Louisa needed a husband, and she needed one soon, because Charity wasn't sure how much longer she was going to be able to keep up this charade. Dressing like a man didn't bother her—quite the contrary. But pretending to be Robbie when the real Robbie was cold in his grave? That was too much. It was a daily reminder of what she had lost, of what she would never have.

Louisa put down her teacup and clasped her hands together. "I'd be glad to go to Bath for a few months. Remember that the Smythe girls found husbands there."

Charity remembered all too well. One of them had married a country clergyman and the other had gotten engaged to an army officer on half pay. She's be damned if Louisa threw herself away like that. Hell, if she had gone through with this farce for Louisa to wind up marrying a curate she'd be furious.

She had to forcibly remind herself that her feelings were immaterial. This was her chance to see Louisa settled in the way Robbie would have wanted. It was only because of the Selbys that Charity was here in the first place, clean and fed and educated, rather than . . . Well, none of that bore thinking of. She was grateful to the family, and this was her chance to take care of the last of them.

"Listen, Charity. When I think of the expense of this London trip—"

"You mustn't call me that," Charity whispered. "Servants

might hear." And if Charity knew anything about servants, which she most certainly did, it would only be a matter of time before one overheard. And then their ship would be quite sunk.

"Oh!" Louisa cried, clapping a hand over her mouth. "I keep forgetting. But it's so strange to call you Robbie."

Of course it was. Not everyone was as hardened to deceit as Charity had become. She had been assuming this role for years, from the point when the real Robert Selby had decided that he did not want to go to Cambridge and would send Charity in his stead. She, at least, was used to answering to his name. But since Robbie had died two years ago, she increasingly felt that she no longer had his permission to use his name. The deceit was weighing heavier on her with each passing day.

All the more reason to get Louisa set up splendidly. Then Robert Selby could fade gracefully out of existence, leaving his Northumberland estate free for the proper heir to eventually inherit, while Charity would . . . Her imagination failed her.

She would figure that out some other time. First, she'd take care of Louisa.

"If all else fails, we'll go to Bath or a seaside resort. I promise." And she flashed her pretend sister her most confident smile.

Chapter Two

"Keep a weather eye out for any of the aunts, Alistair." Gilbert had a playful sparkle in his eye that Alistair was glad to see after their recent disagreements. "Half the ton is out and it's too damned fine a day to have it ruined by the likes of Aunt Pettigrew." The young scapegrace pushed his hat down low over his brow as if that would disguise him from any passing relations.

Alistair bit back a laugh. He shouldn't encourage his brother in such foolishness. But he didn't want to encounter his aunts any more than Gilbert did. Alas, they were likely lurking around here someplace, everyone in London having apparently decided as one to take advantage of weather that seemed to belong more to May than to March.

He slowed his horse to a walk when they approached a knot of carriages. "I've been avoiding the aunts since before you were born. Give me some credit."

"Brace yourself, because Aunt Pettigrew is looking for you. Yesterday she summoned me to her house—"

"And you went?" He had known his brother was flighty,

but a man had to be a confirmed bedlamite to willingly visit Lady Pettigrew.

"Of course not! But then she came around herself—"

"To your rooms?" The image of Aunt Pettigrew, swathed in furs and shawls, calling at Gilbert's bachelor lodgings at the Albany was too absurd to call to mind.

"She sat in her carriage and waited by the entrance to my building until I came out, if you can believe it."

"A siege, then. You have my pity." Here they were, talking nearly like a normal pair of brothers despite the decade that lay between them. "What the devil did she want?"

"She asked if you were holding a come-out ball for Amelia Allenby. I told her of course not, that you're far too snobbish—" He checked himself. "I told her you have nothing to do with the Allenbys, or balls, or debutantes," he amended.

"And so I don't." A ball for his father's illegitimate child. What a revolting notion.

"She went on for a while about harlots and jezebels and the sins of the father and all the rest of the usual rot." Gilbert paused to tip his hat at a passing acquaintance Alistair did not recognize. "Oh, and something about how the hallowed halls of Pembroke House would be defiled by the spawn of sin."

Alistair was stunned. "She actually said that? Hallowed halls and whatnot?"

"Hand to God." Gilbert's eyes were shining with merriment.

"She's madder than I thought." One might have thought that the late marquess's own sister would have known better than anybody that there was nothing hallowed about the halls of Pembroke House.

"I daresay she's annoyed that you didn't engage her grandson when you were looking for a secretary."

Of course she was. There was always somebody who wanted something.

But it rankled Alistair to find that he was in accord with his aunt about the Allenbys. Being allied with such a one as Lady Pettigrew was enough to make one doubt one's convictions.

"Have you thought about my proposal?" Alistair ventured, wanting to change the topic to something he felt surer of. But he saw right away that he had bungled things. He always did where Gilbert was concerned. He watched the smile vanish from his brother's face like the sun disappearing behind a cloud. Damn it. But what was he supposed to do? Let Gilbert carry on in this decadent, aimless manner? Surely not. Indeed, when Gilbert had called at Pembroke House today, Alistair had thought it meant his brother was ready to listen to reason regarding his future.

"I didn't call on you for a lecture," Gilbert said tightly, as if reading Alistair's thoughts. "I thought we'd get some air, behave civilly, refrain from airing grievances or cataloging my faults for a quarter of an hour or so, but evidently I was mistaken."

Oh, for God's sake, did he have to carry on like that? "The living is a good one." It was no less than a sinecure, a comfortable rectory in Kent with a curate already there to attend to the more menial tasks. Gilbert had been disinclined to serve in the army or navy, and that left him with the church, as far as Alistair was concerned. It had been two years since Gilbert had finished at Oxford, but still he had not taken orders. Alistair was beginning to worry that his brother would take after their father in laziness and dissipation.

"I don't think I'm cut out to be a clergyman." Gilbert spurred his horse ahead.

Alistair suppressed a groan and nudged his own horse to catch up. They had been through this at least two dozen times. "But then what will you do? You can't mean to go on in this manner, I hope." Drinking and gambling and going through his quarterly allowance in the span of six weeks. He could marry, but it went without saying that he'd have to marry an heiress, the Pembroke estate being stretched to the limit.

A horrifying thought occurred to him, likely inspired by Mrs. Allenby's visit the other day. "You don't mean to be a poet or something, do you?"

Gilbert let out a crack of laughter, his sullenness evidently gone as quickly as it had come. "God, you make it sound as bad as being an opium eater or a highwayman. No, dear brother, I don't intend to write poetry. Mainly because I'm bad at it. But let your heart rest easy on that score. Nor do I intend to take to the stage or become a prize fighter."

Now Alistair laughed too, despite his better judgment. "A dancing master, then?"

"No, a smuggler. We need the money."

Gilbert was like a toddler, his bad mood forgotten with a bit of silliness. "Why not cast your sights higher, then? Have some ambition, man." Alistair adopted a stern expression that he feared was a near caricature of his usual self. "You could take to the seas as a privateer."

"Or perhaps a . . ." The younger man's voice trailed off. "Who the devil is that girl over there?"

Alistair was about to ask where to look when the answer became immediately clear. A few yards ahead stood the prettiest girl he had ever seen. She was hatless, of which Alistair could not approve, but that afforded them a better view of her perfect features. There was some commotion surrounding her, and her bare head was soon explained when a gentleman ran over to her with a bonnet. If she had let her bonnet loose in an effort to attract notice, she had succeeded. Half a dozen gentlemen were now approaching the man who had retrieved the errant object.

Only then did Alistair realize that the man was none other than Robert Selby. Without thinking, he brought his horse to a stop, joining the cluster of onlookers.

He could hear the clear ring of Selby's laughter as he adjusted the bow under the girl's chin to a rakish angle. She was blushing prettily and seemed flustered by the attention.

"That, I believe, is our father's goddaughter," he said, watching his brother's jaw fall open in astonishment.

Charity could hardly keep from bouncing on her toes. They had done it. After all those futile weeks of angling for invitations and paying afternoon visits to all the decent connections she could scrape together from Cambridge, all it had taken was one badly tied bonnet.

A dozen well-heeled gentlemen gawped at Louisa, likely wishing for an introduction. If even a quarter of them brought cards tomorrow, if even one saw fit to invite Louisa to any sort of gathering, that would repay every farthing they had spent on coming to London.

And Louisa had played it off marvelously—blushing and stammering as if she hadn't a clue what Charity was up to when she tugged on the bonnet ribbon. To be fair, perhaps she didn't know—Charity hadn't exactly informed her beforehand. Some situations called for decisive action, and sometimes gently born young ladies had to be kept in the dark when scruples were to be abandoned. But it hardly mattered, because Louisa behaved exactly as she ought to. She always did.

Charity heard footsteps on the gravel behind her and assumed it was one of Louisa's admirers come to get a closer look.

"You *do* have a situation on your hands." The voice was coolly amused. "My, my."

She didn't need to turn her head to know who it was. Even at Cambridge she didn't often encounter that sort of accent, cold and polished like hard steel.

"My lord," she said, sketching a bow to Lord Pembroke. "I'm not sure I follow your meaning."

"Your sister." With his immaculately shaved chin he gestured toward Louisa. "You were quite right that she's lovely. Too lovely, I'd venture to say. You'll be overwhelmed with offers, but I'm afraid they'll be all the wrong sort."

"You think some fellow will offer her a slip on the shoulder?" Charity bit her lip. Even merely receiving an offer to become a man's mistress could ruin Louisa's chances at a respectable marriage.

If the marquess were put off by her plain speaking, he didn't show it. "Oh, I'm certain of it." He pulled his spectacles from his pocket and made a ceremony of unfolding them and placing them gingerly on his nose. "Luckily for you, I've reconsidered. I'd be most glad to take you and your sister under my wing, as it were."

She was momentarily stunned. Tilting her head back to meet his gaze more fully, she studied his face, searching for any hint of what had caused him to move from haughty disdain to breezy acquiescence in the span of a few days. Whatever the reason, it wasn't kindness. There was no trace of compassion on his chiseled features. "Why?" she finally asked.

"Does it matter?" He raised one eyebrow in a faint display of amusement.

"Frankly, no." And it didn't. But she still wanted to know what had motivated their benefactor.

He laughed softly, without any warmth. Charity had seen sneers that were friendlier.

"At least you're honest," he said.

That she most definitely was not, but she wasn't about to contradict him on that point. "May I ask how you plan to assist us?"

"I will hold a ball. You and your sister will be invited and I will dance with your sister. Not the first dance," he said, as if deciding whether to toss a farthing or a ha'penny at a street sweeper, "but perhaps the second one."

He looked older in the daylight. In that dusty old crypt

of a library she hadn't been able to guess his age. Of course she hadn't needed to guess, since Debrett's told her he was thirty-four. But in the gloom, lit only by the fire that burned in the hearth behind him, he had been reduced to a silhouette of forbidding aristocratic hostility. Here in Hyde Park in broad daylight, she could make out fine lines near his eyes, magnified by his spectacles. But still, he was the sort of man one might say would be handsome, if only he made an effort, if he smiled or made any attempt whatsoever to be agreeable. Likely he had no need to be agreeable, being as rich and powerful as he was.

How utterly repellent. She had to force her face into some semblance of gratitude.

"You'll dance with my sister?" She dragged her attention back to the matter at hand. A single dance? That would never suffice. Why bother making such a show of offering aid when it was so paltry?

"There hasn't been a ball at Pembroke House in decades." He hesitated, and when he spoke again it was with the grudging honesty of a man not willing to participate in anything so base as a half truth. "At least, not the sort of dance to which one invites respectable ladies. Receiving an invitation will be considered a mark of the highest favor, naturally. My dancing with her will cement her position as a person of considerable interest. She will be inundated with invitations and protected from inappropriate offers. That, Mr. Selby, is what I will do for you and your sister."

Had she ever met a man so arrogant? She thought not. "Is that your experience, my lord? That a single dance with a young lady is enough to confer such an advantage on her? I've never met a marquess before so please forgive my ignorance. Is nobility a sort of contagion? Like lice or influenza?"

For a moment she thought he would take offense. His lips pressed together into a thin white line, and for the briefest instant he was the farthest thing from handsome she could have imagined. Then he grinned, a smile so lop-sided as to be wholly out of place amid his severe, aristo-cratic features.

"I dare say, if this is how people act in your part of Nor-thumberland, it explains why my father turned up there. He had no regard for the respect due his station. I once found him holed up in a cowshed with a couple of poach-ers. The poor fellows had no idea if they were going to get dragged before the magistrate or if they had made a friend for life." Lord Pembroke's expression shifted from amused to reproachful, the crooked smile replaced by a frown that matched the small creases around his mouth. "Of course, in the morning he was too hungover to remember any of it."

In light of that fleeting smile, Charity had to revise her opinion of the man. Or at least of his face. Yes, he was in-sufferably arrogant and likely up to no good in his offer to help Louisa. But he was most definitely handsome, damn it. She couldn't quite tell if it was the grin, or the face, or simply some ineffable combination of rank and privilege that cre-ated the illusion of beauty. Would she feel this tug toward him if he were a costermonger or a stable boy? Impossible to say, since he was so wrapped in layers of wealth and rank you could scarcely discern the nature of the man within.

He caught her staring at him and raised an eyebrow in response, and she had to fight off a blush.

Charity knew herself to have a lamentable weakness for handsome men. And now, it would seem, Lord Pembroke knew it too. There wasn't much she could do about it in her current role, and even as a woman she doubted she was pretty enough to attract a man like this one. But it had been so long since she had *been* a woman that she couldn't rightly remember.

He pointedly cleared his throat and she realized that she was still staring at him. She decided that the more gallant course of action was to keep right on looking. Staring might be rude, but looking away would be cowardice.

Also, she was quite enjoying looking at him.

Lord Pembroke held her gaze for an instant, as if he knew exactly what she was thinking. "To answer your original question, before you devolved into impertinence. My dear child, I can't remember the last time I danced with anyone, let alone a chit in her first season whom nobody has ever heard of. If you doubt that my noticing your sister will confer any advantages on her, simply wait and see."

"You don't dance?" He had to be invited to dozens of balls and have infinite opportunities to dance. "Why ever not?"

His eyebrow hitched up once again. "Why would I?"

"Because it's fun?" She danced every chance she had. Of course she only knew the men's parts in most dances, she and Louisa having practiced until they were certain that neither of them would disgrace themselves in London ballrooms. The men did rather less twirling and leaping but it was still more excitement than one was usually allowed to have. "Well, I suppose that if a single dance with me conferred all manner of prestige, I'd be stingy with my dances too."

"Stingy with my—" He broke off and threw his head back in a burst of surprised laughter, forcing Charity to the unfortunate conclusion that he'd still be quite handsome even as a costermonger.

The young man who had been standing nearest to Louisa glanced toward them, evidently startled by the sound of laughter.

"I didn't mean to accuse you of stinginess, my lord," Charity apologized.

"Yes you did. And no more of this 'my lord' flummery. You aren't a servant. Call me Pembroke or—if you discover some hidden aptitude for respect—Lord Pembroke."

He then beckoned to the young man, whom he introduced as his brother, Lord Gilbert de Lacey, and wasn't that a grand mouthful. She, in turn, presented both gentlemen to Louisa, who curtsied so charmingly that one might have thought she practiced the gesture in front of her looking glass nightly.

Perhaps she did, come to think of it. Louisa had approached this season in London with all her usual industry.

Only then did Charity become conscious that the four of them were the objects of significant curiosity. The park was crowded with gentry, in carriages, on horseback, and on foot. Pembroke must not have been exaggerating his consequence because it was plain that the ladies peering out of their phaetons and the gentlemen pulling their horses to a stop all wanted a better look at the strangers who were talking to Lord Pembroke and his brother.

Charity recognized this as her cue to leave, to take Louisa away while interest was at its peak. "Good day," she said, tipping her hat slightly. "And thank you." To her surprise, the marquess caught her gloved hand and grasped it, holding it in place as if he had planned to shake hands and then thought better of it.

"Don't thank me yet, Mr. Selby." His voice was low enough that only she could hear.

Through the layers of leather, she felt the warmth of his palm and the strength of his grip, hotter and more forceful than she would have expected from a man who seemed so cool and haughty. She felt a small thrill travel through her body, the pull of attraction accompanied by a troubling realization: if this nobleman could make Louisa's fortune with a single dance, what disaster would befall them if they got on his bad side? What would happen if he learned the truth about them, or even any small part of the truth?

The seed of a horrible, wonderful idea had taken root in Alistair's mind. This girl, this beautiful blushing country mouse from the wilds of Northumberland, was the answer to his problems. If he managed things right, he could deploy this little miss like artillery fire and rid himself of the Allenbys, of his aunts, of all the dissolute hangers-on that had been plaguing him since he succeeded to the title.

He would hold a ball, something his aunts had been hassling him about from the moment the servants had taken down the black crepe that marked his father's death. But instead of this ball giving his aunts an opportunity to serve as Pembroke House's de facto hostesses, he would use the event to launch lovely Miss Selby into the highest circles of society. He would invite Mrs. Allenby's eldest daughter. But Miss Selby was far, far prettier than Amelia Allenby. In fact, nobody would pay even the slightest attention to any other woman at the ball besides Miss Selby.

In one fell stroke, he would infuriate his aunts, checkmate Mrs. Allenby, and teach a lesson to anyone who ever thought of asking him for anything. He could be utterly proper and even generous to a fault, while managing to shake off all the grasping relations and tawdry connections who wanted to hang on his sleeve.

In the back of his mind lurked the suspicion that this would not play out terribly well for Miss Selby. There was no way that she was prepared to go straight from a country schoolroom to the circles of society that he was dropping her into. It would be a matter of weeks before she made a misstep; he neither knew nor cared what kind of error she would make, only that it would cast her out of society and that he wouldn't lift a finger to assist her.

He smiled to himself. Nobody would ever ask him for a favor again. The estate he had worked so damned hard to restore and the reputation he had dragged out of the gutter would both be safe.

"What the devil was that about?" Gilbert asked when they returned to Pembroke House. "Father had a goddaughter? You're having a ball? This has to be a hoax."

"Perhaps I'm feeling magnanimous." Alistair swung off his horse and handed his reins to the groom.

"Ha!" Gilbert landed lightly on the ground and followed Alistair inside.

"You scoff, but maybe I envision myself as a sort of genie in a lamp, granting the wish of everyone who asks." And it would work out precisely as well for the Allenbys and Selbys as it did for those poor sods in the story.

Gilbert snorted. "Oh, definitely a hoax, then."

"You'll receive your invitation in a few days and then you can decide for yourself whether it's a hoax." He tugged off his gloves and handed them to a waiting footman.

"Selby, though. Never met him before. His sister says he went to Cambridge, which explains why we've never crossed paths. But he seems a likable fellow."

Wrong. He seemed like an overgrown schoolboy, all gangly limbs and untidy hair, to say nothing of the epidemic of freckles that covered the bridge of his nose. His manners, while pretty, lacked polish. He had utterly failed to acquire the tone of tactful boredom that all London gentlemen adopted, his clothes were indifferently tailored, and he had the nerve to approach a total stranger to ask for favors.

And yet, Alistair had the unsettling sense that if there had been better light in the library the other day, if he had a chance to properly see Selby, he would have gladly granted the impertinent boy's slightest wish.

It was not a comfortable thought. Likely this was how his father had ruined himself, throwing his money and reputation away on any charming personage who crossed his path.

No, that was not right. Alistair was made of sterner stuff than his father. He could do what was required of him, he could behave like the gentleman he was. He could resist temptation. It didn't matter in the least that when he closed his eyes he had a vivid picture of Selby's slight frame stretched out beneath Alistair's own, of Selby whispering impertinent requests into his ear.

He would let this temptation pass, as he let all temptations pass.

Chapter Three

By all rights, the evening ought to have been predictable to the point of boredom, just another dinner party at Pembroke House. Alistair hadn't even given it two consecutive minutes of thought since telling his secretary who to invite. He took it for granted that his cook would prepare dishes that were sufficiently grand, that the butler would uncork something appropriately impressive, and that the rest of his servants would do all that was needed. As for his guests, they would also do what was expected of them, which in this case was to carry home the tale of who else had sat around Lord Pembroke's table. Alistair had gathered the principal players in his little scheme, a sort of dress rehearsal for the ball he was holding the following month.

Amelia Allenby was there, looking indecently like their father, and talking Selby's ear off about some Greek or another. No, make that a Roman. Tacitus, by the sound of things, so at least it wasn't one of those fellows who wrote about nothing but orgies and so forth. Selby, to his credit, was holding up his end of the conversation, as if Roman historians were in any way a normal thing to discuss around a

Mayfair dining table. The girl's mother had been quite right to worry about her becoming a bluestocking.

Gilbert was supposed to be sitting next to one of Lord Martin's very marriageable and sufficiently dowered daughters, but somebody had made mischief with the place cards. Instead he was deep in conversation with Selby's pretty sister. A handful of other gentlemen eyed the pair jealously.

Alistair was coming to understand that Louisa Selby was not a country bumpkin, nor was her brother an overgrown schoolboy. Dressed in unrelieved white, her hair in a simple twist that ought to have been the height of dowdiness, she was almost too beautiful to look at. All she had to do was smile and nod and she would have been considered the toast of the ton, but she seemed to be holding up her end of conversation.

What precisely she had talked about, Alistair could not say, because he had been too busy studying the lady's brother.

Robert Selby was charming.

He was disarming.

Alistair, unfortunately, could attest to Selby possessing both those qualities because he found that he was both charmed and disarmed. It was embarrassing, but there you had it. Every time he let his gaze stray toward Selby he felt the corners of his mouth twitch up inanely.

Surely he ought to be above such things.

After the ladies left the table, Alistair watched Selby lean back in his chair, idly taking long puffs off a cheroot that he held between two fingers. He was listening to young Furnival prattle on—the two of them had been to Cambridge together—and occasionally laughing in response to whatever his companion was saying.

Selby's laugh was like the sound of champagne being uncorked, startlingly sudden and bright, the sort of sound that made everyone in the room turn around and take notice. Alistair felt like he heard it not with his ears but with his entire body.

Furnival said something about a horse he had running in Newmarket, and Selby laughed again. Alistair noticed a few other gentlemen smiling in response, as if Selby's laugh was contagious, like typhus or scarlatina. Hell, Alistair realized he was smiling too.

This had to stop.

"What club do you belong to, Selby?" he called down the table.

Selby instantly turned to answer his host. "I haven't joined one."

"I'll put you up for White's," Alistair offered. Why was he doing this? What did he care whether Selby joined his club?

A crease appeared on Selby's forehead. "White's? Isn't that a Tory club? I don't think I'm—"

Alistair waved his hand dismissively. "That's not of the slightest importance."

"But—"

"My dear fellow. I don't care if you're a Whig or a Jacobite or an outright revolutionary. The fact is that you must join White's if you wish to make the right sort of connections." Another fact was that Alistair didn't like the idea of Selby joining some other club and laughing like that when Alistair wasn't around to hear it.

Furnival and Lord Martin, both members of White's, murmured their assent.

"That settles it," Alistair said, gesturing for the footman to refill the brandy glasses.

Selby laughed again, causing a lock of hair to tumble forward onto his forehead. He pushed it back, wreaking havoc on his hair, not that it had been terribly orderly even at the start of the evening. Really, he ought to cut it. It had no business falling onto his collar like that, flouting all standards of decent grooming. Surely that was why Alistair wanted to smooth it into place using his own hands.

Later, in the drawing room, Alistair leaned against the door frame, watching Selby charm a dowager countess while his sister played the pianoforte. Maybe Selby sensed Alistair's gaze, or perhaps he was just tired of talking to Lady Edgeware, because the next thing Alistair knew, Selby was striding across the room to him.

"Thank you for inviting us tonight," Selby murmured, too low to interrupt his sister's playing. "It was kind."

It was nothing of the sort. "That's not why I asked you."

"Oh, I know that. Did we pass muster?" Selby asked softly, with a sly look up at Alistair.

"What's that supposed to mean?" Alistair retorted. He fumbled in his coat pocket for his spectacles, which he hadn't worn at dinner. It always felt slightly ludicrous to wear spectacles while in evening clothes, as if he might be called upon to balance an account book at any moment. But he'd be damned if he'd pass up a chance to see this impertinent fellow in sharp focus.

"I assume you asked us here to make sure we weren't barbarians who would disgrace you at your ball. You wanted to make sure we knew how to act in company."

Now that Alistair had his spectacles on, he could fully appreciate Selby's impish grin. He wished he had left them in his pocket. It was impossible to retain a sense of gravity while looking at that impudent mouth, that pert chin.

"No," Alistair said slowly, trying to master himself. "That's not why I invited you." Strictly speaking, the Selbys would satisfy his needs even if they had barnyard manners. "I thought to let a few people get a glimpse of your sister, to set the stage for the ball."

"To let people know what kind of show they're in for? Like when the circus sends a boy into town ahead of the caravan, shouting about all the oddities one can see for a penny?"

Alistair had to choke back a laugh. "And who is the circus freak in that metaphor? It can't be your sister."

"Oh, I don't know," he said, affecting a mock-philosophical tone. "Perhaps we're all circus freaks at the end of the day."

"Is that from Tacitus too?" Despite his best efforts, Alistair felt a smile tug at his mouth.

"Were you listening to us?" Selby asked brightly. "Miss Allenby is brilliant. She reads Latin, which is remarkable enough, but she also reads Greek."

Alistair did not care one jot who read Greek and who didn't, and momentarily forgot why he had invited the Allenby girl in the first place. "Miss Allenby is my father's natural child," he said, suddenly conscious that he was trying to warn Selby off Amelia Allenby. What did he care if the lad made an unfortunate match? It would serve him right for being so impertinent, after all. And wasn't that what Alistair wanted to do, teach all these hangers-on why they shouldn't beg him for handouts and favors?

Selby didn't seem surprised at the revelation, though. "That explains the resemblance."

Alistair was taken aback. "Resemblance! I think not. She has orange hair and freckles."

"Your eyes—"

"Her eyes are blue, and mine are brown. You're having me on." But he'd let him have his little joke, if it kept him nearby.

"I meant the shape." His mouth was twitching in a repressed smile. "And of course your hair. Your hair is almost black, but it has a reddish tint, especially near the bits of gray."

He must have looked affronted, because Selby hastily continued. "No, don't look like that," he protested. "It's handsome! Very distinguished."

Alistair was about to sarcastically offer his thanks when Selby touched him lightly on the arm and said, all earnestness, "It goes well with the title and the money. Stern lord of the manor, and all that."

Once again, he had to stifle laughter. "Why, you insufferable wretch. Indeed, one would never know that you had only recently arrived in London. All the best people discuss a marquess's graying hair in his own drawing room. Very polished manners. Very refined. The freak show metaphor is seeming increasingly apt."

Selby laughed, another pop of champagne, and Alistair felt gratified out of all proportion that he had amused the fellow.

And that Selby thought his infernal gray hair *handsome*.

Only after his guests had left, and Alistair was surveying his now-empty drawing room, did he realize that he had sadly underestimated both of the Selbys. If their success tonight had been any indication, they would take the town by storm. No doubt his dinner guests would spend tomorrow spreading word of Lord Pembroke's charming protégés. By the evening of the ball, everyone would be falling over themselves to meet brother and sister. They would have vouchers to Almack's and invitations to all the season's best events. No doubt they could even rustle up some connection to present them at court if they put their minds to it.

It also occurred to him that their names were going to be inextricably tied up with his. He had, he realized belatedly, taken a risk in associating himself with such unknown, untested figures. His scheme of using them to deter future requests did not depend on their manners, but if either of them erred in the slightest, it would reflect on his judgment.

He had been so caught up in his own petty desire to score a point off his aunts and Mrs. Allenby that he had lost sight of what truly mattered—his name, his family reputation. He had worked tirelessly to restore the honor his father had discarded.

And he had let a momentary whim cause him to jeopardize it entirely.

Charity wasn't surprised to discover that at White's, the gentlemen threw money around like they were emptying the contents of an ash can. She enjoyed cards as much as the next person, but when the lordling sitting across from her tossed three golden guineas into the center of the table, she felt positively puritanical in her distaste.

Or maybe she simply was jealous. Imagine having enough money to wager pound after pound on a silly game of vingt-et-un.

Imagine living a life so comfortable that losing a few pounds at a game of cards seemed exciting. It was nothing to the gamble Charity and Louisa had taken.

"I'll sit the next hand out," she said, sliding her chair back from the card table.

She made her way to an unoccupied settee in a dark corner of the room, intending to render herself as unobtrusive as possible for the rest of the evening, until she could make her excuses and return home to Louisa.

"Wise," said a gravelly voice. Lord Pembroke lowered himself beside her, and she wondered how long he had been watching. She felt the seat cushion sink towards him under his heavier weight. "It's only a matter of time before they're too drunk to hold their cards and begin wagering on what color waistcoat will be worn by the next man who walks up the stairs."

Charity had heard of such goings-on at White's, but had never thought she'd see those antics with her own eyes. "I daresay if I had a bit more money I'd act the same," she mused. There was no sense in trying to hide her lack of funds from Lord Pembroke. He had surely divined that the Selbys would have no need of his assistance if they had unlimited resources.

Pembroke must have made some discreet gesture to a waiter, because Charity soon found herself being presented with a glass of brandy delivered by a white-gloved hand. She took a grateful sip.

"If you were to flip through the pages of the betting book over there," he said, gesturing across the room with his own glass of brandy, "you'd find a good number of wagers placed by my father. One day when I was feeling especially sorry for myself, I added up the amount he had lost, and I discovered it would have been enough to purchase an establishment for my brother and disencumber a number of properties that were weighed down by mortgages."

It was hard for Charity to accept that a peer of the realm with a house on Grosvenor Square and a horse as fine as the one he had ridden in the park the other day could have much cause for self-pity, but when she turned her head and studied his austere profile, the stern set of his jaw, she knew he was sincere about his troubles. "You speak freely of your father's vices," she observed.

"I'm simply bringing you up to snuff. I haven't told you anything the rest of London doesn't already know." He took a long sip. "My father was quite infamous," he added grimly.

He was serious-minded, this hard-featured aristocrat. It wasn't simple arrogance that made him look down his nose at others, but full-blown moral rectitude. Charity would have bet that he was positively up to his ears in self-reproach too. All that rot ought to have gone out of style with the Crusades, as far as Charity cared.

"I don't hold with gambling," was all she said. And it was true, insofar as she felt sick at the thought of gambling away money that didn't belong to her. If she had her own money—well, that was never going to happen, was it?

They were so near, inches away from one another, that they could keep their voices quite low. Charity wasn't sure if she could actually feel the heat coming off his body or if her own body was playing tricks on her. All it would take would be for her to shift the smallest margin to the side and their hips would be touching, their boots rubbing against one another's.

At that moment Pembroke slung an arm across the back of the settee. She could feel the fine wool of his coat brushing against the hairs on the back of her head. Paralyzed by awareness, she couldn't decide whether to sit up straighter to free herself from the closeness, or to lean back into his arm.

It was only a companionable touch, one man to another. Men were always jostling and backslapping, treating one another with casual friendliness like so many puppies. She had participated in this easy camaraderie time and again, but there was nothing casual or easy about being near Lord Pembroke. Not only because of his rank and power, but because she wanted him, and she couldn't disregard the sparks of warmth that seemed to travel from his body to hers.

This was the hard part of being a man. Six years ago, when she first put on Robbie's taken-in clothes, she had felt silly, like she was in a costume. That had lasted all of five minutes, and then she felt righter than she had in her entire life. She was *supposed* to be wearing breeches and top boots, riding jackets and cravats. Her hair was meant to be cropped.

When she absolutely had to dress as a woman—those visits home from Cambridge when Robbie was still alive—she usually borrowed one of Louisa's shabbiest and most faded gowns. She felt like a mummer, like an actor in a farce, and longed for the next chance she'd have to resume her breeches and waistcoats.

But this proximity to a man she desired was very hard to manage. And there was no denying that she did desire Lord Pembroke, despite all his arrogance and hauteur. Or, hell, maybe because of it. He was just so bloody sure of himself, of his place in the world. And why shouldn't he be?

It was useless to think of him in that way, though. She had had her share of women—and men, for that matter—interested in her, but what was she supposed to do about it when they were under a misapprehension about who and what she truly was? They thought they were attracted to a young country squire, not a former housemaid dressed in her dead master's castoffs.

She sighed, an action that caused her to tilt back in her seat and accidentally settle against Pembroke's arm. She stilled, wondering if he would pull his arm away. Instead she felt his fingers in her hair.

"You really ought to do something about your hair," he said softly, and she thought she could actually feel the vibration of his voice where his hand touched her. "It's too long by half." He fiddled with the ends, where her hair curled a bit around her collar.

She turned her head toward him, not enough to dislodge his hand, but enough so she could gauge whether his expression was amused or reproachful.

It was neither. His eyes were narrowed, his mouth curved up slightly in the faintly indulgent expression he seemed to adopt only when addressing her. He looked . . .

He looked like he wanted to touch her as much as she wanted to be touched. God, she was lonely. And a little bit drunk. Even the friendly, sisterly touches she had used to share with Louisa were now strange and rare, hampered by the civilities of London society. She wanted to feel another person's hands on her.

No, she wasn't being quite honest with herself. She wanted to feel this man's hands on her.

She took another sip of brandy and watched as Pembroke did the same, his hand still on her head, his eyes never leaving her face. He wanted her. Lord help her, but she wouldn't have guessed Pembroke to be that sort of fellow. Not that she cared one way or another, except that it made her current situation a good deal more difficult.

And more interesting.

His hand slid into her hair, massaging the back of her scalp. She suppressed a groan of pleasure. Now, why in hell did it feel so good when other people rubbed one's head and so pointless when one did it oneself? But this felt more than good. She felt like she needed a bucket of water dumped over her, but still she couldn't summon up the self-control to pull away, to come up with any excuse to leave this settee, to return home, anything.

"Robert," he said in that low, intimate tone. "Odd, but you don't seem like a Robert. What do they call you at home?"

Now, how could she answer that? Robbie hadn't seemed like a Robert either, which was why everyone had called him Robbie. "At school they called me Selby," she answered truthfully. "Louisa calls me all manner of things." This, too, was true.

"Hmm," he murmured, his hand momentarily still on her head. "Robin. That's what I'll call you."

"Like Queen Elizabeth's Robin," she commented, only realizing that comparing herself to a queen's supposed lover was not perhaps quite the thing.

That must have brought him to his senses, because he removed his hand and said, "Indeed," in a much less intimate tone. "Robin suits you, though. Much less serious than Robert."

She couldn't disagree, and she liked the idea of having a name that hadn't belonged to poor Robbie nor been impersonally bestowed on her by the vicar's wife. Charity Church, for heaven's sake; it was more a designation of origin than a proper name.

The card game broke up, and they were joined by a handful of gentlemen. Some of them Charity knew either by name or face from Cambridge, but the rest seemed to take her presence at White's or her proximity to Pembroke as a sufficient recommendation, proof enough that she was part of their world.

They were talking about a friend of theirs, somebody

Charity had never met, so she was able to drink her brandy and observe the gentlemen without anybody paying her much attention.

Well, strictly speaking, she was observing only Pembroke.

He had a bit of dark stubble on his jaw. She would have figured him for the type of man to appear only clean shaven in public. Or perhaps his beard simply grew in too fast to avoid stubble by this time of night. Surely that notion shouldn't make her feel suffused with warmth. There was, after all, nothing so remarkable in a beard. But she wanted to reach out and feel its coarseness under her fingertips.

His hair appeared very dark in the dim light of the club, the strands of silver only the faintest sparkle. His spectacles must have been in his pocket. Indeed, when she let her gaze roam lower, she thought she could see their shape beneath the fine wool of his coat. She could also make out the outline of lean muscles.

It was time to leave before her thoughts went farther in this direction. She stood up, but she must have moved too fast, or perhaps she had had too much to drink, because the room began to spin around her. Her field of vision narrowed and blurred, and the next thing she knew she felt a strong arm wrap around her waist.

"Steady now," Pembroke murmured, his voice a rumble in her ear. "The brandy here may be stronger than what you're used to."

"Must be," she said faintly, but she rather thought it was the presence of this man who had clouded her thoughts, and not the drink.

"Do you have a carriage waiting for you?" he asked. "Or, if I put you in a hackney, do you have anyone waiting for you at home?"

"No carriage," she said. That was an impossible expense. "And I daresay Louisa has been in bed for hours."

"Then I'll drive you home in my carriage." Pembroke steered her toward the door after bidding good night to the other gentlemen.

He kept his arm around her, hauling her against him, as they descended the stairs. She let herself enjoy the feel of him solidly next to her. He smelled good, too, like books and brandy.

"Up you go," he said after his carriage was brought around.

"You didn't have to worry," she said. "I'm not drunk, and even if I were, I can hold my liquor. I wasn't going to embarrass you."

"You're probably nine stone with your boots on. I doubt you can hold three glasses of wine."

He was right about that, but she wasn't going to admit it.

"Besides," he continued, "I didn't think you were going to embarrass yourself, let alone me. I wanted to go home and didn't care to leave you in the company of those gentlemen."

Oh. "Thank you?"

He laughed, low and soft. The carriage pulled up in front of her house and she opened the door.

"Don't thank me," she heard him say as she descended to the street. "I seldom do anything that merits gratitude, Robin. I am always correct, but never benevolent. Remember that."

She hurried into the house without daring so much as a glance back over her shoulder.

Keating opened the door for her. "Miss Louisa is waiting for you." His arms were folded across his chest.

"It's two o'clock in the morning." She handed him her gloves and coat. "She ought to be asleep."

"So should you. It's no hour for a young lady to wander about London." These last words he spoke in a barely audible whisper. Keating, of course, was in on the secret. He had been with Charity since Cambridge, ostensibly as a manservant but more often as an accomplice and an ally. And tonight, a mother hen.

She kissed him on his grizzled cheek. "Good old Keating."

"Be off with you, pet."

When she reached the top of the stairs, she could see a light coming from under Louisa's door. She scratched lightly on the door, quietly enough not to wake Louisa if she had already fallen asleep.

But there came the sound of slippered feet padding across the bare floor, and the door to Louisa's room was flung open.

"I thought you were dead in a ditch." The candle Louisa held was nearly burnt down. She had been waiting up for hours, then.

"I was at the club Lord Pembroke had me join."

"Until two in the morning?" Louisa sniffed. "And positively reeking of brandy."

Charity didn't know what bee Louisa had in her bonnet—it had nothing to do with brandy or late hours—but there was no sense in getting into it now. "The night lasted rather longer than I had thought it would. Next time I'll send word, if you like."

Louisa wrinkled her nose. "And this is a Tory club, is it not?" She, like her brother before her, was a staunch Whig.

"Yes, Pembroke insisted—"

"Pembroke!"

Charity was surprised by the vehemence in Louisa's voice. Louisa was usually so mild, so easy to get along with. "He's done us a great favor—"

"I sincerely doubt it," she retorted, her blue eyes glittering by the light of the candle she held in her hand. "He doesn't seem the sort of man to do favors."

That observation was uncomfortably in accord with what Pembroke himself had told her not five minutes earlier.

"Regardless," Charity said, "it would be odd if I refused his invitation to join his club. I didn't drink all that much, and I didn't lose any money at the tables. I promise that there's nothing for you to worry about." At least, nothing more than the usual. "Besides, since when do you object to a gentleman having a bit of harmless fun?"

Louisa stared at her, mouth hanging open. "Charity, you are *not* a gentleman," she whispered.

Charity felt herself blush. It wasn't as if she could protest, but the fact of the matter was that she felt more like a gentleman than she did anything else. Cheeks hot, she said, "You know what I meant."

They stood there for a moment, regarding one another—

Louisa in her white dressing gown and hair in curling papers, Charity in rumpled evening clothes, cravat rakishly askew.

"What are you going to do after I marry, Charity?" Louisa asked, breaking the silence.

"I don't know." Charity glanced away from Louisa's face, taking in the peeling paint on the door frame. "There's the gamekeeper's cottage at Fenshawe. I could stay there," she said, knowing it for a lie.

Louisa wrapped her dressing gown tightly around her. "But we won't own Fenshawe after Cousin Clifton inherits."

The "we" was generous. Charity had never owned anything, least of all the estate of Fenshawe. Robbie had owned it. And since it had been entailed, it ought to have passed to his cousin. But when Robbie died, Charity had already been attending Cambridge under his name. Her thoughts muddled by grief and confusion, it didn't seem so terrible to keep quiet about Robbie's death and step into his shoes at home as well. The cousin, living in Dorset, could be kept in ignorance.

Sometimes when Charity was having a hard time falling asleep, she tried to think of exactly how many laws she had broken, how many ways she ought to have been hanged or transported. But Robbie had scarcely any property that wasn't entailed. Louisa, not yet sixteen, would have been destitute and homeless. For the two years since Robbie's death, they had stinted and scraped together enough money out of the estate's income to fund this season in London and put together a modest dowry for Louisa. The plan was for Louisa to marry and then they would figure out a way to set things right, to let the cousin inherit and to allow Charity to go back to being herself.

Whoever that was.

"I could live with you, after your marriage," Charity countered, already knowing that it could never happen.

"I'd love nothing more," Louisa said, and Charity believed it. "But I just realized that whoever I marry will recognize you as my brother. You can't very well put on a gown and hope nobody notices the resemblance."

Charity had known that from the beginning. There could be no happy ending to this deception. Even when Robbie was alive and healthy and brash and persuasive, she had understood that if she went to Cambridge in his stead, there would be no going back to being plain Charity.

Even if there were, she didn't want any part of it. There would be no more gowns, no more floors to scrub.

Neither could she continue as Robert Selby one minute longer than strictly necessary. Charity didn't have the stomach for it.

She would be alone, adrift, with no name and no friends. She would, in fact, be in much the same situation she had been in before arriving at Fenshawe over fifteen years ago. The only difference was that this time her aloneness would be the result of her own choice, a sacrifice she had made to protect the one person who was left to her. She looked fondly at Louisa.

"Charity, where will you go?" Louisa asked with her eyes wide. "What will we do?"

She leaned forward and kissed Louisa on the cheek. "Never mind that, my girl. I have it all in hand," she lied.

CHAPTER FOUR

Every time Charity turned around, the silver tray in the front hall bore a new assortment of calling cards and letters.

"Another batch." Keating unceremoniously dumped a pile of invitations onto Louisa's writing desk.

"Do try to behave like a respectable butler, Keating." Charity adopted an arch tone. "You're serving in a very fashionable household now."

"I sometimes forget. Can't imagine why. Could be that I can't be arsed to care." The two of them were alone in the drawing room, so they could speak freely.

"Or it could be that you're a scoundrel and a reprobate."

"Takes one to know one." He threw a pointed glance at Louisa's mountain of invitations. "I hope you know what you're getting into."

All Charity knew or cared about was that the drawing room was full to bursting nearly every afternoon. After having lived in virtual isolation at Fenshawe since Robbie died, this was a welcome change. The two most frequent visitors were Amelia Allenby and Lord Gilbert de Lacey. They often arrived together, Lord Gilbert bringing Miss Allenby in his curricle. Lord Gilbert's purpose was ostensibly to call on Mr. Robert Selby, but any fool could see that he was there to moon over Louisa.

As for Amelia Allenby, Charity looked upon her as a gift from the gods. She had never had a female friend besides Louisa, and as much as she loved Louisa, that was more a family connection than a friendship born of common interests. Miss Allenby, though, was somebody Charity could talk to on any number of subjects. She had read all the poetry that had been popular among the undergraduates in Cambridge and was even on familiar terms with a number of the poets.

"Tell me about your mother's salon," Charity said later that afternoon. "What does one have to do to get an invitation?" Seeing the girl flush, she hastily added, "That's likely crass of me, angling for an invitation so shamelessly. But after being marooned in Northumberland I have no conduct at all."

Miss Allenby tittered nervously. "You don't need an invitation. But I'm not sure my . . . Lord Pembroke, that is, would approve . . . ah." She cast her gaze desperately around the room, looking anywhere other than at Charity. "It's a delicate situation, you see."

"You mean that your brother is very stuffy and might not like it if his protégés associated with his father's mistress," Charity offered. "Oh no. Now you're blushing. I told you I have a sad lack of conduct."

"It's not that," she protested immediately. "Your conduct is simply lovely. But I don't wish to displease Lord Pembroke."

Charity dismissed this concern with a wave of her hand. "My attending Mrs. Allenby's salon can be of no importance to him. I won't bring Louisa, not out of any benighted notions of propriety but because she'd be bored silly. Besides, Pembroke can't object to my knowing your mother, when his own brother is so open about the connection."

They both turned their heads to look at the gentleman in question, who was at that moment deep in conversation with Louisa. Snippets of conversation drifted their way.

"The issue is the *quality* of the manure," Louisa was saying.

"What do you know about drainage?" asked Lord Gilbert. He was writing in a small notebook he had withdrawn from his coat pocket.

Miss Allenby shot Charity an incredulous glance. "Are they discussing agriculture?"

"Likely so. Louisa's had the running of the home farm for years." Even before Robbie died, Louisa, still in pinafores and braids, had implemented improvements and economies. "I'd have left it all up to the steward but she has definite opinions on these things."

"How admirable," Miss Allenby murmured, and seemed to mean it.

"Now that Lord Gilbert has asked about drainage she'll go on for hours. She has a passion for it." Perhaps if Louisa hadn't been such a beauty, she would have stayed in Northumberland and eventually married a farmer, and spent her days bossing him about regarding turnips and guano. Charity dismissed that thought as lunacy. The girl was going to make a brilliant match and lead a life free of worry.

"I'm not entirely clear what drainage even is," Miss Allenby confessed, "and I'd like to keep it that way."

They both giggled at this, and only stopped when they were interrupted by the butler announcing the arrival of Lord Pembroke.

Every time she saw him, she was struck anew by how imposing he was, but here in their shabby little rented house, he seemed grander still. He was like a crystal goblet on a table filled with clay jugs. Too fine for everyday use.

He had never visited them before. For a moment, he stood at the threshold of the room, presumably surveying the arrangements and finding them lacking. Charity watched as the briefest flicker of assessment crossed his face. The room suddenly revealed itself to Charity as being too small, the furniture too worn, everything a bit too dirty and sad-looking. She felt the inadequacy of everything she had worked for, the madness of the gamble she was taking. She had wagered her entire identity, her safety, her future, and come up with a few hundred pounds, a leased house, and some faded upholstery.

But then his gaze met hers and he crossed the cramped room in two strides. All her concerns were swept away by the force of his nearness.

After giving a desultory bow to Miss Allenby, he turned to Charity. "I had to see what the fuss was about," he said in his customary haughty drawl. "It seems that half the ton has already visited. I thought I ought to make an appearance lest you think me remiss."

"As if such a thing were possible." She snorted. "I'm sure you've never been remiss in your life."

"Well," he said with a shrug, but didn't deny it.

She smiled at that show of arrogance. "Come see Louisa."

If he were dismayed to find his brother tête-à-tête with Louisa, he didn't show it, but Charity had to guess that he wouldn't want to see his brother make calf eyes at a nearly penniless girl from an unknown family. And Charity was confident that sensible, practical Louisa would allow her head to be turned only by someone with a bit more money and stability than Lord Gilbert.

Louisa was perfectly, blandly civil, but Charity could tell that she did not like Lord Pembroke. So after Louisa had poured out tea, Charity took him by the arm. "Now come meet your actual hostess."

"Oh—it can't be." He had a wicked gleam in his eye. "Am I finally to meet the aunt?" He had several times now asked where the Selbys were keeping the aunt who served as their nominal chaperone.

"Yes." She squeezed his arm in reproof. And if she enjoyed the feel of his muscles rippling under her touch, then what of it? "Try to contain your delight."

"This reminds me of the first time I met the king. Do I look all right?" he teased, making a great show of smoothing his lapels.

"Oh, shut up." She led him to the corner of the drawing room, where Aunt Agatha was dozing behind a potted plant. Agatha Cavendish, Louisa's great aunt from her mother's side, was of course in on their deception. When told about the entail, she had responded that entails were precisely the sort of thing she'd expect men to come up with, Selby men in particular, and had promptly gone back to sleep. She was exactly the chaperone they needed for this trip: she paid no attention to anything that happened in the house and scarcely ever ventured outside it.

"Aunt Agatha, may I present Lord Pembroke?" Charity spoke loud enough to wake the old lady.

"Eh?" Aunt Agatha answered, momentarily startled. "Oh, so you're the marquess. How nice for you." And then she closed her eyes.

Charity looked up at Pembroke's face to gauge his reaction, but his face was impassive.

"Precisely like the first time I saw the king, in fact," he said dryly. "He, too, asked if I was a marquess and then fell back asleep."

Charity let out a bark of laughter.

"But seriously, Robin, she can't be your sister's chaperone. Find someone more . . . alert, will you?"

She was taken aback. "I most certainly will not, not that it's any business of yours."

"Like hell it isn't. Your sister—"

"Is a woman of sense. She doesn't need some interfering busybody she hardly knows hovering over her." Surely she ought to be more diplomatic to the man who was serving as their sponsor into London society, but she'd be damned if she'd allow Pembroke or anybody else to freely criticize her household.

Pembroke straightened his back, putting some distance between the two of them. When he spoke his voice was frosty. "I'm less concerned about your sister's behavior than what people would say if they discovered she was scarcely supervised."

"Well, you can stop being concerned because it has nothing to do with you. It was gracious of you to give Louisa an entrée into society, but that doesn't mean you can muddle around in our lives." Charity took a deep, steadying breath. "She's my sister, and I have the situation in hand. Now if you'll excuse me, I've left Miss Allenby on her own for too long now."

It was all lies, of course. But she didn't need Pembroke—in his magnificently tailored coat and glossy boots, so very splendid that he made these surroundings even drearier by comparison—to tell her so.

Was he supposed to apologize? Was criticizing one's choice of chaperone the type of insult a man had to atone for? Alistair was not accustomed to making apologies of any kind, let alone over this sort of triviality. Especially since he was most obviously in the right. Nobody with eyes and ears could suppose that ancient lady asleep in the corner to be capable of chaperoning a girl in her first season. But Robin had seemed put out, and Alistair didn't want a rift between him and his new friend.

Even thinking *Robin* and *friend* in the same sentence gave him a pleasant thrill. He wasn't used to thrills being pleasant rather than unsettling.

For that matter, he wasn't much used to friendship.

Surveying the room, he saw Gilbert very cozy with the beautiful Miss Selby. He didn't like that one bit, but he wasn't enough of a fool to do anything about it. If he suggested to Gilbert that perhaps he might want to chase after a girl in possession of more than two shillings to rub together, the pair of them would likely fall madly in love. So Alistair didn't even let his gaze linger on the couple, instead turning his attention to where his half sister sat with Robin.

He didn't like that either, oddly. They were looking at a new translation of something or another, and their heads were bent conspiratorially together over the open book.

Leaning against the wall, he watched them. Was this a romance? If so, why did it make him want to hurl his teacup against the wall? Surely it would be just deserts for Mrs. Allenby to see her eldest daughter wed to a minor Northumberland landowner whose income—according to the solicitors Alistair had charged with the task of looking into the Selbys' background—amounted to less than two thousand pounds a year. Alistair ought to be delighted.

As he watched, Robin pushed that infernal hair off his forehead. Never in the history of polite society had a man so badly needed a haircut, and never had Alistair been so grieved at the prospect of a man's hair actually being cut.

He knew that what he felt for young Selby was a kind of desire. And he knew himself well enough to understand that he felt this kind of desire for men as well as women. Thus far, he had been able—for the most part—to ignore this inconvenient urge when it applied to men. And so he would ignore his desire for Robin. Therefore, he assured himself, it could have no bearing on his distaste for the idea of Robin being married to Amelia Allenby or anyone else.

But when Gilbert rose to take his leave, bringing Miss Allenby away with him, Alistair felt a surge of relief.

"If you'll excuse me," Louisa said, dropping a curtsy, "I need to speak with Cook about dinner."

That left him alone with Robin.

"I'm sorry," he said as soon as the door shut, while the urge to make things right was still stronger than his sense of rectitude. "I shouldn't have said anything about your aunt. Even though I'm right. But it's your decision. A bad decision, but yours to make."

For a moment Robin was silent, regarding him with an expression Alistair couldn't read. "That's your idea of an apology?" he said finally.

"Did I not do it right?"

"No, Pembroke. No, you did not."

"Well, I've never done it before, so perhaps I want practice."

"You've never—" he shook his head in disbelief. "I'm honored to have been your first, then."

And damn it all to hell, but Alistair felt his cheeks heat.

"Your horrible apology is accepted," Robin continued, finally smiling. One of his eyeeteeth was crooked, and he had a small gap between his front teeth. Alistair couldn't figure out which imperfection he liked more.

"Thank you," Alistair managed. He took a step closer. "Miss Allenby's mother—my father's mistress, of course— was no older than your sister when she met my father." Why the devil did he have this compulsion to air his family's linens in front of Selby? "I may have exaggerated notions of what protection is required by young ladies."

Robin watched him for another moment, his eyes boring into him. "Understandable."

"I meant no insult to your sister by comparing her to Mrs. Allenby, of course."

Another pause, and Robin moved a step closer, close enough so that Alistair could discern the maze of freckles on his face, close enough that he could see that Robin's eyes, which he had at first supposed to be gray, now appeared to have flecks of every color. The closer he got, the more glimmers of blue and green and amber he could discern. And he wanted to get a good deal closer.

"I didn't think you did," Robin said.

"Why does she not like me? Your sister, I mean."

Robin opened his mouth, and for a moment Alistair thought he meant to deny it. "Louisa thinks I'm overawed by your rank, that I do whatever you say because I'm cowed by all your wealth and consequence."

A month ago, Alistair would not have been dismayed to learn that an acquaintance was impressed with his standing. In fact, he would probably have thought it his due. Hell, it *was* his due. But the idea that Robin Selby was humoring him, accepting his weak apology, listening to his shameful explanations of his father's disgrace, for no reason but to ingratiate himself? That made his heart sink.

"Is it true?" he asked.

Robin regarded him steadily with those disconcerting eyes. "Do you want it to be?"

"No, of course not. Besides, if you're toadying up to me, you're doing a mighty poor job of it. I've seen nothing but cheek and impertinence from you."

Robin laughed, a single mirthful crack that seemed to

warm the room by several degrees, and Alistair found himself smiling in return. Here, in this shabby room, he was happier than he could ever remember being.

"I have in the new novel from the Minerva Press, if you care to take a look," Alistair said as casually as he could manage.

"Do you really?" Robin asked brightly. They were lurking near the back wall of Lady Pettigrew's music room, whispering like schoolboys, while a Swede imported specifically for this occasion performed on the cello. Alistair usually attended his aunt's entertainments out of obligation mingled with something like mortification of the flesh, as if he might invest himself with virtue by enduring a night of tedium. But with Robin for company, he hadn't been bored once.

"It arrived in this month's shipment from the bookseller." He omitted to mention that the bookseller had sent the novel only because Alistair specifically asked for it, which he had done after overhearing Robin and Miss Allenby discuss their shared love of Gothic novels. "I haven't had a chance to look at it yet, but you're welcome to borrow it. I'll send a footman with the book in the morning."

"Do you mean it?" His eyes lit up. "Don't bother with the footman. I'll come by your house tonight, after I bring Louisa home. If that's all right, that is."

"You're more than welcome. The place is all at sixes and sevens in preparation for the ball, but the library has so far been spared."

Robin hadn't been to Pembroke House since the day

he had come begging for favors. That seemed like years ago now, and Alistair felt strangely giddy and nervous to think of Robin in his house.

Perhaps that was why Alistair had that extra glass of brandy. And then the one after that.

By the time he arrived home, he was in a state of nervous anticipation. He found himself puttering around the library like the worst kind of housemaid, stacking and restacking piles of books and papers, lighting a branch of candles, stoking the fire until it blazed.

And all this for the visit of a man who was of no consequence, a lad of four-and-twenty whom nobody had ever heard of before last month.

He poured himself another glass of brandy and drank it in one gulp.

When the butler announced Robin's arrival, Alistair was in the state his father had called "pleasantly well-to-live." This, according to the late marquess, who anyone would have to concede was an expert on all matters related to drink, was a state of intoxication somewhere in between "a trifle disguised" and "outright foxed." Alistair, who rarely drank more than a single glass of brandy or wine, only knew that his insides felt warm and his mind mercifully clear of his usual cares.

This, he suspected, was how everyone else felt all the damned time.

"Good evening, Pembroke!" Robin called cheerfully as he entered the room. He was dripping wet.

"What the devil happened to you?" Alistair's voice

sounded thick and remote to his own ears. "It looks like you've been thrown into the Thames."

"I brought Louisa home and sent the hackney on its way, thinking I'd walk here. But by the time I reached Oxford Street it had started to rain, which of course meant there wasn't a single hackney to be had."

"Take off that coat and give it to Hopkins," Alistair ordered. "And come sit by the fire." A footman, who had no doubt been alerted to his lordship's guest's alarming state, was already standing by with a sheet of toweling.

"Don't trouble yourself," Robin said. "There's no sense in my drying off and warming up when I'm only going to get soaked again on the way home."

"You'll do no such thing. You'll take my carriage."

Robin still hadn't taken off his dripping coat. "It's only water. It rains in Northumberland too, you know."

"I'm certain your constitution is admirable, but my book is less hardy, and if you intend to bring it with you, you'll do so in my carriage." He used the tone that brooked no disobedience, precisely how he'd command a stable boy to do as he was bid. He would not stand in his own house and allow Robin to go off and catch a chill. "Moreover, the carpet you're standing on didn't need to be doused this evening, so kindly remove that dripping garment, let Hopkins restore it to some semblance of correctness, and sit down by the hearth immediately." Alistair knew he was being overbearing, but Robin was shivering.

With a great show of reluctance, Robin peeled off his sodden coat and handed it to the butler, promptly wrapping himself in the towel and kneeling by the fire. Alistair stayed where he was, a safe distance half a room a way, too far to reach out and attempt to dry Robin's dripping hair or make any other foolish mistake. There were so many foolish mistakes that he'd make if only given half a chance. Robin had been sent from his dreams—or maybe his nightmares—to tempt him into making every single one of them.

Robin was thin, very thin. Of course Alistair had known that the lad wasn't sturdy—that much was plain even through several layers of linen and wool. But with his damp shirt clinging to his arms, Robin appeared so slight as to be almost delicate, like he could blow away as suddenly as he had drifted into Alistair's life.

"I revise my opinion," Alistair said. "Not nine stone."

"Pardon?" Robin turned his head, and Alistair could see that the man's lips were blue.

"You weigh eight and a half stone, at the utmost, and that's including your wet clothes. You appear in need of a good meal."

Robin looked away, but not before Alistair could see the expression of hurt in those many-colored eyes. "Don't make me feel self-conscious," he said.

"I didn't mean—" Alistair stopped himself. "I'm sorry." His second apology. He stood and made his way over to the fire, standing beside where Robin still knelt on the rug. "I worry," he said after a minute.

Robin stood and looked up at him, the towel draped around his slender shoulders. "I know you do. I wouldn't have thought you had anything to worry about, what with all this." He waved a hand around, indicating his surroundings. "But you've got this line here," he reached up and traced a single cold finger along Alistair's forehead. "I don't know what you fret about, but I know you do it."

"I worry about everything," Alistair confessed. And it was true. "I worry about Gilbert. I worry that somehow all the work I did to repair the estate will be undone. I have—" Was he really going to admit this? "I have a recurring dream that my father is still alive, plunging the estate further into decay." He laughed, a bitter sound. "What a terrible thing, to dream that one's father lives and to count it a nightmare." Sometimes Alistair dreamed he was as bad as his father in every way and then some. That was even worse.

"It's not terrible." Robin cupped Alistair's cheek in his palm, stroking his thumb along the cheekbone like one might to do a confused child. No, like one might do to a lover. Alistair leaned into the touch. "It's hard to be the one on whose shoulders these things fall," Robin said.

It was. It really was, and it was a relief to hear it spoken aloud. He turned his face and pressed his lips into Robin's palm—not quite a kiss, but almost. "You know about that too," he said, understanding dawning. Sometimes he forgot that other people had crushing responsibilities and fears and expectations. He was not alone, not in his burdens, not in his life, not in this house—not tonight, at least.

"A little," Robin said, not moving his hand. "I won't tell you to stop worrying, that there isn't anything to worry about, because that never works. And it's never true. There's always something to eat you up."

"You don't seem to be eaten up." He was always smiling, always laughing, charming everyone around him.

"I've found the fears are there whether you fret or not. So I sweep them aside and try to enjoy myself while I can."

While he could? That didn't make sense, but Alistair knew this wasn't the time to ask. "That's why calling you Robin sounds right," he said, before he could reconsider the wisdom of what he was about to say. "You're like spring. When you came here, when I met you. It was like . . . light, like the coming of spring, even though I hadn't known it was winter." Oh God, he *had* had too much to drink. Either that or he belonged in Bedlam. What a thing to admit out loud. "I'm afraid I'm a maudlin drunk."

Robin looked up at him for a long moment, his expression unfathomable, then pulled him into a hug, letting the damp toweling fall to the floor. "Hush," he said, and Alistair knew it meant *I'm here*, and not *Be quiet*.

Alistair felt Robin's still-damp head settle beneath his own chin, as if it were the most unobjectionable thing in the world for the two of them to be standing here thusly. But Robin felt cold and smelled sweet, so Alistair wrapped his arms around his friend, the wet fabric of shirt and waistcoat chilly under his hands. He felt Robin let out a breath and sink against him, the younger man's weight scarcely registering as a pressure against his chest.

There was a sound in the hallway and Robin abruptly stepped back. Alistair could have told him it was only a housemaid refilling the coal scuttles and that nobody would disturb them in here.

"If someone came in they might get the wrong idea," Robin explained, not quite meeting Alistair's eyes. He was fiddling with the hem of his waistcoat.

"Would they, now?" Alistair retorted. If this hypothetical intruder concluded that the Marquess of Pembroke was behaving like a lovesick swain, he would be quite correct, damn it.

Robin blushed but didn't plead ignorance or make any move to change the topic, or do any of the other things he might have done if he didn't know exactly what Alistair was talking about. "As a man who prides himself on his correctness," Robin said patiently, as if Alistair were five years old and not particularly bright, "it wouldn't do for you to be seen in the arms of another man."

Suddenly Alistair felt furious. Not at Robin, not even at himself, but at everyone who gave a damn whose arms he was in. "I'm the bloody Marquess of Pembroke and I'll do what I please with my arms, thank you very much. I'd like to see anybody stop me." He knew he sounded infernally arrogant, he knew those very words had likely been spoken by his own father in justification of his exploits, but he didn't care.

"Besides," he continued in a calmer tone, "I haven't done that sort of thing since school." He straightened his cravat, as if that would restore his dignity. "With a man, I mean." He was deliberately opening a door that didn't need to be opened, and he was going out of his way to do so.

Robin turned to him with a startled grin. "Neither have I, for that matter."

Only after Robin left did Alistair realize they had both forgotten the book.

CHAPTER FIVE

Charity knew she ought to refuse Pembroke's offer to let her have the use of one of his mares. He framed it as a favor: the animal was very skittish, his new groom had not yet proven himself trustworthy, and so forth. But she had known it was a sham. She had stupidly mentioned that she missed the morning ride she had become accustomed to taking in the country, and he had maneuvered her in such a way that she couldn't refuse.

And this from a man who said he never acted out of benevolence.

What would happen when Louisa was married and Robert Selby disappeared? Would Pembroke wonder why he had been so suddenly dropped? Or—worse—would he make an effort to find her? When Charity had planned and schemed all those months ago, this sort of entanglement had been the furthest thing from her mind. But now she felt like she was mourning her own death, mourning the death of Robert Selby all over again. Mourning things she had no right even to think of.

"I'll race you to the Serpentine," Pembroke called over his

shoulder. It was only eight o'clock and the park was almost empty.

Without answering, she spurred the mare, passing Pembroke and effectively giving herself an unsporting head start. She heard the hooves of Pembroke's stallion approaching behind her, and crouched lower in her saddle. His mount was undoubtedly faster, but she was so much lighter. She tucked her hat under her arm, not wanting it to blow off, and nudged the mare faster. The horse, she guessed, was enjoying this unexpected freedom as much as she was. A chance to test her limits, a chance to let herself go.

She reached the Serpentine a full length ahead of Pembroke.

"Scamp." Pembroke was breathing heavily. "Scoundrel and cheat. You little wretch."

"Guilty as charged." She placed her hat back on her head at a rakish angle.

"You ride hellishly well. Do you ride to hounds in Northumberland?"

"We have a hunt somewhere nearby, but I don't ride in it." How could she? The local gentry would know she wasn't the real Robert Selby. She had to hole herself up at Fenshawe, only venturing out for solitary, early morning rides.

"Who taught you to ride? Was it your father? Or was it a groom? If so, I ought to steal him away. Now, why the devil are you blushing? You're a damned fine rider and that's nothing to be ashamed of."

"It was a friend who taught me." It had been Robbie, of course. He had taught her to ride, she had taught him Latin and arithmetic and geography. A number of other things they had simply worked out together, in the way healthy young people often will when living under the same roof with scarcely any supervision. There was no way to think of those things in the presence of this man without blushing.

"A friend," Pembroke repeated, and Charity realized he was considering that information in light of what she had implied the other day about not having dallied with a man since her school days. That had been no more than the truth, even if it had been misleading.

She was doing her best to be honest with him despite the essential lie underpinning everything. Surely there was some way she could be her true self—whoever that even was—in spite of all the things she could never be honest about. She didn't know if that was the right thing to do, or if *right* was even an option in this situation.

"What happened to this friend?" Pembroke continued, shooting her a sidelong glance.

"He died a little over two years ago." She looked away when she saw a flash of sympathy in his dark eyes. The last thing she could accept was any sympathy about Robbie's death, not when she had taken such shameless advantage of it. "We ought to get these horses back to your stable," she added before he could say anything kind.

They rode to Charity's house first so Pembroke could pay his respects to Louisa and Aunt Agatha. He seemed determined to win them over, which Charity found both endearing and hopeless.

Charity was surprised to find a man standing on the pavement, looking up at the street number and then consulting a piece of paper, as if confirming that he was at the right location.

"Can I help you?" Charity asked as she drew the horse up.

"That depends," the man said. He was about fifty, with gray hair and a plain brown coat. "I'm looking for Robert Selby. My name is Maurice Clifton."

Charity fought the urge to run inside, to slam the door behind her. But cowardice wasn't on her long list of sins. "I'm Robert Selby," she lied, smiling brightly. "And you must be Cousin Clifton."

Now, why should the lad look like a startled rabbit? What kind of monster was this Clifton fellow for Robin to be looking at him that way? Alistair wanted to exert all his authority, send Clifton packing, and whisk Robin away from here. Instead he assumed a stony, watchful silence. That was his greatest asset as a marquess—simply existing, like a loaded and cocked pistol.

He watched Robin shake off that fearful look and manage a tolerable imitation of his customary lighthearted cheer. "Forgive me for not recognizing you, sir. I think I only met you once, when I was eight or nine."

"Quite right, quite right, young Robert. No matter. I scarcely recognize you, myself. I didn't expect to find you in town, Cousin. What brings you so far south?"

"My sister wanted a season. To be honest, so did I." He smiled broadly, and Alistair wondered what Clifton had to be made of not to be susceptible to such a grin.

But the man remained unmoved, his mouth set in a grim line. "I wouldn't have thought Fenshawe yielded sufficient income to support this sort of indulgence."

No, that was simply too much. Strangers, no matter whether they were related, did not question one another's finances. Alistair coughed.

"Oh, I nearly forgot. How could I! Lord Pembroke, this is my cousin, Maurice Clifton of Dorset."

The cousin looked suitably impressed to be encountering a marquess. Good. Let him remember that if he thought to cause Robin any unpleasantness.

Alistair took his leave, parting with a cool nod for the cousin and a warm handshake for Robin, passing the mare's reins into the hands of the groom who had followed them from the park.

Desire was one thing—bad enough, really. But this urge to rescue Robin, to prevent him from experiencing even the slightest inconvenience—that was something new. Something unsettling.

He felt protective of Gilbert but that had more to do with hoping his brother found some purpose in life and didn't take after their father. There wasn't a lot of affection or warmth between them. Alistair didn't have a lot of either quality in his life and never had. Until he met Robin he hadn't thought it possible.

He wanted time to turn this over in his mind, to discover what these unaccustomed feelings meant, but when he returned home he found Gilbert waiting for him in the library.

"Gilbert," he said, ringing for tea. "Did we have an appointment?"

"No, I didn't think I needed—" Gilbert shook his head. "Never mind. I wanted to see you. I have a question and could use your advice."

Alistair prayed that it did not involve a pregnant opera dancer or an investment scheme. He sat in a chair. "Go ahead," he prompted.

Gilbert squared his shoulders and set his jaw, looking like a man about to send his horse over a wall he knew to be too high. "How much money would I need to marry? I have four thousand pounds."

"You can't marry on that," Alistair said immediately. Too immediately, perhaps, because his brother looked like he had been slapped.

"No, of course not. What I mean is, how much would a girl need to have for me to be able to keep her comfortably?"

"Six thousand." He had run over these figures many times. "You could live respectably but only in the country."

Gilbert swallowed. "But what if I used my four thousand pounds to buy a small property—"

"No." Alistair held up his hand to stop his brother. "It's not safe." Did the man not read the papers? "Crop prices—"

"But wouldn't a good-sized farm provide enough income to keep myself and a wife?"

"And what of your children? What is to become of them? I hardly need to remind you that our own father is an example of what happens when a man fails to provide for his children. That's why we're having this conversation in the first place. By all rights, you ought to have money of your own."

And not a paltry four thousand pounds, either. "But father squandered your inheritance."

"I'm not sure about that." Gilbert shifted uncomfortably in his seat. "A lot of that money he spent went to the care and keeping of the Allenby girls, and they're his children too."

Alistair had no response to make to such nonsense. The entire point, as far as he cared, was that one ought not to have children one could not provide for. He tried a different tack. "If you took up that living in Kent, you'd have the rectory and a comfortable income. If you kept your four thousand pounds safely invested, that would, in due course, provide for your children."

This was precisely what he told himself whenever he considered Gilbert's future—that with the living and the investment, there would be just enough for Gilbert to have a respectable, comfortable future, and he was not going to countenance his brother's throwing that away.

Gilbert nervously picked at the seam of his gloves. Today's visit, Alistair realized, had not been about a hypothetical question. He knew he ought to ask if Gilbert was all right, if he needed any immediate assistance—advice or a bit of money or even an excuse to leave town for a fortnight. But he couldn't bring himself to say the words. If he opened his mouth, what would come out would be a litany of criticisms—against their father, against young men who would not take holy orders and settle in new-built Kent rectories, against all the moving pieces of the universe that did not comport themselves in an orderly and proper manner.

So he sat silently, until finally Gilbert gave up and left.

The clock chimed, and then after a while it chimed again, and Alistair still sat alone in his library.

"I don't think it's as disastrous as you do, Charity." Louisa was calmly sewing a flounce onto the hem of a walking dress. "He came to Fenshawe once, maybe twice, and Robbie was only a child. Your coloring is similar enough to Robbie's for nobody to remark on a difference."

Charity paced back and forth in the cramped drawing room. "But *he* looks like Robbie. How can that be? I don't recall your father looking much like either of you. It was so unsettling, Louisa." It was like seeing a ghost, an especially cruel sort of spirit, showing her what Robbie might have looked like if he had been allowed to grow old.

Louisa glanced up, a moment of concern flickering across her perfect brow. "I can see that it would be. I hope I don't have to meet him."

So did Charity. She hoped neither of them had to meet him again. But they would. Of that she was certain. A man didn't go out of his way to find relations and then not follow up on the connection. He likely thought he was being kind by renewing the relationship. "I felt like a thief. Fenshawe ought to be his. That's thousands of pounds that should have gone to him, and instead—" She stopped herself when she saw Louisa's frown deepen. They had undertaken this entire charade to secure Louisa's future, and Charity didn't want her to feel responsible, especially since the girl hadn't even been sixteen when they had come up with this scheme.

But all the same, they could both swing for it if it came to that.

"I thought he never went to London," Charity said with a renewed sense of panic. "I thought he stayed in Dorset."

"That's what Aunt Agatha told us." Louisa resumed her sewing, calmly smoothing the fabric into identical gathers.

Aunt Agatha. What a fool Charity had been not to find out for herself if the old woman's memory was correct. "Perhaps we ought to leave. We could go to Bath after all," she suggested.

"No!" Louisa cried, dropping her needle.

"All right, all right," Charity said, falling to her knees to find the needle. "I only suggested it because you had seemed keen on the notion a few weeks ago."

"Yes, but that was before . . ."

"Ah! Here it is." Charity held up the needle. "Before what?"

"Before the season started," Louisa said, squinting to rethread her needle. There was a note of desperation in her voice. "We're so enjoying ourselves, are we not?"

They were, not that it mattered a jot how delightful it all was if ultimately they were to be exposed, tried, impoverished—

"I think I'll go for a walk," Charity said.

"At this hour?"

Charity had no idea what hour it was, only that the sun hadn't yet set, and that she was going to wear a path in the already threadbare carpet if she didn't stop pacing. She might as well walk outside, where at least she wouldn't trouble

Louisa any further. There was nothing Louisa could do to help, nothing she could say to set Charity's mind at ease, so there was no sense in plaguing her with doubts and worries.

"There's always India." Keating was waiting by the door with Charity's greatcoat. "Or South America. I could have us on a ship this time tomorrow."

That would never do. Keating was nearly fifty, with a bad leg and one ear that was completely deaf after years spent in the boxing ring. His only skills were being an indifferent servant, an aged prizefighter, and a loyal friend. She had hoped that Louisa, once married, could find a place for Keating in her gatehouse or stables.

"Thank you," she said. "I know you mean it."

She walked all the way down to the river, and then followed it up to Westminster before her nerves turned to outright misery. What was to become of all of them? She stopped at a sweet shop and bought a packet of lemon drops, immediately popping one into her mouth. The burst of tart sweetness did nothing to distract her from her worries.

When she looked up she had reached St. James's Park. In only a month this city had become as familiar to her as Fenshawe, which she had always considered the nearest thing to a home she was ever likely to find. From there she walked to St. James's Square, only then realizing that she was too close to White's and would doubtless run into someone she knew. She hardly felt capable of polite, cheerful conversation.

What she really wanted was a friend. Someone to sit with, share space with, someone who would understand if she needed to spend the evening grumpily pitching wadded up balls of paper into the fire instead of being entertaining.

She walked to Grosvenor Square without pausing to consider whether Pembroke actually fit that description, but held steadfast to the hope that he might.

She found him sprawled on the settee by the fire, book in hand, spectacles slipping down the patrician slope of his nose. He glanced up and grinned when he saw her. She attempted a smile in return but must not have carried it off because his own, genuine smile immediately dropped away, replaced by a look of concern.

"What's the trouble?" he asked, crossing the room to stand before her. He tipped her chin up so she had to face him, and the familiarity of the contact sent warmth through her body. "Anything I can help with?"

She shook her head. "I'm not feeling at all the thing. I shouldn't have come here."

"Ridiculous. Of course you should have. I was reading that book you wanted to borrow. Since you're here you might as well take it off my hands."

"No, you finish it first. I have a headache and won't be reading much of anything until tomorrow at best."

"That bad, is it?" When she didn't answer, he gestured to the settee that still held the book, spine up. "I'll read it out loud to you, then."

"You don't have to—"

"Of course I don't," he sniffed. "I don't have to do a damned thing. But I will anyway. Sit." He folded his long frame into one corner of the settee, leaving her the remaining three quarters, an absurd amount of space given their relative sizes. This, she guessed, was to prevent her from getting any ideas of hugging and petting him the way she had the other night. Her face went hot with mortification. She on the opposite end of the settee, her hip pressed against the arm. When she glanced shyly over at him, he was regarding her with a raised eyebrow.

"I'm not going to eat you," he said, his voice low.

"Likewise," she managed, and felt the flush spread from her face down to her chest.

He flipped back to the beginning of the book and started reading from the start, despite how boring it must have been for him to reread the pages.

She let herself get carried away by the tale. Mad nuns and locked passageways, that was exactly what she needed on a night like this. What was a case of stolen identity, impending poverty, and criminally fraudulent behavior compared to murderous bandits in pursuit across swamps and over mountains? It put one's own trials in perspective.

She had read these sorts of tales to Robbie and Louisa. That was how she had come to be friends with the Selby children. Just the three of them—sick old Mr. Selby hardly counted, and the cook and other servants seldom left the kitchen—in the middle of nowhere. It was hardly to be wondered at that they sought companionship in one another.

Charity had come to Fenshawe when she was eight, right after Mrs. Selby died, and had taken to telling stories to calm Louisa, who was little more than a lonely baby. Some were stories of her own devising, some were local fables, and some were from books she brazenly took from the library once she realized there was nobody at Fenshawe who cared to stop her. Robbie had at first listened at the nursery door, then edged in closer and closer until he too begged Charity for his nightly story.

But nobody had ever read to her. Robbie had never been much for books and Louisa preferred to sew while Charity read aloud. Tonight was a rare treat. And Pembroke even did different voices for the characters, which she might have thought beneath him if she had ever thought about it at all, which she certainly had not.

He also offered wry asides for her amusement. He would pause, glancing up over the rim of his spectacles. "She never even considered selling the emeralds and hiring a solicitor to find her missing half sister. Instead she gads about through tombs. Deplorable."

"Too right." Charity yawned. "Do they not have pawnbrokers in Italy? I have to say I'm rooting for the nun. She at least has some ambition."

A low rumble of a laugh. "You *would* root for the nun, you wretch."

The nervous energy that had fueled her walk through London began to evaporate, leaving her spent and exhausted. She leaned against the corner of the seat and closed her eyes, letting Pembroke's rich voice and the drama of the story lull her nerves into something like peace.

She must have fallen asleep, because when she opened her eyes again, Pembroke was no longer reading. The book was open in his lap, but he was silent, regarding her instead of the pages.

Embarrassed, she sat up abruptly. "How long was I—"

"Shut your eyes and go back to sleep," he said softly.

"I ought to go—"

"There's no need." He reached out and pulled her against him with one strong arm, easing her head against his shoulder. "Rest."

As if that were a possibility. She could have laughed at the lunacy of such a command. How could she rest with her body next to his, with her cheek pressed against the fine wool covering his shoulder? With each breath she was confronted with the friction of her body against his, a reminder of all the places they met and all the places they didn't.

Not moving her head off his shoulder, she glanced up at his face and saw that his eyes were open, but he wasn't reading. Instead, his gaze was fixed on some spot on the wall opposite him. Letting her eyes roam lower, over the inky stubble of his jaw, down to his throat, she saw his pulse beating quickly, his Adam's apple working as he swallowed. He was no more at ease than she was.

"I can't," she said, but she didn't pull away. "I can't rest like this."

She felt him exhale, a sound somewhere between a sigh and a laugh. "No, Robin. No more can I. This is the least restful I've felt in my entire life."

His fingers began tracing a circle on her shoulder. It was that easy circle that did her in—it seemed so of a piece with everything that had come before, the talking and riding and chatty bantering. It made her believe, for an instant, that what came next might also be a part of their friendship. It would be the two of them, only more so. It wouldn't be a lie.

She breathed in the scent of him, which she now realized was the scent of this room. Books and brandy, a fire burning low.

God help her, she looked at the placket of his trousers. And really, what did it say that she felt no pang of conscience, no sense of remorse, nothing? She looked at the bulge in the Marquess of Pembroke's trousers as incidentally as she might look at the wall hangings.

And he caught her looking. She could have died of embarrassment, or maybe desire, or maybe both those forces were working in concert.

"Indeed," he said, and now he was not laughing, not at all. He was looking down at her very seriously, and his arm had tightened around her shoulder.

That was all the prompting she needed. What was she, made of stone? He was warm and solid and he wanted her. Or rather, he wanted Robert Selby, but in this fuzzy state between sleeping and waking, none of it mattered. All that mattered was the way his breath hitched when she reached up and, with shaking fingers, gingerly plucked off his spectacles.

He captured her wrist midair and looked at her with those dark, dark eyes for half an instant before closing the gap between them. His lips were warm, his stubble scratchy against her own smooth skin. She kept still, seized by the sense that if she actually kissed him back she'd be stealing the kiss. It would be taken on false pretenses. She, mere Charity Church, would have intercepted a kiss meant for Robert Selby.

But that was before his tongue stroked her lower lip and all her finer feelings went up in smoke. What was true, what was virtuous, and who the hell could bring themselves to care? Not Charity, not Robin, not anyone else she might be.

His tongue met hers and that was all that counted. She wrapped her arms around his neck, pulling him down to her. She bit his lip, and when he groaned she felt the vibration against her mouth. So she did it again. He liked what she was doing and by God, she liked it too. Any further analysis was beyond her.

"You taste like lemon drops." He smiled, and she could feel the quirk of his lips against her own.

She kissed the corner of his mouth, then kissed her way down to his jaw, before pressing her lips to the soft part of his throat where the stubble gave way to smoothness.

"Christ," he said, his voice a baritone rumble, his hands threading through her hair.

And so she sucked gently on that very spot that had made him blaspheme, using her hands to push his perfectly tied cravat out of the way. Had he avoided a dinner engagement in order to stay with her? She didn't care about that either. She cared about the pulse under her lips, beating wildly. She cared about the fact that the Marquess of Pembroke was whispering her name—or close enough—in her ear in between curses. She cared about the big hands that were sliding up her sides, tugging at the linen of her shirt—

No, that would not do. She had only enough presence of mind to remember that what lay beneath her clothes was not what Pembroke expected.

"Wait," she panted. "Wait. No."

His eyes were wild, his expression confused, but he took his hands away from her body immediately. He was a gentleman and she was a shameless deceiver.

Surely that knowledge ought to tamp down her desire, but it did not. She still wanted him. And she would continue to want him, even after tonight, even after this season, even after she had disappeared from his life, from his world.

She let herself skim her fingertips along his jaw one more time before dashing from the room.

CHAPTER SIX

If Alistair had known Robin was going to act this way, he wouldn't have kissed him in the first place. He didn't go around kissing men willy-nilly. Or at all, for that matter. It was a delicate business. One couldn't go about throwing one-self at men unless one wanted to be brought up on charges of sodomy or—at best—shunned by decent society and known as a criminal deviant.

Besides, Alistair would rather have Robin present and unkissed than Robin absent under any circumstances. The wretch hadn't been at the park this morning, nor yesterday morning. He had also been conspicuously absent from their club ever since that blasted kiss.

A scratch at the library door, an apologetic cough, and Hopkins announced Mrs. Allenby. She had visited twice since the day she first requested his help, both times with inane questions relating first to the color of hothouse flowers Alistair intended to order for the ball (apricot) and then pertaining to the number of waltzes he planned (two). He had humored her, and he knew that was partly because he was distracted by other matters.

It was Robin who had driven him to distraction. Where was he, and why was that place not here, by his side?

He was a blasted idiot.

"Oh, you poor dear," Mrs. Allenby said from the door. "Gilbert said he thought you were coming down with some sort of spring ague and I dare say he had the right of it. You don't look at all the thing."

Spring ague? He had never heard of such a malady, let alone contracted it. If he looked out of sorts, it was because he missed Robin. What was Gilbert thinking, telling tales about his health, and since when did bloody Mrs. Allenby have the right to fuss over him? She didn't—heaven forfend—think that as his father's mistress she had standing as some sort of mother figure, did she? She was only a few years older than he was, for God's sake.

Yet here she was, looking at him as if he were a child with a troubling rash. He folded his arms and glared down at her.

"I'm perfectly well, *Lord* Gilbert is an interfering busybody, and if you're worried that I'll take ill and cancel the ball you have no cause for concern. I've told Hopkins that even if I drop dead he's still to roll out the awnings and ice the champagne."

This recitation evidently did nothing to convince her of his well-being, because she frowned more deeply. "If you say so, Pembroke."

"I do say so. Do you have Aurelia's gown finished?" He was delighted that he thought to misremember the girl's name.

She paid this rudeness no attention. She never did, damn

her. "The modiste sent it over last week. She'll never be a beauty but she'll have nothing to be ashamed of."

Nothing to be ashamed of! The child of a—well, never mind. "Mr. Selby finds nothing amiss with her appearance. I dare say Angelica has mentioned him to you?" How many *A* names could he think of, he wondered?

"Mr. Selby? Of course Amelia mentioned him. Everyone has. I've never heard anyone mentioned as often as Mr. and Miss Selby, not even when Byron's friend ran off with that poor girl."

Alistair neither knew nor cared about Byron's lecherous friend; as far as he knew, that entire set crawled from bed to bed and Mrs. Allenby ought to know better than to associate with them. "It doesn't bother you that your daughter might fall in love with a nobody from Northumberland? I doubt he has two thousand a year."

She was silent for a moment, regarding him with a look he couldn't decipher. "I'll be glad to see my children settled happily and honorably, my lord. I had heard that you were particular friends with Mr. Selby, so I'm surprised to hear you refer to him in those terms. In fact, I came here today to see if you knew any reason why I ought to warn Amelia away from him."

He felt his cheeks heat with shame and anger. She was right, this infernal woman. He shouldn't refer to Robin in such a way. "I know of no reason why he wouldn't be an eligible husband," he forced himself to say. It was a lie, but he couldn't very well go about announcing what he and Robin had gotten up to on the settee the other night.

She nodded. "Thank you for that."

"Has he made an offer for her?" He felt like he was wrenching the words out of his chest, but he had to know the answer. Could that be why Robin had been avoiding him?

"No, no. Nothing like that. As far as I know he isn't even courting her." Her voice held a note of something altogether too much like reassurance, too much like sympathy.

Still, relief washed over him. If he had, even inadvertently, dallied with a person who had been promised to another, he would have been brought to a new level of shame. That particular transgression was a bit too similar to his father's misdeeds.

He rang the bell for a footman to see Mrs. Allenby out. He didn't trust himself to remain civil any longer today, and doubted whether he had managed it terribly well so far.

The troubling thing was that even if Robin didn't marry Amelia Allenby, he'd marry someone else. He'd have to. That godforsaken estate in the wilds of Northumberland was entailed. Robin needed an heir, otherwise the property would pass to that red-faced cousin. The idea of seeing Robin betrothed or married was enough to make him feel sick. Was he jealous of some future Selby bride? How lowering.

He sat back down at his desk and attempted to write Robin a note. Something brief and friendly, just the sort of thing you write another man after licking his tongue on your sofa.

When Hopkins announced another visitor he was entirely relieved to have an excuse to stop. It was his solicitor, Nivins.

"It's about Miss Selby," Nivins said, sitting too stiffly in the chair across from Alistair. "A delicate matter, you see."

Alistair suppressed a groan. "She's only 18. Has she managed to get herself involved in a scandal already?"

The solicitor let out a breath that almost sounded like a whimper. "Ah, so she is 18. That was what I came to ask."

"Yes, she turned 18 in this past November, according to her brother."

"My lord, that would put the date of her birth as November 1799."

"And what of it?" Alistair could add and subtract as well as the next person. He didn't pay his solicitor for that service.

"The late marquess was, if you recall, not present in England at the time. He left in 1798." He shuffled through the sheaf of paper he had on his lap. "Here is a letter in his own hand from November of 1799 written in Padua, directed to my office. Here is another in December of that same year from Milan. And several written in the first part of the year 1800, all from various parts of Italy."

And all undoubtedly requesting funds. The solicitor's recitation of dates meant something, but try as he might Alistair couldn't grasp the point. The meaning eluded him.

Nivins placed the letters on Alistair's desk with an unsteady hand. "As you no doubt recall, he did not return to England until the autumn of that year."

Of course Alistair recalled. He had been in his first year of Oxford and utterly mortified to learn that his father had established a household with the mistress and infant he had brought back from Italy. Mrs. Allenby and Amelia, of course.

Nivins blinked a few times, obviously hoping Alistair would speak and spare him the trouble of saying whatever words were on his tongue. "He could not, therefore, have been Miss Selby's godfather," the solicitor finally said.

Only decades of self-control and finely honed aristocratic restraint prevented Alistair from gasping. How could he not have realized this? Robin—goddammit, *Robin*—had told him his sister's age. Why had Alistair not gone to the trouble of subtracting one sum from the other and arriving at the essential impossibility of the situation?

Robin had lied to him.

"I see," Alistair said, his voice sounding as if it came from a great distance. "I daresay the Selbys were mistaken about the nature of their father's connection with the late marquess. Thank you kindly for drawing my attention to the matter."

Nivins patted the stack of papers he left on Alistair's desk. "I'll leave your father's letters with you in case you wish to check for yourself—"

"No!" Alistair barked. "Take them with you." He forced his voice into a cooler register. "As you said, I recall the events myself."

Robin had lied. He was no better than any of the beggars and cheats who attempted to wring money and favors from the estate.

And Alistair should have known, he ought to have figured it out for himself. But he had been too caught up in their friendship—ha!—to apply rational thought to the matter.

There was, however faint, still the possibility that what he told Nivins was actually true. Perhaps Robin and his sister had been misled by their father.

He dismissed Nivins and called for a footman. "Get me Selby," he said. "Bring him to me. Tell him it's urgent."

Charity ran nearly all the way, straining to keep up with the stride of the much taller footman. Had Pembroke taken ill? Why would the footman not tell her what was the matter? At Pembroke House, she slipped past the butler and ran up the stairs. He'd be in the library. He always was.

She found him, his back against the fireplace.

"Is everything all right?" she asked, out of breath. "Your footman said . . ." Her voice trailed off as she saw his face. He was furious, the kind of fury that was all the more terrifying for how tightly leashed it was. His fists were clenched, his jaw was tight. And his eyes—she had never seen them so cold, not even that first time she had been in this room. "No, I can tell things aren't all right." She took a step towards him. "Can I help?" Dare she hope that he had sent for her for the same reason she had come here the other night? For comfort, for friendship?

His icy glare checked her progress and she froze in place.

"My father was not your sister's godfather, was he? You lied, did you not?"

She was momentarily stunned. Of all the lies she had told, it was bitterly absurd for that to be the one to cause her trouble. Charity had dim, childish memories of the late marquess visiting old Mr. Selby, even after Mr. Selby's days of hunting and riding were long over. The marquess would sit at Mr. Selby's bedside and play cards for farthing stakes. He had sent a ham after the funeral. Charity remembered slicing it while wearing a black armband, and giving the choicest bits to a teary Louisa. Saying that the marquess had been Louisa's godfather was such a minor stretch of the truth as to hardly matter, at least in comparison to all the much greater and more dangerous lies she told.

She gripped the back of the nearest chair, if for no other reason than to give her something to do with her shaking hands.

"I lied," she whispered. "Your father was not Louisa's godfather." She watched as his expression slipped momentarily from fury to sorrow, and then just as quickly back to fury.

"So. What was it you wanted from me?" His words were clipped and frigid monosyllables. "I assume you planned to blackmail me with the events of the other night?"

"No!" She had to gasp for air.

"How much do you want? Let us dispense with the preliminaries and proceed to that stage of the transaction." His voice was a cold, sharp knife. "How can I buy your silence, Mr. Selby? And your future absence, I need not add."

"It's not like that," she protested. "I would never blackmail you." How could he think she had kissed him for such a purpose? She couldn't bear to know that he thought of her in such a way.

"Do forgive me if I find it hard to trust your word. In my experience, liars lie. They lie about big things, they lie about little things. They lie even when there's nothing to lie about.

And you, Mr. Selby, are a liar. I have no doubt that you are also a blackmailer."

"No," she whispered, but even that was a lie. She had indeed gotten used to lying. Every day when she got dressed, when she left a calling card, when she let everyone around her believe she was someone she was not. It didn't matter that she was coming to believe that the lie was more real than the truth.

Pembroke's mouth was a rigid line. "You will have a draft on my bank for a thousand pounds. That ought to be enough to rid me of the pair of you."

"I won't take your money." She couldn't let him think she had set out to hurt him. The lie about his father being Louisa's godfather was harmless. All her lies were harmless, unless you counted Maurice Clifton, and she would set that right as soon as she had a chance. "Everything that happened between us—I meant it all in earnest." Without intending to, she darted a glance at the sofa.

His lip curled in revulsion. "Spare me the protests, Mr. Selby."

He didn't call her Robin. She felt that her heart would split in two. Behind his icy anger she could hear the pain in his voice and knew she had put it there. She had made him doubt their friendship. She couldn't stand it.

But there was something she could do. There was one way she could convince him that she had not intended to blackmail him, at least.

She spoke before she even drew another breath. "I'm not Robert Selby. That was a lie too. My name is Charity Church."

His expression was totally blank and his silence stretched out so long that Charity wasn't sure he had understood her. "But that's a woman's name," he said finally.

"I'm a woman." This, the miserable fact of the matter, felt more dishonest than anything she had thus far told him. "A foundling. I went to live with the Selbys as a housemaid. When Robbie died, Louisa would have had nothing because the estate was entailed." And because nothing had been set aside for her, but she wasn't going to speak ill of Robbie. "So I pretended to be Robbie. For Louisa." The explanation was so shabby, so inadequate, when put so baldly.

"You are a *woman*." He stared at her, plainly incredulous. "*You* are a woman." He ran his eyes over her body, so slowly and searchingly that she could not hold back the blush. "Why are you telling me this? Can you possibly think that my knowing of this additional—and far greater—deceit will absolve you of the lesser one?"

"No," she protested, her hands gripping the back of the chair so hard she could barely feel her fingers anymore. "I wanted you to know that I meant you no harm, never intended to harm you. I'm a woman," she explained, the words sounding pathetically feeble, "so there could be nothing to blackmail you about, you see."

"Nothing to blackmail me about? You see nothing in this situation that might reflect poorly on me? Nothing that might bring me shame? Good God. Your sister—" He shook his head rapidly. "*Not* your sister. Miss Selby, I mean. She had to know of this deception."

He meant to destroy Louisa. "She was only a child when

it started," she said hurriedly. "I went to Cambridge instead of Robbie when he and I were only eighteen, and Louisa had nothing to do with it. She's blameless, I promise you that."

"Oh, and I'm quite confident that your word is very valuable, Mr.—" He let loose a single bitter laugh. "Miss Church. You say you went to Cambridge under the name of your master when he was still alive."

To hear Robbie referred to as her master was enough to force tears into her eyes, but she would not cry, she would do nothing that would seem to ask for this man's pity. "Robbie was never interested in book learning, so we agreed—" But Pembroke didn't give a damn how they had come to the arrangement. He only wanted to know the extent of her deceit. She lifted her chin, forcing herself to meet his glare. "Yes, I lied to everyone at Cambridge as well."

He narrowed his eyes. "You must have been . . . close . . . to your employer."

That was meant to be an insinuation, but whatever he was insinuating was nowhere near as complicated as the truth. "It was Northumberland," she answered. "Very close to Scotland," she added, irrelevantly. "Servants often play alongside their employers' children."

"Next you will tell me that stealing the name and fortune of one's dead employer is also an ancient Northumbrian tradition."

He was mocking her now. She resolved to get through this with all the dignity she could muster, then somehow, later, figure out the rest of her life. For now, she simply would not cry. "We were friends."

"I should damned well think you were."

More mockery, then. She would force herself to bear it. "I look on Louisa as a sister. She is my only family." She would tell the truth even though he could never understand.

"Miss Church." His voice was so venomous as to practically be a hiss. "But you are not Miss Selby's only family. She has, I recall, a cousin. Mr. Clifton. Am I correct that he was Robert Selby's heir?"

For a moment, Charity thought she might actually faint. Oh, why did today have to be the day she finally developed feminine sensibilities? She should not have told him about her masquerade. She saw that now, but it was too late. Now he would destroy her and Louisa too. Louisa would have nothing—no reputation, no friends, no money. She'd be in a worse position than if they had simply let Mr. Clifton inherit, and it was all Charity's fault.

"Well?" His voice was a poisonous drawl.

She watched the firelight flicker off the signet ring he always wore. He was a marquess, a peer of the realm, and he could ruin her and Louisa with scarcely any effort. Oh, why had she not taken his offer of a thousand pounds? That would have padded Louisa's dowry and funded Charity's disappearance. How very stupid she had been to confess to this powerful man, and for no better reason than because she was too fond of him.

"Yes." She met his icy gaze. "He ought to have inherited Fenshawe. And he will, once we stop."

"Once you stop? Good God. Let me tell you, Miss Church, that I've had the misfortune to deal with all manner of confidence artists and swindlers since my father died and left me to pick up the pieces of the estate. But never once have I met one as hardened and shameless as you." He shook his head, as if in disbelief. "I have not decided what I'll do with you. For now, be gone."

At least she reached the street before the tears came.

CHAPTER SEVEN

Alistair had never been in such sympathy with his father. He would have liked nothing more than to follow the late marquess's example and get mightily drunk, run off to some Mediterranean idyll, and proceed to thoroughly abandon his responsibilities. He settled on a few glasses of brandy, which did nothing to improve his outlook and only solidified his gloom into a hard ball of anger that seemed to settle in his stomach.

He couldn't take comfort in any of his usual pursuits. He could not ride his horse in the park or seek solace at his club lest he run into Selby. And the reason Selby—Miss Church, rather—might be in those places was that Alistair himself had put him—her—there in the first place. Alistair had practically rolled out a red carpet to make his new friend at home in this world. He had been so charmed and blinded that he had failed to protect himself.

Nor could he flee to the country, because—mortification of mortifications—he realized that he would have to go through with his blasted ball. The invitations had long since been sent out, and even now the house was swarming with servants, polishing and preparing for a ball there now was no point in holding.

The only way out would be to feign grave illness, but the hint of fraudulence reminded him a bit too much of Selby. *Miss Church*, he reminded himself very firmly, although it was impossible to think of him—*her*—as such. There was nothing for it but to stand his ground, survive the next few days, and then retreat to the country as soon as the last guest had left the ball.

He considered rescinding the Selbys' invitations, but that would look very strange indeed after he had gone out of his way to take them under his wing. Perhaps Miss Church would behave like a gentleman—oh dear, the irony—and decline to attend. He could tolerate Miss Selby as long as he didn't ever have to look upon Robin again.

Robin. Oh God.

Of course, he could tell the truth, make a frightful scandal, and have Miss Selby and The Impostor cast out of decent society as pariahs. That would be their just deserts, after all. But he would look so foolish. Alistair had too much pride to let himself become the butt of any jokes. He had too much respect for the name and title he had salvaged from the last generation's misdeeds to cast it back into the trash heap of ruined reputations. He had been so blinded by his affection for this deceitful conniver that he had nearly destroyed all his work. He was furious with Miss Church and he was furious with himself.

He needed air, though. There had to be a way to exercise himself without encountering another human being. He could pace through the gardens, perhaps. Decided, he flung open the library doors and descended the stairs, causing duster-wielding housemaids to scatter like bats. His servants were all even more timid and apologetic than usual. It was never a good sign when the master of the house holed himself up for days on end. Some of these servants had served the family long enough to know precisely how bad it could get. Well, then, he would show his face among them for long enough to make it clear that at least this Marquess of Pembroke was sane and sober.

He cast his mind around, looking for something to say that would reassure them. "The . . . ah . . . carpets look very well beaten," he tried.

Wide eyes, hasty curtsies, a flurry of milords, and he was in the garden. He took a deep breath, the first fresh air he'd had in days. There was nothing much in the garden yet, it being only April. And he'd be well out of here by the time the place was properly in bloom. He'd be in Kent, or perhaps Shropshire, where he'd stay until he could trust himself to behave reasonably.

Charity Church. He kicked some gravel off the path. Why even bother naming a child if that was the best one could come up with? She had been a foundling, she said. Presumably one found at the door of a church and committed to the charity of that institution. Charity Church, indeed. Not that he could manage to wrap his mind around the idea that his Robin was in fact this stranger with the dreary name.

A part of him, the part he had failed to silence with brandy and righteous anger, shouted that he'd be willing to call this person by any name he or she wanted as long as he got to hear that laughter, see that welter of freckles.

But no. His mind was playing tricks on him, as surely as it had when he let himself overlook the impossibility of his father's attending Miss Selby's christening. He was . . . bewitched. There was no other word for it, even though the unreason behind the sentiment was something he'd expect from his father or Gilbert or the madwoman who told fortunes at the Crown and Lion. He held himself to a higher standard, but he had let himself be brought to the edge of madness—for what was it but madness to overlook facts that ought to have been as plain as day? Enchanted by their friendship and intoxicated by an attraction that seemed to be mutual, he had managed not to notice that the person in question was not what he seemed to be.

He found that he didn't care terribly much whether Robin was a man or a woman. That was quite secondary, compared to the fact that Robin was a fraud and a cheat.

Surely the fact that he didn't care spoke badly of his faculties. There were men who preferred other men, and kept damned quiet about it, and there were men who preferred women. To not take a stand one way or the other seemed wanton. Greedy. Not at all like the sober, measured gentleman Alistair wanted to be.

He kicked the gravel again, only to realize that this would likely cast the undergardeners into frenzies of confusion. In preparation for the damned ball, they had raked the gravel so evenly that the tiny stones looked like butter neatly spread on scones.

Kneeling, he tried to smooth the surface. But he didn't have the knack of the thing. No matter what he did, he kept exposing patches of soil, bald and forlorn. A gentleman's hands were not meant for setting such earthy things right.

"No need for that, my lord," said a voice behind him. It was the gardener.

Alistair was mortified to have been caught, although he wasn't sure what his infraction was. Kicking the gravel in the first place, demeaning himself by attempting to remedy the situation, or having made such a poor job of it?

"Ah, yes," he said, as if he had behaved quite normally, in a manner befitting a marquess. "Thank you, Grimes."

In a manner befitting a marquess. Yes, that's what he'd hang on to, that's how he would get through the painful atrocity that would be this ball. He was a bloody marquess. If he held a ball, it would be, by definition, everything that a ball ought to be. He would cling to the dignity of his station, to his birthright.

A marquess, as long as he behaved like one, could not be diminished by any grasping charlatans or shameless frauds. Or penniless foundlings driven to extremes to help their friends—

He would not let his mind travel down that path. No more would he indulge in this sort of sentimental flight of fancy. He would not tarnish his standing out of misguided sympathy for the criminal classes.

Alistair brushed the dirt off his gloves and went back inside.

Charity had retreated to the tiny, musty study at the rear of their rented house, the room where Louisa wrote letters to the Fenshawe steward and Keating hid from the rest of the staff. For days now, Charity had avoided the drawing room. She couldn't bear to face anyone. Leaving the house and risking running into Lord Pembroke was entirely out of the question. Aunt Agatha, grumbling but compliant, had risen to the occasion and accompanied Louisa to the park and on afternoon calls.

The door creaked noisily open, revealing Lord Gilbert standing on the threshold. Some confused servant must have sent him back here, to what had to be the shabbiest room he had ever graced with his aristocratic presence.

"This is dashed awkward, but can I ask you a favor, Selby?"

"Of course," she managed, attempting what she hoped might pass as a smile. "Anything."

"It's my brother. He's a . . . well, you know." He fidgeted uncomfortably on the hard chair. "I hardly need tell you. On the best of days he's a bit hard to take. All grimaces and lectures, you know."

She did know. Only a few days ago she had found it charming, possibly because it was so plainly a front, and who better than she to know a front when she saw one? The real Lord Pembroke wanted to read lurid novels and cuddle on the sofa. All this lord-of-the-manor business was because he was embarrassed by his father's excesses and anxious about providing for those who would have been cut off without a groat if he hadn't stepped in to shore up the estate's finances. And one of those beneficiaries was none other than Lord Gilbert, who surely ought to know better than to complain about the brother who kept him in shiny boots and ample brandy.

"He has high standards," she said, knowing full well that the cause of their rift was the fact that she did not meet those standards and never could.

"Of course," Gilbert said quickly, his handsome face contrite. "But I don't reckon he needs to be quite so insufferable about them. This morning he threatened to stop my allowance if I don't take holy orders and move to Kent."

Charity privately thought that nobody ought to be a clergyman if they didn't feel called to it, but at the same time considered Gilbert a total ingrate. If he couldn't put his mind to making himself *feel* called, surely he could figure out some way to earn a living without his brother's money. "And what can I do to help?" she asked, not sure where she came into this.

"Well, like I said, it's an awkward business." He gazed around the room, as if his surroundings would offer some clue as to what to say, some path through whatever doubtlessly minor awkwardness was troubling him.

Charity knew the exact moment he noticed the peeling plaster, or maybe it was the faded draperies or threadbare carpets, because he snapped his gaze back to her. He was embarrassed to be here—he was embarrassed to have noticed what kind of place this was. He only tolerated the drawing room because Louisa was in it, a sufficient ornament to compensate for acres of worn upholstery.

"Whatever falling-out you've had," Gilbert continued, his cheeks reddening, "do you think you could see your way to patching it up?"

"I'm afraid I don't—"

"I don't blame you for it," he said, the words coming out in a rush. "He's so prickly, it's a wonder we all don't quarrel with him. But he was so much . . . happier, I suppose, when you were around. If he wants to cut off my allowance, that's fine. I'll manage. But I don't think he'd want to do that unless he was miserable. Do you see?"

Charity did see. And she agreed—that did sound like the action of an unhappy man. But knowing that Pembroke was miserable, and that it was her fault, only poured salt on her wound.

And what did it matter that she *enjoyed* this sham, this fraud? So what if by now she felt more at home as Robert Selby—*Robin*, she thought with a pang—than she did as Charity Church? Miss Church was a poor creature, a housemaid, with no family and no future, no possessions beyond the drab gray dress she wore to clean the floors of a house she was allowed to live in only on sufferance. Robin Selby, though, was free. Robin danced and laughed, was at ease with lords and ladies, and was able to take care of the people he loved.

But in a few months, a year at the utmost, there'd be no reason for her to keep up this charade. Once Louisa was married, Charity would have to give up this life.

Sooner, if Pembroke chose to expose her. The possibility of exposure had always seemed vague, contingent. But now she felt like a prisoner listening to the beams of a scaffold being hammered into place outside her cell. Her one hope was that exposing her deceit would create precisely the sort of scandal that Pembroke would want to avoid.

Lord Gilbert coughed, forcing her thoughts back to the present. "Do you think you could just make it up with him? He'll never apologize for whatever it is he did to keep you away, so perhaps you could take the matter in hand?"

But he *had* apologized to her. Twice. First for criticizing Aunt Agatha, then for commenting on her thinness. What must it have cost him to so uncharacteristically swallow his pride? And how must that memory compound his outrage, to know he had lowered himself to begging pardon of the very person who had duped him?

"I'm afraid I'm the one who owes the apology," she admitted.

Lord Gilbert laughed, a startled and embarrassed sound. "Oh, I doubt that. You're so agreeable, you and your sister. I can't imagine either of you provoking a quarrel. But it's kind of you to take the blame. Do you think you could pay a call on him this afternoon? Just to show him that you mean to go on as you have?"

She tried to imagine showing up at Pembroke House and acting as if the events of the other day had never happened. He'd have her committed to a lunatic asylum.

She felt the blood drain from her face when she realized that this was an actual possibility. A man with his connections might very well cause a woman of her crimes to be sent to Bedlam or worse. And then what would become of Louisa?

No. She would simply have to depend on his distaste for any kind of scandal, and refuse to consider whether there were methods a peer of the realm might employ to dispose of her quietly and without any notoriety attaching to his name.

"Are you quite all right, Selby?" Lord Gilbert had come to kneel by Charity's side. "You looked like you were about to faint."

He was a kind man. Harmless, despite being aimless and spoiled. She couldn't even bring herself to resent his unearned good fortune or the part he might play in this unfolding disaster.

"I'm coming down with something, I dare say," she lied.

"Oh, no. You're not going to get sick." He rose to his feet. "If you don't show up at my brother's ball tomorrow, I'll come here and fetch you myself, even if you have typhus. There are too many people who are counting on you and your sister to be there—"

"We'll be there," she said. She wanted to lock herself away in this cheerless room, but that would do no one any good. They would have to go to the ball. There was no way around it. It was either that or they might as well give up London entirely. A few more weeks and one of the gentlemen who had been infesting the drawing room would offer for Louisa. Pembroke's ball was exactly what they needed to bring this sham to a close. Each suitor would realize how very in demand Louisa was, and would hurry to win her hand before any of his competitors.

A fortnight at the utmost, another month before a wedding could take place. During that time she would count on Pembroke not wanting a scandal.

And then she would disappear, as if by a conjurer's trick.

Revenge was beneath the Marquess of Pembroke. Revenge was best left to cuckolded farmhands and medieval popes, jealous fishwives and mad Plantaganets. Gentlemen who wore perfectly tied cravats and whose account books were testaments to rectitude had no need for anything so base as revenge. For such gentlemen, the mere knowledge of their superiority, their ability to outrank and outclass everyone around them, ought to afford sufficient comfort.

So why was it that Alistair spun himself yarn after yarn of how he would bring The Impostor low? He had one very sustaining fantasy of having that fraudulent creature tossed onto a ship and sent to the icy reaches of Canada, where there would be nobody to swindle or beguile but great white bears and bloodthirsty French trappers. It was cold there, and dark. Wintry and barren and silent.

A sun-kissed face and an infectious laugh would be quite wasted. Useless, in fact. Charm couldn't protect one from frostbite. There, The Impostor would be quite as cold and alone as Alistair felt now, as Alistair had felt two months ago.

Robin. The coming of spring, he had once said.

Alistair wished he were the sort of man to smash glasses,

to throw crockery at the wall, to swear at servants. Perhaps those men had the right of it—one explosion of anger followed by an embarrassed return to normality.

No, Alistair did not wish that. He was levelheaded, he was both rational and reasonable. He neither threw nor swore.

He fantasized about sending people to Canada. No trace of madness there.

"Fuck!" he attempted. Nothing. His anger and sorrow had not dissipated. "Damn!" he tried, vaguely embarrassed to raise his voice in an empty room. Still no use.

"Alistair?" came a hesitant voice from the doorway. The longer he spent in this library, the more timidly people addressed him.

Mortified, he slowly pivoted around. It was Gilbert.

"Everything all right here?" his brother asked, quite unnecessarily. There were babies in their prams, minnows in the brook, stars shining upon distant planets who could look at the Marquess of Pembroke and tell that things were far from right.

"I was conducting an experiment," Alistair said, likely compounding the inanity of the scene, but he was speaking the truth and that had to count for something. "I wanted to see if swearing made me feel better."

"Did it?" Gilbert looked genuinely curious.

Alistair tried to look like a detached, impartial man of science. "It did not."

"Ah. Doesn't work for me either. Worked a charm for Father, though."

Alistair had forgotten that. It was a dark day indeed when Alistair found himself emulating his father.

He remembered what had transpired the last time he had seen his brother. "Did you consider my proposal?" It was high time Gilbert established himself at that rectory, settled down, and lived responsibly. Alistair needed to see Gilbert safe, provided for, with some direction to his life.

"That's why I came. I'll always be grateful that you offered it to me, but I have to decline. I'm sure there are many worthy fellows who'll be happy to have such a good living. Give it to one of them. But not me."

Idiot. *Idiot.*

Alistair sighed and sank into the chair by the fire. It was warm for April, but the fire was blazing. Likely the house-maids lacked the temerity to question his cranky lordship about whether he still required a fire. Gilbert poured them both glasses of brandy and pressed one into his hand, a kindness Alistair knew he did not deserve.

He tried to school his voice into some semblance of calm, as if it meant nothing to him to cast his brother adrift. "I don't dare hope that you have some reasonable, alternative plan for your future," he said after a sip of brandy. It was not a question, merely an observation. He had given up trying to figure out the man.

"Well, actually . . ." Gilbert began.

Alistair hastily drained his glass. Had any sensible observation commenced with "Well, actually"? If so, Alistair had never heard it.

"I was thinking of trying my hand at farming."

"Oh my God," Alistair said. This again. The younger son of a marquess becoming a farmer. The mind reeled. Of course there were some gentlemen who made a hobby of improving the farms connected with their estates, and were forever writing letters to publications that one could evidently subscribe to if one wished to pursue that particular mania. But these were great landholders, operating on a scale that Gilbert could not aspire to. Alistair feared Gilbert had in mind a mule and a plow, a straw hat and a watercolored rustic idyll.

"I shan't ask you for anything," Gilbert said, a mite too stiffly. "I'll do this on my own."

And when he inevitably failed, Alistair would bail him out. They both knew it, but it wouldn't do to say it aloud. "I see." Alistair tipped his head against the back of the chair and studied the motes of dust that were caught in the lamplight. "I wish you luck."

"What happened between you and Selby?" Gilbert asked.

"Excuse me?" Alistair straightened so abruptly he nearly injured his neck. "I have no notion of what you mean. What have you heard?" Only after he saw the stunned expression on his brother's face did he realize that those last words were only heard from the mouths of guilty men.

"It's only that I noticed that he hasn't been here or at the club, and when I called on him this afternoon—"

"You went there?" Alistair could feel his cheeks heat and took a deep breath, trying to calm himself.

"I often do," Gilbert replied evenly. "Anyway, he hasn't even been in his own drawing room these past few days, so I nosed around the house until that strange butler of theirs brought me to him. I asked him if the two of you had a falling-out—"

"You *what?*" Alistair roared.

"I was concerned." Gilbert seemed not to notice that his brother was practically foaming at the mouth. "I know how awful you are about admitting when you're in the wrong, and thought to tell him so. That way he didn't think it was personal. But he said that he was the one in the wrong, and—"

Alistair laughed, dry and joyless. "Oh he did, did he? How noble. How very generous-minded of him."

Gilbert was now regarding him in plain astonishment. The fellow could never make his face do anything other than advertise his thoughts. "What on earth happened?"

"I'm not at liberty to—"

"Please don't hide behind moral superiority." This was the first hint of frustration with his older brother's foul mood that Gilbert had betrayed today. "If you know anything about the Selbys—Miss Selby in particular—that you believe renders them unfit for our friendship, you'd do best to tell me."

Alistair curled his lip. "Why, are you going to call me out?"

"Alistair, just listen to yourself! I'm asking because I intend to marry Louisa Selby and if there's some reason I shouldn't, you ought to tell me."

"And you'd listen to me for once? I doubt it. But have it your way. I can think of nobody less suitable to be your wife than Miss Selby. Marry whom you please." Hell, if he were to be a farmer he could sink as low as he liked. "But not Miss

Selby. Anyone else. I couldn't bear it." Those last words he hadn't meant to speak out loud. But they were the truth—he didn't know how he could endure a constant reminder of The Impostor. Of his own loss.

"Ah," Gilbert said after a long moment. "I see."

Alistair truly hoped that he did not.

CHAPTER EIGHT

Miss Church—Mr. Selby—Alistair had quite given up on the matter—danced every dance, fetched drinks for spinsters and wallflowers, and in general charmed and delighted a ballroom filled with jaded and cynical members of the ton.

A week ago, Alistair would have been proud, would have considered it a feather in his cap to have discovered such a fellow. Not only that, but he would have shared in his friend's triumph.

Now he only marveled at the layers of deceit involved in this performance. It was absolutely impossible to look at Miss Church and see a woman. From the way she walked, to her manner of speaking, to the gallant way she brought ratafia to the ladies, she was every inch the fashionable young gentleman.

In the natural course of things, somebody ought to be fetching *her* ratafia, oughtn't they? He tried to envision The Impostor wearing a white muslin gown and graciously receiving a proffered beverage, but the image proved quite elusive.

One who had made a less thorough study of her over the last month would have thought that tonight she was the happiest of God's creatures. Her smile never slipped, her laugh—perhaps a trifle flatter than the champagne pop that had won his idiotic heart—still cut through the hum of music and chatter. And yet he knew from Gilbert's report that she was not happy. She was quite possibly as distressed as he was, and indeed she had more reason for sorrow: they both knew perfectly well that he had the whip hand. The one time she had let her gaze stray to her host, he saw a flicker of fear on her open countenance. And rightly so. He could ruin her and her sister without even going out of his way, without using up a fraction of his power and esteem.

He surveyed the ballroom, glittering evidence of that power and esteem. A royal duke danced with a Russian princess. The prime minister stood by the door to the card room. Thousands of beeswax candles burned in highly polished chandeliers and sconces, their light sparkling off the jewels that the country's most important families had retrieved from their vaults for the sole purpose of wearing tonight. This was, as he had known before even sending the invitations, the event of the season.

The longer he watched, the more his eyes dazzled, the dancers dissolving into sparks of light—a ruby necklace gleamed here, a beaded gown there. And in the middle of the glittering whirl, no matter where he looked, was Charity Church. His eyes couldn't stop resting on that one person out of all the hundreds, his gaze snagging every time on that one crooked smile, that one bird's nest of hair.

Even the reason she was present in this room tonight was rooted in a lie. She had begged a favor from him on false pretenses, although that lie now seemed almost comically insignificant in comparison to having masqueraded as a dead man and stolen another man's inheritance. Falsifying a godparent seemed quaintly naughty as opposed to feloniously corrupt.

But, no, that wasn't the real reason she was here tonight, was it? Alistair was too accustomed to honesty to ignore the fact that he had invited the Selbys for his own purposes. He had intended to make them into a cautionary tale about what happened to those who pester the Marquess of Pembroke for favors. He meant to use Louisa Selby's beauty to crush Mrs. Allenby's plans for her daughter and to annoy his aunt.

That was all before he and Robin had become friends, though. Had that friendship been a lie? Had he been deceived about that as well?

"She's quite lovely." Furnival had appeared at his shoulder.

"Who is?" Alistair asked.

"Miss Selby, of course." Furnival laughed.

And so she was. Objectively, Alistair knew this, although the sight of her brought him no joy. Her gown was—well, her blasted gown was in annoying proximity to The Impostor, so he hadn't quite gotten a look at it. "She's a fine-looking girl," he said.

"A dozen men would see your 'fine-looking girl' and raise the stakes with gold rings and wedding vows."

He didn't doubt it. As long as Gilbert wasn't the bridegroom, he'd be glad to see Miss Selby wed and far the hell away from him. Were any of the contestants American? Canadian, perhaps? "I'll wish her happy," he said.

"That's not what I heard." Furnival's voice was a childish singsong.

What on earth had the man heard? Had Gilbert confessed his intentions to this fellow? Alistair brought his voice to its chilliest and most aristocratic register. "Whatever you've heard, I assure you I wish the lady no ill will."

"I didn't think you did." Furnival had his head cocked to the side, like a dog not quite understanding his master's command.

He suddenly had an idea. "What do you know about them? You went to Cambridge with Selby, didn't you?"

"Selby? He's always been exactly as he is now. You'd think that coming from the middle of nowhere he'd have been bashful or awkward, at least at first, but he wasn't. He seemed so dashed happy to be there, as if he had waited his whole life to sit in a freezing lecture hall and then sneak out of lodgings to have a pint at the pub. You never regretted running into him, if you know what I mean."

Alistair most certainly did, more's the pity. "He didn't succumb to the usual undergraduate vices—gambling and women?"

Furnival made a dismissive noise. "He didn't have enough money for any of that. And I don't know why, but I had the sense that he had a sweetheart waiting for him back home."

Ah. That was a notion Alistair had not thought of, but it added quite a dimension to the picture he was putting together in his mind.

"I have to . . ." He gestured vaguely around the room, hoping that Furnival would infer that Alistair had to attend to a host's duties.

He watched Miss Church lead Miss Allenby off the dance floor. Really, it was a sad indication of his mindset that he could summon up only the merest whisper of disapproval at seeing that Allenby girl, the spit and image of their late father, present at Pembroke House. He was even able to acknowledge that she looked quite suitably pretty.

But then all the glittering, dazzling movement in the ballroom seemed to slide to a stop as he caught The Impostor using her teeth to pull off a glove, finger by finger. It was the sort of thing one didn't do in a ballroom, remove gloves with one's teeth. No, it was something boys did when well out of sight of governesses and tutors. Captivated by the graceful, boyish—yes, boyish, there was no way around it, however disorienting he found it—charm of the action, he reached for his spectacles to get a better look. She began with the other glove, starting with the thumb.

By the time she reached her littlest finger he was in a dangerous state of arousal.

That would not do. Not at all.

She was passing through the wide French doors to the garden, so that was where Alistair went too.

It was ideal weather for a ball. Not so cold as to discourage forays into the garden, but chilly enough that a lady in gossamer fine silk might have to nestle close to a gentleman for warmth. But Charity Church was not wearing a gauzy confection. She wore an indifferently tailored coat and a waistcoat of silvery blue. Her pantaloons were snug to the point of indiscretion, to the point that his gaze skimmed along them, trying to divine a clue as to what lay beneath.

Which really was not something the Marquess of Pembroke ought to do at a ball, examine the contents of his guests' pantaloons. No matter how snug.

She turned to face him, her pointy little chin held high. "Why did you follow me out here?"

"Perhaps I wish to see my own gardens." Perhaps he wanted to prove to himself that he was capable of acting like a gentleman, regardless of his anger, or his desire, or any bizarre combination of the two.

Or perhaps he was simply running mad.

"I doubt you could identify a single plant," she retorted. "It's beneath you."

He raised an eyebrow. "Indeed, my horticultural ignorance does seem to be the most remarkable aspect of this little tableau." He let his gaze rake up and down her body. When he reached her face, he could tell even in the moonlight that she had blushed.

"If you're going to expose me, I wish you'd get it over with." She dragged one ungloved hand through her hair, disheveling it even further. "I've spent the entire evening wondering if you'd do something horrid."

He had wondered much the same thing, but had concluded that the Marquess of Pembroke behaved impeccably to his guests, even the most disgraceful among them. But he didn't feel like relinquishing the upper hand quite yet. "If I'm going to *expose* you, Miss Church, I'll damned well take my time."

Her blush became even darker, until the freckles and flushed skin blended together. When had he developed an aptitude for double entendre? That seemed more in his father's line. Perhaps it was in the blood. He took a step closer, wondering what other interesting propensities might be in the blood.

She took a step back and he heard her dancing shoe crunch along the gravel that the gardeners had so painstakingly smoothed.

Was she afraid? Did she think he would strike her? Abuse her in some other way? God almighty. "I'm not going to assault you, for heaven's sake."

"I know that, Pembroke," she snapped. "I mean to go further into the shrubbery, so that way if you call me by name again we won't be overheard."

They retreated further into the garden, through masses of plants he most certainly could not name, until they were far enough from the ballroom that the music drifted unevenly on the breeze, sounding as if it came from underwater. She turned and faced him, her jaw firm and her eyes sparkling. She was brave, he'd give her that. What an undertaking this was, after all.

He remembered the shadow of fear that had crossed her face when they saw one another across the ballroom. She had given him the power to ruin her. She hadn't needed to tell him about her masquerade or the full extent of her fraud. She had, in fact, done so only to assure him that he was safe from being accused of having sodomitical inclinations. She could have let him worry about that, but she hadn't. It was only right and proper for him to offer her the same service.

"I'm not going to expose you or your sister, or do anything to harm you." He spoke so gravely that it felt like an oath.

Her eyes went wide. "Why not?"

"Revenge, like horticulture, is beneath me."

She laughed, a small and startled sound, a mere echo of the champagne pop but close enough to make Alistair smile helplessly in return. Even when she clapped a hand over her mouth, evidently deciding that this was not a laughing matter, he still smiled. God above, he had missed her. He had missed *this*.

He was a bloody fool.

"Miss Church," he started.

"Nobody's ever called me that," she said. "The Selbys all called me Charity—I was their housemaid. Then at Cambridge . . ." She fixed him squarely in the eye, as if daring him to take issue with her frankness. "I was Selby. I've literally never heard myself called Miss Church. It's quite unnerving."

Alistair remembered the first time he had been called by his title. That had been mortifying, considering the many ways the last holder of that title rendered it a byword for licentiousness and profligacy. But "Miss Church" had no such connotations. It was a blank slate. She ought to be grateful. Then, as he regarded the dashing figure before him, he understood what she was saying. "You do not wish me to call you Miss Church."

She crossed and uncrossed her arms, as if she didn't know what to do with her limbs. "I . . . I don't know that what I wish is material in this situation."

Did she think that now was the time for deference? "A month ago I demanded that you stop calling me 'my lord' and you complied."

The silence stretched out between them. "But I have no other name for you to call me by," she finally whispered.

He took a step closer. "Robin," he said softly. He was close enough now to catch the scent of lemon drops and greenery that always seemed to mark the air around her.

"Don't," she said, shaking her head.

He stopped. "Don't do what?" he asked. He certainly had no idea what he was planning to do, so it would be helpful if she at least told him what he could not do.

"Don't call me that unless you mean to be my friend."

Friend. "Robin." He heard her sharp intake of breath. "I've tried, but I don't think I can stop being your friend."

She couldn't tell if he was teasing her, toying with her. Perhaps calling her his friend was part of his revenge.

He didn't look vengeful, though. He looked like his usual haughty, disdainful self, sizing her up like she was a horse he didn't think stood a good chance of winning at Newmarket.

"Why are you looking at me like that?" she asked.

He lifted his gaze to meet hers and raised a single eyebrow by way of answer. That eyebrow did all kinds of things to her that eyebrows weren't supposed to do.

She felt her cheeks heat. "Are you looking for signs of . . . femaleness beneath my clothes?" She wanted to fold her arms over her chest but decided to brazen it out.

His smile was slow and sinister and maybe a little wondering. "I think we both know that I don't give a damn what you have beneath your clothes. Would that I did." He paused, as if letting that sink in. "I am merely admiring how the blue of that waistcoat matches your eyes."

"But my eyes are gray," she said.

"Not when you're wearing that waistcoat, they aren't."

His gaze was even more unnerving now that he was looking at her eyes. "I'm sorry about having let you believe that I'm something I'm not. I feel dishonest and I wish—"

"Pardon my ignorance, but I would imagine that you're well practiced in feeling dishonest."

So he was not to let her off easy. "About the estate, of course I do," she said, not wanting to mince words. "But not the clothing. I've been dressing this way for so long that it feels right. It always has, really." She looked at him expectantly, hoping to read some sign of understanding on his face, and seeing only confusion. But he nodded, at least showing her that he accepted her answer, even if he didn't understand. Hell, she wasn't sure she understood either.

"Well," she continued, "there was one time I felt dishonest about . . ." She made a sweeping gesture that could have indicated either her clothes or her body, whichever he chose to believe. "That night in your library." She forced herself to look him in the eye when she said it, expecting to see distaste or anger. Instead she saw his eyes darken ever so slightly.

"As I said, I don't give a damn about . . ." He made the same gesture, sweeping his hand vaguely through the air between them, and she imagined that she could feel his touch on her skin. "Never have." He shrugged. "I don't like being deceived, though." There was something uncertain, slightly hesitant, in the tone of his voice that told her it was a request, not a chastisement. "But I don't suppose anyone does."

"I am sorry I lied about your father being Louisa's godfather." But that wasn't what he needed to hear, what she needed to say to make things right. "I won't deceive you again."

"Somehow I doubt that you're an open book, Robin." His name for her sounded like a caress, like a reproach, like a promise.

"That's not the same thing," she protested, but he had closed the gap between them and grasped her hands in his own.

She had to tilt her head back to meet his eyes now, because the top of her head only reached his nose and that was when she was standing ramrod straight.

"Robin," he said, and she couldn't tell if it meant *I missed you* or *Why are you putting me through this?* Or maybe it meant something else entirely. One of his hands let go of her own and came to rest on the back of her head, gently cradling it.

She closed her eyes as his lips skimmed over hers. His other hand settled on her hip. There was no pressure in any of it—both of his hands rested lightly against her, his lips barely touching hers. It was the ghost of a kiss, not nearly enough. She didn't know whether it was because he was being respectful or simply ambivalent.

Wrapping her arms around his neck, she deepened the kiss. Maybe she was too eager, maybe she was too bold. She was, as he had pointed out, no stranger to deception, but it was beyond her powers to pretend that she didn't want this man.

His shoulders felt strong and broad under her touch, and she could feel his muscles shifting when he tightened his grip on her, drawing her closer against him, fitting their bodies together. When his tongue stroked her lower lip, she couldn't help but smile.

"Is there something amusing I ought to know about?" He was doing that haughty aristocratic thing with his voice again, but she could tell he wasn't serious because he was smiling too.

"Pembroke—"

"Absolutely not." He kissed the corner of her still-smiling lips. "The time for that has come and gone. It's Alistair, or you can gracefully sidestep the name issue."

"Alistair," she breathed. "Get back to kissing me."

And so he did. One of his hands stole inside her coat and waistcoat and she could feel it, hot like a brand against her lower back, separated from her skin by only the thin linen of her shirt.

She kissed his jaw. Really, she could spend all night appreciating the way that coarse stubble rasped against her lips. Every inch of him was so impeccable, polished and refined and perfectly coiffed, but then there was that stubble, hinting at vast wells of ungentlemanliness. She nipped at the soft skin of his neck and he muttered an oath, his hands clamping down on her hips like a vise.

This was probably another level of deviance to add to her ever-mounting list, but she wished she could see them. She wanted to see him in his perfect evening clothes and barely rumpled hair, his strong arms wrapped around her own similarly but less elegantly attired body. What she would have given for a looking glass.

She wanted more of him. She needed more. She leaned

into him, trying to press her body against his, chasing the sensation she was craving. He groaned at the contact, and she felt the proof of his desire hard against her belly.

Good. She liked that, knowing that he was as far gone as she was. If she dropped to her knees and worked open the front of his breeches, he wouldn't stop her. But she wouldn't do that to him, wouldn't ask him to take his desire off its short leash. Not in the garden at his own ball, at least.

She eased back, letting some cool night air slip between them. She lightened her kisses until they were merely what was strictly necessary to maintain contact between her lips and his body.

And then she finally took her lips away too, and dared to look at his face. Would he look scandalized? Regretful? She promised herself that she wouldn't care what she saw there.

He looked slightly dazed, as if he had been spun around a few too many times in a game of blind man's bluff. She waited for him to say something. "I . . ." he started, and shook his head. Still looking faintly distracted, he took her hand and pressed it into the placket of his breeches. The gesture was so coarse, the very last thing she would have expected from him. "I've never been this hard in my life, not without actually, you know."

You know? She was delighted by this coyness. "I *do* know," she said, gripping him through the fabric and feeling his erection leap in approval. "But we'll leave that for another time." She patted it consolingly.

The sound he made was practically a growl, and she thought her face would split in two if she smiled any more broadly.

A few bars of music drifted in from the ballroom. "You ought to go back. Somebody will notice that you're gone," she suggested, wanting to give him an easy excuse. They couldn't stay out here all night.

"Not so fast," he murmured. "This is a waltz. Nobody in their right mind would expect me to waltz when I've avoided all the other dances."

She would never understand why he didn't dance. "I love to waltz. Louisa and I practiced it for hours."

He took her hand and drew her back toward him. "Dance with me," he whispered in her ear, resting his other hand on her waist as he steered her into a slow circle.

It didn't feel even remotely right, and she realized that it was because she was used to dancing the gentleman's part. But she tried anyway, with the result being that they trod on one another's toes and bumped gracelessly and repeatedly into one another.

"This isn't working," she said, frustrated. Their bodies had fit together so seamlessly when they had kissed, but now it was a shambles. "I don't know how to dance the lady's part."

"Neither do I, I'm afraid."

As if he'd ever offer to dance the lady's part. She made a dismissive sound and shook her head.

"Try it like this." He tugged her close again. They stood still, listening to the strains of a song they could barely hear, unable to work out the steps to a dance they shouldn't have been attempting in the first place.

She rose onto her toes and pressed a kiss to his cheek, before slipping away toward the ballroom.

CHAPTER NINE

When Charity was about ten, she went with the Selbys' cook to the market at Alnwick. The cook wanted to buy a special cheese to tempt old Mr. Selby's appetite, and she brought Charity so she wouldn't have to carry her own parcels or do her own sums.

Charity had never seen so many people in one place, or perhaps even cumulatively over the course of her short life. At Fenshawe there were a bare dozen people, even when the cook's niece came from the village to help with the laundry. The tiny village church near Fenshawe might hold fifty people, and that was on Easter Sunday. At the dimly remembered parsonage, where she had been brought as a baby and kept until the vicar died, there had been scarcely anybody at all. She remembered quiet, dust, and the vicar's patient lessons.

Alnwick had been a revelation. All those people, loud and purposeful and fast-moving. She had never even dreamt of such a thing. Coins flashed in the sun, exchanged for mustard and apples and sharp new needles. She had clung to the cook's apron, not out of fear of being lost, but so she wouldn't be tempted to run off and join the throng.

Looking back, she supposed there had been perhaps two hundred people present that day in the market square. But that was more people than Charity had conceived of existing in the entire world.

That was how Louisa's drawing room seemed on the day after Pembroke's ball. It was a magnificent crush. There were, according to Keating, carriages all the way down the street. The ladies wore gowns the value of which Charity would not allow herself to calculate, the gentlemen had a degree of polish that Charity could never attempt to emulate, and they all had the unmistakable lightness of people who had never worried about where their next meals would come from.

And they were all here for Louisa. Well, technically some of them left cards for Robert Selby, but they were here for Louisa and everybody knew it.

After Charity fled from the garden, Alistair upheld the promise he made last month and stood up with Louisa, while Charity watched the news of Lord Pembroke's dance with the beautiful Miss Selby ripple through the crowd.

They made a completely unobjectionable pair: his rank and wealth matching her grace and beauty, his dark good looks contrasting pleasantly with her golden loveliness. "A striking couple," the ladies murmured. "I dare say he's done for," the gentlemen jested.

Charity had never been so jealous of another human being as she was that moment of Louisa. And she hated herself for it—to be jealous of Louisa was like being jealous of a field of daffodils. It simply made no logical sense. All the same, she felt almost sick at the sight of how they danced perfectly together—it was a minuet, nothing so intimate as a waltz, but still it happened, which was more than she could say of her own attempted dance with him.

But at the same time, this was her own triumph. These whispers of curiosity, these sighs of admiration, they were all signs that their gamble hadn't been for nothing. Louisa would be safe, protected, provided for. They had done it.

Almost.

First they had to entertain a swarm of ladies and gentlemen, a Northumberland village's worth of people contained in one tatty drawing room. She caught Lord Gilbert's eye and gave him an apologetic wave. It would be impossible for her to make her way through the crowd to talk to him.

She loved it. She adored the hum of well-bred chatter, the lively banter, the press of people around her. Louisa sat prettily on the sofa, pouring tea—Keating was going to wear himself out carrying up all the hot water this gathering would require—and acting only vaguely surprised by the attention. Perfect.

Charity was tempted to rub her hands together and cackle in the manner of a villain in a play.

After that long-ago visit to the Alnwick market, she asked Robbie whether he had known that there were positively hundreds of people in Britain. She was helping him with all those verbs he could never seem to properly conjugate, and he had looked up at her with a curious tilt of his head.

The next day he taught her to ride so she could get herself a bit farther than the borders of Fenshawe. "We'll take a peek at the sheep-shearing over near Harbottle," he had said, as if it were a perfectly reasonable suggestion. Indeed, the house was in a state of perpetual disarray due to the master being so ill, so nobody noticed the absence of the heir, a housemaid, and a pair of horses.

They had been fast companions until the day he had sent her off to Cambridge. "I can't leave, not when Daisy's in foal. Besides, what's the use of your knowing all those Latin verbs if you're not going to university?" he had insisted, as if Charity were the one being annoyingly stubborn in suggesting that she instead stay at Fenshawe to sweep out the grates and beat the carpets.

It had been the market day at Alnwick that had sealed her fate, she now realized. She had gotten a glimpse of the world and of the people in it. They were everywhere, laughing and working, and she could never be happy again at sleepy, isolated Fenshawe, no matter how much she loved the Selbys.

And she *had* loved the Selbys. She had changed Louisa's nappies, she had spoon-fed old Mr. Selby his last meal. She would never run out of tears for Robbie.

Even if she hated every minute of this sham, she would have done it anyway if it meant Louisa would be taken care of. But she loved it. And by God, she was not going to feel guilty about the pleasure she was taking in this masquerade and all the freedom it afforded her.

"Have you seen my brother?" Against the odds, Lord Gilbert had managed to reach her side.

"No." She raised her voice to be heard over the din. "I didn't expect him, though."

"Really? After that dance, I'd have thought he would have nowhere else to be."

There was an edge to his voice, something faintly hostile and disapproving. It took Charity a mortified moment to realize that of course he was referring to Alistair's dance with Louisa, not his waltz with Charity.

"Oh, he would never allow himself to be one of a crowd," she said lightly. But, come to think of it, why *wasn't* he here? Not for Louisa, but for Charity herself? Surely he could have predicted what today would bring for Louisa and what it would mean for Charity. After the intimacy they had shared—she absolutely would *not* blush—did he not want to see her?

Evidently he did not, and the realization was enough to dampen her joy at today's success. He had likely woken up this morning and been overwhelmed with more kinds of shame than he even could identify.

Shame was a luxury of the rich, as far as Charity could tell. Everybody else had to worry about getting food in a way that didn't land them in a noose, but marquesses had time and pride to spare. She wondered what aspect of their connection he found most regrettable. Was it that she was a thief, a foundling, a former servant, a liar, or simply that she dressed as a man? Likely she was objectionable in ways she hadn't even thought of yet.

The knowledge of his shame shouldn't bother her. Shame wasn't contagious. His disapproval couldn't make her think less of herself. Charity had always known that she wasn't one of those blessed few who had the luxury of keeping their hands clean.

But she hated being the dirt that soiled the Marquess of Pembroke.

Alistair's ancestors were not renowned for their exploits on the battlefield or in Parliament. The fact that there were still de Laceys owed more to their talent in avoiding beheadings than it did to any greatness. While other noblemen were killing one another for power and proximity to the throne, the de Laceys were eloping, seducing, and scandalizing. Alistair's grandfather and great-grandfather had had the knack of keeping their heads down and their breeches fastened, but they were the black sheep of the family; theirs were the lone portraits in the gallery at Broughton that didn't exude a palpable air of dissipation.

Considering this mainly unbroken lineage of womanizers and inebriates, it was especially galling that Alistair could not, for the life of him, figure out what to do about Robin.

That was not quite true. He had many ideas of what he'd like to do with Robin, but not a single notion of how to bring those dreams to fruition without compromising everything he believed in.

He did not want a mistress. He did not want to make a Mrs. Allenby out of his Robin. The very idea revolted him enough to nearly kill his desire, and the thought of siring a bastard on her made his blood run cold. On the other hand, the Marquess of Pembroke could not very well marry the likes of Charity Church. It was quite impossible. A housemaid turned impostor could never be the Marchioness of Pembroke. God forgive him for even formulating the thought.

So he quite gave up on trying to find a solution, and

instead determined to calmly explain to Robin that anything between them was utterly impossible. They could—must—be friends, but not the sort of friends who dance in the garden and grope one another. She was charming, she was lovely, and they would never touch one another again.

As simple as that. When all else failed, he could still rely on his aptitude for self-denial.

But first he had to find her. He considered paying a visit to her at home, but Gilbert had complained that the Selbys' house was a veritable anthill of would-be suitors. He caught a glimpse of her riding in the park—not on his horse, he realized with a stab of irritation—but it was too crowded to do more than salute her from a distance.

"Where the devil is Selby keeping himself?" he asked Gilbert one morning when the younger man had come for breakfast.

"He has his hands full with Miss Selby and Amelia," Gilbert responded in between bites of ham.

"Amelia?" Alistair repeated, his fork poised halfway to his mouth.

"Yes, our sister." Gilbert slammed his own fork back onto the table. "You've heard of her?"

"Don't be absurd. I only want to know what Selby has to do with it."

"The Selbys and Amelia are friends, and they go about together, as friends do," Gilbert explained, as if friendship were a concept that Alistair was too slow to comprehend.

It wasn't like Gilbert to be quite this testy, but Alistair didn't know how to broach the topic. He was glad that Gilbert was here at all, and didn't want to make a muddle of things the way he usually did with his brother.

"He'll be at Portia's salon tonight, if you really want to see him," Gilbert continued.

By Portia he meant Mrs. Allenby, of course. Alistair had never set foot in her house, and few people had the temerity to mention her salon in his hearing. It was hardly respectable, packed with would-be revolutionaries and badly dressed poets, from what he gathered. But Gilbert looked strained to the breaking point—perhaps he had discovered that farming required actual knowledge, as well as manure and other unsavoriness—and Alistair didn't want to irritate him any further. Their relationship was not as warm as it ought to be, he was realizing, and that was starting to feel like a loss. Moreover, it was starting to feel like his own fault.

"Very well, then. I'll go to the salon. I'll pick you up in my carriage." Alistair took a long sip of tea. "What does one wear to one of Mrs. Allenby's salons? Is evening attire acceptable, or must I fashion a pair of sans-culottes?"

Gilbert made a derisive noise, but Alistair could see the beginnings of a smile cutting through the gloom, so he kept on going. "Does one bring one's own opium, or is there some sort of communal . . . I don't know, tureen?" Now Gilbert was openly smiling, albeit sardonically. "Do the orgies commence promptly at eight, or—"

"Stop, stop!" Gilbert laughed. He threw his napkin on the table and rose to his feet. "I'm leaving before you change your mind."

Victory. He had amused Gilbert out of his sullen mood, and

better still, he was going to see Robin. The prospect seemed to make the light shafting through the windows all the brighter.

They were drinking champagne while listening to a man in a velvet dinner coat read a poem about rats.

"I think the rats are a metaphor," Charity whispered.

"Something to do with the Corn Laws, I gather," Amelia mused.

Charity was about to disagree but nearly yelped when her friend elbowed her in the ribs.

"Over there," Amelia whispered. "Look. By the door."

At first she thought she had hallucinated. The room was hot, and even though she hadn't had much champagne, a drunken imagining seemed more likely than Alistair actually being present at Mrs. Allenby's salon.

"Oh God, just look at him," she breathed, and received another jab in the ribs from Amelia. But how could she *not* admire the man? He was wearing one of his most uncompromisingly tailored coats in unrelieved black. His waistcoat was also black, his cravat a masterpiece of simplicity. She couldn't see his breeches but knew they'd be perfectly fitted and spotless. He stood out like a beacon of gentlemanly correctness in this colorful gathering.

She wanted to run her hands over every inch of him. And then she wanted to do the same thing with her tongue.

God help her, but she was going to have to add a mania for subdued tailoring to her list of depravities.

"Stop staring," Amelia hissed.

Charity didn't stop. She didn't care who caught her staring. That was one of the nice things about this sort of gathering. These people prided themselves on their raggedy manners, which Charity privately thought rather silly, but she'd gladly take advantage of the freedom it gave her.

The freedom to stare at the Marquess of Pembroke like he was a roast dinner.

And he was staring back, but not at her. He was regarding the motley assemblage as if he were at the zoo. How long before he pulled out his spectacles? Ah, there he went now, reaching into his pocket, polishing the lenses on his handkerchief, and coolly placing them onto the bridge of his nose. Over a dozen times she had seen him perform that same series of gestures, every movement dripping with hauteur and breeding and privilege, and she could watch him do it a million more times.

"Stop it *now*." Amelia pinched Charity's leg. "Even if you don't care about your own character, have some care for his. He'd die if he knew he was being ogled by a man in public, and in this house of all places."

Quite true. Alistair lived and died by his bloody reputation, and everybody knew it. So instead of staring, she would go over there and have a perfectly gentlemanly conversation with the man.

Making her way across the room, she could tell the minute he noticed her. His mouth quirked into approximately one-sixteenth of a smile—you would need a protractor to be sure it had really happened—and his left eyebrow shot up as if to say, *What in God's name am I doing in this place?*

Charity could have asked him the same question, but she didn't care what he was doing here, only that he was here at all. She went over to where he stood, not noticing who she had to squeeze past to get there.

When she reached his side, he dipped his mouth close to her ear. "There's a man over there with a cat inside his coat."

She could feel his breath against her skin and didn't know how she was going to keep her composure. She kept her eyes focused on the poet at the front of the room, who had now lapsed into French. "They're only people," she whispered. "And clever ones, at that." The man with the cat was some kind of astronomer.

"At least you didn't bring your sister."

That made her whip her head around to face him. "Yes, but *your* sister is right over there." Really, she had had enough of his disdain for the Allenbys, especially after Amelia had shown such care for Alistair's precious reputation. If Charity were lucky enough to have a sister she would do anything to keep her close, and here Alistair had three sisters he had hardly met and a brother he scarcely seemed to know.

At first she thought he would take offense—hell, he was meant to—but he only set his mouth into a grim line for the merest instant.

"I'm insufferably arrogant." He brushed some imaginary dust from his sleeve. "Ask anyone."

She snorted. "Do you want me to introduce you to people?"

"God, no," he sniffed. "I'm not here for that."

"Are you here to mock and scoff, then?"

"No, you daft brat, I'm here because I was on the horns of a dilemma. If I want to see you I have to either come to this den of vice or experience whatever circle of hell your drawing room is these days. Gilbert complains that you're under siege by every bachelor in Mayfair."

He had come for her. He had brought himself to what had to be the last place in London he would choose to visit. And he had done it for her. She felt warmth spread through her body. "Why didn't you send me a note? I would have come to you at Pembroke House."

She felt his shoulder jostle against hers. "I know you would, Robin." His voice was a low rumble. "But I recalled the last time I sent for you, and didn't want you to think you had been summoned to the headmaster's office."

He hadn't wanted her to worry. "So instead you stayed away for days? I didn't know what to think." She shifted her stance, causing the back of her hand to stroke the side of his thigh. Oh, there were a thousand ways two gentlemen could touch one another in public without drawing suspicion, and Charity intended to explore every one of them before the night was through.

He caught her hand and squeezed it, keeping his eyes fixed on the poet. His grip around her fingers was strong, a warning, not a caress. She could feel his signet ring pressing into her skin, a reminder of who and what this man was.

"Do not toy with me, dear Robin." His voice was wonderfully sinister. "Or I will take you into one of those alcoves and do awful things to you."

He dropped her hand and she chanced a sidelong glance

at him. He didn't look like a man propositioning a lover, not even in jest. No, he had a frankly wondering expression, as if he had just now come to the not-so-welcome conclusion that he would indeed take her into the alcove despite all his best judgment.

"There are a good many alcoves here," she observed conversationally.

He sniffed. "This room appears to have been designed for couples to slip away discreetly. It probably was, come to think. I can imagine the lady of the house and my dear papa deep in consultation with the architect."

She would ignore that comment. "That passageway over there, for example," she said, gesturing with her chin to a narrow vestibule, "leads to the music room."

The sound he made came from deep in his chest, more a growl than anything else. "And what would you have me do in the music room, you wanton?"

"I haven't quite settled my mind on a course of action, sorry to say." She slid one of her feet over so her boot touched his. "I'm afraid I'm sadly indecisive. It's as if you brought me to your library and asked me to choose only one book. I'd be paralyzed by the variety. I'd want to read them all, you see, but there isn't time for that."

She glanced at him out of the corner of her eye and saw his own eyes widen. "Then I will make the decisions." His voice as cool and remote as it ever was, despite the fact that she could plainly see the throbbing pulse in his neck. "That reminds me," he added, with a degree of composure that only the Marquess of Pembroke could hope to attain, "if you're so overwrought by the library at my London house, you'd be brought to fits of insensibility by the library at Broughton Abbey."

"I'll take your word for it." There was no possibility she'd ever see his family's principal seat for herself. Whatever her faults, she wasn't delusional.

At that, he turned to face her, but she kept her eyes on the front of the room, where the cat-carrying astronomer was talking about his observations of one planet having passed in front of the other earlier that year.

"Do you follow this?" Alistair whispered after a moment.

"Yes," she said. "I went to Cambridge. I took a double first. Ask anyone." She saw his eyebrow lift as he realized she had echoed his own words. "Perhaps you found Oxford less rigorous?" she asked innocently.

"Oh, the devil take you." But his eyes were dancing.

"Mrs. Allenby is coming this way." She leaned close enough to breathe in the scent of his soap. "Either you be civil to her—you are a guest in her house, Alistair—or I'll step away so I'm not tainted by association with your rudeness."

"Tainted by—Oh, that's terribly rich coming from you, scapegrace."

But when Mrs. Allenby drifted over, he bowed very properly and asked after her health.

The lady looked from Alistair to Charity and back again. "Thank you for coming, Pembroke. Very kind of you."

Alistair opened his mouth to answer, but Charity cut him off. "You can't thank him for anything. He'll only start telling you that he doesn't mean to be kind, and before he's done you'll quite believe him."

"You have a sad lack of gravity," Alistair said after Mrs. Allenby had moved on.

"It's a failing," she said merrily. "But I get along."

He nudged her with his shoulder. "Robin, I came here tonight to tell you that I can't see my way to finishing what we started in the garden."

Just as she expected. She refused to let her heart sink.

"But," he continued, "I thought about what you told me that night you arrived dripping wet."

"I'm surprised you remember anything that happened that night, as soused as you were."

"I remember." His hand brushed idly against the small of her back. "You said that you put your worries to the side and enjoy yourself while you can. I want to do that. With you."

She needed to speak up before she became lulled by the feel of his hand on her. "I don't want to be something you have to force yourself not to be ashamed of."

"Robin." His voice was a murmur, a rumble, a thing she felt in her belly. "I don't feel ashamed when I'm with you."

He was as good as telling her that he'd regret it only after the fact. But his eyes were dark and intent, his body warm and solid next to her.

"Let's go," she said.

CHAPTER TEN

It didn't matter how tempting that music room sofa looked. Alistair wasn't going to defile Robin in the house his father had built for a mistress. He was respectable. He had standards.

No, he was going to defile Robin in his own goddamned bed, as if that made it right.

This plan of laying aside his principles long enough to enjoy himself, to enjoy Robin, seemed dubious at best. But he hadn't been lying when he said he didn't worry around her. He worried a hell of a lot about how this thing between them could result in anything but a disaster, but he did his worrying when she wasn't around. When he was in the same room as her, all he could think about was freckles and laughter and how much he wanted to get his hands all over her, have her hands all over him.

"Let's go." The whisper of her voice set his nerves on end.

"Out," he said from between gritted teeth, and made for the front door. He would have grabbed her by the arm and hauled her out if he didn't think it would cause a stir, and besides, she was following along quickly enough.

His carriage was waiting. Robin hopped in as soon as he opened the door, flashing him a smile over her shoulder. Christ, she *would* be happy at such a moment. Well, for that matter, so was he, but not a smiling sort of happy.

No, he was a doubt-ridden and vaguely nauseated kind of happy, which he hadn't realized until now was a possibility. His emotions usually landed on one side of the fence or the other: one side was relief, the other anxiety. What he'd give for a fraction of the rapture Robin felt listening to a lunatic poet or embarking on a misguided affair.

After he slammed the door behind him and rapped on the roof to signal to the coachman, he looked over to see her pulling off her gloves. His cock jumped, the predictable bastard. "Did nobody ever tell you not to use your teeth?"

"Of course they have," she said blithely. "Louisa tells me every day. I have all manner of terrible habits, you know."

He seized one of her hands in his and started to pull off the glove properly. "First of all, you do not know where those gloves have been—"

"Of course I do. They've been on my hands. My hands don't go capering about town without me. That's what wrists are for."

He had freed one of her hands and now held it firmly in his own, running his own gloved thumb over the wrist in question. "This is sophistry. I expect more from a Cambridge scholar." Even in the dark of the carriage, he thought he could see her eyes darken at his touch, at the caress of leather over the soft skin on the underside of her wrist. "Secondly," he continued, "you'll ruin your gloves if you keep biting them."

She opened her mouth as if to present him with a counterargument, but then shut it again. "I need my hand back," she said after a moment.

He let go immediately. Ah, yes, all right then. She was going to be the reasonable one. He ought to be relieved that at least one person in the carriage had some sense. Very well.

But then he felt her hand cup his jaw. "That's why I needed them off, you see. I wanted to feel this."

"Feel what?" His wits were slow tonight. He needed everything spelled out for him.

Her fingers stroked along his cheek. "The scratchiness."

Oh. "You probably need me to take off your other glove so you can properly appreciate both sides of my face." Her fingers were warm and soft and he wanted all ten of them to himself.

She shook her head slowly, then swiftly pulled the other glove off with her teeth. *Hell.* "Not enough time." That hand, once free, landed in his hair.

"Like hell there isn't. You're coming home with me, aren't you?" Wasn't she?

"Do you want me to?"

He hauled her onto his lap. Christ, but she was light. "Figure it out, scholar." He pulled her against him, letting her feel how hard he was, just from a bit of glove removal and stubble stroking.

"Do you want me to?" she asked again.

"Yes, for God's sake, come home with me." The carriage was slowing down. "Please."

"And what will we do when we get there?"

"I'll draw you a picture once we get inside."

She shook her head. "I need to hear you say it."

Ah. "Come to bed with me, Robin." And in case she needed him to be more direct, he added, "Let me touch you. As much or as little as you like."

"And do I get to touch you in return?" Her lips skimmed over his own.

"Please." His voice sounded hoarse, ragged. "Please."

Alistair had no recollection of what nonsense he told Hopkins. Something about how Mr. Selby was borrowing a book and the servants needn't wait up. And Robin, the little deceiver, was as cool as could be, asking after Hopkins's gouty leg.

At the top of the stairs, Alistair possessed himself of her elbow and marched her past the library to his own bedchamber. The room was dim, lit only by a low-burning fire. That wasn't enough, not by half. He wanted to see every inch of her. He lit a taper in the hearth, then used it to light the candles that were over the chimneypiece, near the bed—

He noticed movement out of the corner of his eye. Robin was untying her cravat.

"In a hurry?"

"Yes, frankly." She unwound the cravat, exposing her pale throat.

He set the taper down and sat on the edge of bed, not daring to go any closer. Besides, he wanted to watch how she disrobed. That way he'd know what to have her doing in his fantasies.

"Good." His mouth went dry.

She didn't step any closer, but turned so she was fully facing him. Her coat dropped silently to the carpeted floor. The only sound in the room was the crackling fire, Robin's fingers flicking open waistcoat buttons, and Alistair's own shallow breaths.

Alistair felt his control begin to slip when he watched her shrug nimbly out of her waistcoat. Her shirt was the usual thin linen, perhaps a trifle overlaundered, and through it he could see the outline of her silhouette. She was slim, the straight line of her braces scarcely interrupted by the slight curve of her breasts. He hadn't allowed himself to wonder what she did about her breasts to keep them hidden in her disguise, because he feared that once he let his imagination travel down that path he'd never be able to talk to her in public without becoming visibly aroused. But somewhere in the back of his mind he had supposed she wore something to bind or constrict herself.

But it was plain that she did not. He could see her nipples through the filmy fabric of her shirt. All this time, she had been walking around with her breasts simply *there*, framed by braces and scarcely covered by a waistcoat and coat? Riding in the park, lounging at the club, her breasts had been loose under a few scant layers of fabric? He dug his fingers into the edge of the mattress.

"Come here," he rasped.

She stepped between his legs, no trace of coyness about her, and thank God for that. Gingerly, she took off his spectacles, which he had forgotten he was wearing, and reached over to place them on the bedside table.

"Robin." He slid the braces off her shoulders and settled his hands at the nip of her waist. He felt the slide of her hands against his jaw. There was no accounting for tastes, and if she wanted to paw his stubble he wasn't going to dissuade her. Then her hands threaded through his hair and he closed his eyes, feeling her fingers caress the back of his neck, his shoulders, his arms. Her lips were on his, another mere dusting of a kiss.

But then she pulled away, leaving him searching pathetically for her mouth with his own. "I meant what I said." Her voice was firm, and with one hand she tipped his head back so he had to look her in the face. Her chin jutted out, like a boxer ready to take a punch. "If you have any regrets about this, or your better angels give you hell for enjoying yourself for once in your life, then I don't want to hear about it. You keep that to yourself."

He smiled, more at the fierceness of her tone than at her words. "All right." At the moment, he didn't care about anything but her, and that lightness was rare and fragile, precious and all too temporary. "I promise."

He needed to see her. He untucked her shirt and bent to plant a kiss on the smooth, warm skin he had just exposed. Sliding the hem of her shirt higher, he kissed his way up from her ribcage until he reached the underside of her breasts. She let out a breathy sigh, and took the shirt out of his hands, tugging it over her head.

Thank God he had lit the candles.

"You can't stare at me like that." She brushed one of her wayward strands of hair behind her ear.

"Like hell I can't." He'd stare all he pleased, and then he'd run his hands along her skin. Then his mouth. He'd take his time, get every drop of pleasure out of this night. "You're beautiful."

"You're missing your spectacles."

He skimmed his hands down her arms and felt her shiver in response. She was all hard angles, sharp lines. Bones and sinew covered in silky skin. "I see you perfectly well."

She snorted in response and he smiled at how unladylike—indeed, ungentlemanlike—the sound was.

She had no freckles below her chin. He cupped her breasts in his hands—truly, he had much more hand than she had breast, but that only meant he could possess all of her at once—and heard the hitch in her breath. He looked up at her face and saw that she had closed her eyes, but her jaw was set. Keeping his eyes on her face, he ran his thumbs over her taut nipples, and saw her eyes fly open.

"You like that." He did it again. And then again, until she moaned. Good. This knowledge was enough to work with. He leaned forward and drew one of her nipples into his mouth, sucking gently, then harder, then worrying the tip with his teeth and tongue. Her breathless sounds of pleasure and need went straight to his cock.

"I'm not feeling patient." Her voice was strained.

"What are you feeling, then?" he murmured, before bringing his mouth to her other breast. He slid his hands down her sides, past the slight dip of her waist to her hips and lower. He squeezed her backside through her breeches, soft under his grip on her otherwise spare frame.

She was quiet, and he thought she had lost her train of thought. Understandable, given the circumstances. He could feel her heart racing, feel her breaths quickening.

"I've wanted you for a while." Her voice was serious, so he pulled his mouth away. Her breasts were wet from his mouth, reddened from where his coarse stubble had chafed her.

"I know," he said. And he had. He had known almost from the beginning that there was an attraction between them, shared and dangerous. "I've wanted you too." He pulled her closer against him, between his legs, letting his arousal press into her thigh.

She let out a helpless little moan. "Don't make me wait. Please. Let me . . . make me come soon, Alistair."

He felt a rumble in his chest. Was he growling? Christ. Did she think he would say no to such a request? He opened the fall of her breeches, tugged them down around her hips, and fell to his knees before her.

Charity wasn't sure she had ever imagined a sight more erotic than Alistair kneeling before her, still dressed in his perfect evening clothes, his lips against her most sensitive flesh. She wove her fingers through his sleek, dark hair. Even in the candlelight, flecks of silver were visible among the black, which somehow added to the pleasure she was taking from the sight. Another item to add to her list of depravities.

Feeling his tongue slide in between the folds of her flesh, she tried in vain to part her legs for him. But she was still in her damned boots and breeches, and there was only so much she could move. His stubble rasped against her inner thigh, and if he didn't make her come soon, she was going to do it herself. Then, thank God and all his angels, he slid a finger inside her—only one finger, which shouldn't have been enough but somehow was because it was *his* finger—and she felt her pleasure rise.

"Yes," she whispered. "That's it." He was stroking her with his tongue exactly where she needed it, filling her with his finger, and it was perfect. It was so simple, it was the easiest thing in the world, this rush of pleasure that was washing over her. "Yes," she said again, and it dissolved into a moan of pleasure as her climax overtook her.

He kept his mouth on her, his finger stroking inside her, until her last wave of pleasure subsided. Then he had one arm around her shoulders and the other behind her knees, and he was throwing her bodily onto the bed.

"Robin," he rasped, "do I need to be careful?" He had shucked his coat and was unfastening his breeches, but other than that he was fully dressed, hardly even rumpled.

"Careful?" She was still dazed, and it took her a moment to understand. "Do you mean about babies? Yes, please."

"No, no, that goes without saying." He tugged off one of her boots and then the other. "I meant . . ." He grabbed her breeches by the waistband and peeled them off, leaving her completely naked. "God." He stared, but by now she understood that his stares weren't critical. When he spoke, his voice was a rasp. "You've done this before, I think? Or do I need to take care?"

She smiled and flopped back onto the pillows. "You don't need to take care. Please don't, in fact."

"Very well." He pulled himself out of his opened breeches, and she propped herself up on her elbows to get a better look. She licked her lips.

He pushed her legs apart and knelt between them, still wearing all that clothing. Oh well, she'd just have to get a look at him later. His hair was disordered from where she had run her fingers through it, and his expression was almost solemn as he gazed down at her. With one hand, he slowly stroked himself and with the other, he absently caressed her thigh.

She reached out, pushing his hand away so she could touch him herself. She wrapped her fingers around his shaft, letting her thumb slide across the slit. He groaned, and she felt a drop of moisture bead on the head. Tilting her hips up toward him, she guided him toward her core.

Now he brushed her hand away. They were going to tussle over this, were they? That was fine by her. More than fine. He braced himself over her with one arm and positioned his cock so the head breached her entrance.

"Yes." She raised her hips to meet him, reveling in the stretching and fullness as she surrounded him. As he entered her.

She had forgotten how good this could be. It was so basic a pleasure, so obvious, like drinking cool, clean water on a hot day. It felt so uncomplicated, so right, to have him inside her in this way, filling her and brushing against all those places that came alive with sensation.

"Fuck," he growled once he was fully seated inside her.

That was the coarsest language she had ever heard him use, and now she wanted to hear more. She clenched around him, and was rewarded with an incoherent sound accompanied by a thrust.

Yes. She already felt her desire begin to coil up inside her again. So simple. So easy. They ought to have been doing this for weeks now. Maybe if they had done this earlier—although that was impossible, because of her disguise and his propensity to self-flagellate—maybe this act wouldn't have so many layers of meaning. It would have been two acquaintances, two bodies, a sufficient amount of mutual desire and the accompanying actions. Instead, every time he thrust into her, every sound and breath, every brush of his lips against her neck—it all added up to something more than that.

She could smell his hair, clean and scented with whatever he used to keep it so neat. His starched collar was tantalizingly rough against her naked skin, and she tugged it aside in order to kiss his neck. She smoothed her fingers down the silk of his waistcoat to the wool of his breeches, feeling his muscles flex as he worked his body relentlessly into hers. She shifted her feet on the bed and felt her ankles brush against the cool leather of his boots.

Surely, the fact that he was so thoroughly dressed shouldn't add to her pleasure? It ought to be demeaning, or even absurd, to be lying here naked, getting swived into the mattress by a man who was dressed from cravat to boots, the only exposed part of him the very part that was inside her body. But it wasn't. It was simply Alistair, and of course Alistair had on a pair of perfectly tailored breeches while he was fucking her silly.

"Are you laughing, Robin?" *Thrust.* "Scamp." *Thrust.* "No

sense of gravity at all." His voice was warm and rough, barely more than breath, and so very close to her ear.

"Maybe." She tightened around him again, just to hear him swear. And then her pleasure began to crest again, so she let it, and she did laugh. Just a little, and mainly from happiness.

He let himself go then, pounding into her hard and fast, a few quick thrusts before withdrawing on a curse and taking himself in hand. She watched him spill onto the sheets beside her.

Instead of lying down, he knelt there, seemingly dazed. He was wonderfully disheveled now, his cravat a wrinkled mess and his shirtsleeves askew.

"We ought to have been doing this for weeks," he said, and the way his words mirrored her own thoughts made her sit up and climb onto his lap. She straddled his legs, lowering her mouth to his and unfastening every button she could get her hands on. She stopped kissing him only when he was as naked as she was and they were sprawled side by side.

She traced her fingers along the furrow of his chest, playing with the dark hair that dusted his lean muscles. But as her heart slowed to a normal rhythm and her body cooled off, she started to feel an uneasiness steal over her.

"You're not about to throw me into the street in a fit of regret?"

He shook his head. "I couldn't throw you into the street under any circumstances. You ought to have grasped that by now."

"Not even because I'm a fraud?" It was likely pathetic,

this need for reassurance, especially since she couldn't imagine what he could possibly say to reassure her.

He stared at the ceiling, the moment stretching out perilously far. "You aren't a fraud." His words came slowly, consideringly. "I don't know what the right course of action was in your circumstances, so I don't know that you've chosen the wrong one." He pulled her closer, until her head rested on his shoulder and his arm wrapped around her, strong and sure.

She wasn't done yet, though.

"Not even because I'm low-born? A housemaid, a foundling."

"Ha! I wish you were anything as dignified as a foundling." His voice was somehow both lazy and haughty, and his hand absently stroked her back. "I've quite made up my mind that what you are is a changeling. Some very proper and well-behaved child was snatched away by the fairies and you were put in the cradle in her stead. That's the only explanation for the mischief you've wrought among us mortals."

A changeling. She liked the sound of that, as silly as it was. She had been in between for so long. Neither man nor woman, neither servant nor gentlefolk. Neither fraud nor honest.

"Seriously though, Robin. What more do you need me to tell you? I'm not good at guessing games. Tell me, and I'll say it."

There wasn't anything. There couldn't be. She climbed on top of him. "This," she said, leaning down for a kiss. "Only this."

CHAPTER ELEVEN

Alistair went to Broughton with the hope that being at his ancestral seat would bring him to his senses.

He ordered his post chaise almost as soon as Robin left his bed, so early that the sun had hardly risen. The horses were hitched, the portmanteau was packed, and Alistair, settled against the squabs, could still smell Robin on his skin. He took a deep, reluctant breath. It was her usual green scent, like a spring copse, but this time mixed with sweat and desire. So this was the scent of everything he'd never have, of everything he didn't even know how to wish for.

On second thought, he wasn't sure if the scent was on his skin or only in his imagination. It hardly mattered. Olfactory hallucinations weren't any more troubling than the fact that he had thrown caution to the wind for an entire night. He had not only gone to bed with Robin, but lying in bed with her afterward, talking and touching, he had allowed himself to believe they could go on in such a way. Worse, he had allowed her to believe it too.

He arrived at Broughton Abbey long after nightfall, stiff and cold and very irritated with himself. He had chosen

Broughton rather than the place in Kent despite the journey to Shropshire taking an entire day and the house itself lacking nearly all comforts. For most of the year the chimneys smoked and for the rest of the year the house reeked of damp. He had never known a meal to arrive on the table while still hot, the ancient kitchens being located far from the equally ancient dining room. One of the wings was literally a crumbled ruin, which had been entertaining to explore as a child but he now understood to be little more than a breeding ground for vermin.

But this was the de Lacey family seat, in the family's possession since the monks had been tossed out some centuries earlier. Alistair hoped the cold gray stone and drafty passageways would remind him of what he owed future generations of de Laceys: honor, security, living up to one's obligations. These things mattered more than pleasure, more than whatever he had let himself feel with Robin in his arms.

The housekeeper was exceedingly pleased with herself for having kept a few rooms in a state of readiness. Alistair was pleased with her as well, because there was a fire blazing in his bedchamber and freshly aired linens on his bed. He drank his wine—his father had, if nothing else, kept the cellars stocked—and climbed into the vast oaken monstrosity of a bed.

Some forgotten de Lacey ancestor had caused the family coat of arms to be painted on the wall facing the bed. It was the usual dragons—or were they unicorns?—and some coronets. *Nil Penna Sed Usus*, the motto read. The translation, as far as Alistair could tell, was "Not the pen but its use," but he had always been fairly certain this was a Renaissance-era cock joke. Leave it to the de Laceys to let it all come back to that. Penises and comedy. Quite possibly this enormous bed had been constructed for orgies—and *now* how was he supposed to sleep? Perhaps coming to this house had not been the right idea.

But no. He was not looking to the past but to the future. He had rescued his name and his legacy, he had paid off creditors, he had honored pensions and annuities. He had taken up his seat in the House of Lords and presented himself around town as a respectable gentleman. Now that the property was reasonably solvent, he would finance grammar schools and new cottages, repair the roads and put new steeples on the churches.

He would leave no bastards, no string of discarded mistresses. There would be no disgraceful marriage, no rumors attached to his name.

There was no room for Robin in this plan.

He rolled over, trying to find a comfortable place on the bed, but he already knew there was none. Had he come to this monument to failed nobility and aristocratic dissipation as a kind of penance? Were the abominable chimneys and lumpy mattresses a way to atone for the pleasure he had last night?

Last night. His cock twitched at the memory. So much for penance. He had wanted to hold her forever, to sink into her body again and again, to make her laugh and moan and shudder. He wanted his fill of whatever comfort she was offering, and he wanted to give the same to her.

For his entire life, whenever he encountered a fork in the road where duty and righteousness lay to one side and pleasure to the other, he took the path of duty. He always chose the path he thought his father would not have chosen. It was little more than a primitive reflex. He had prided himself on his strict adherence to propriety, but now saw that there was nothing noble or praiseworthy in such a rote response. And suddenly that did not seem like a good enough reason to take a path that led away from Robin.

What would happen if he tried to steer a course toward his own notion of rightness, rather than always leaning hard on the rudder away from what his father had done?

With a sigh of frustration, he rolled over. He wouldn't idly dally with Robin, but his heart—which organ he had evidently finally determined worthy of notice—insisted that it was wrong to abandon her. Marrying her, though . . . he tried to imagine Miss Charity Church beside him in this awful bed, gazing up with him at the lewd motto of the family she had married into. He wasn't even entirely sure who this elusive Miss Church was—she didn't feel like Robin in his mind—but whoever she was, she would hardly be the most objectionable feature in this appalling room.

He was all too aware that this was not a strong argument in favor of a future wife, a future marchioness, no less. But he was Lord Pembroke, and if he determined that Miss Charity Church was to be his, then he pitied anybody who got in his way.

Six days without so much as a note. Charity was quite proud of herself for having bypassed sorrow and gone straight to irritation.

She had told him that she didn't want any part of his regret or shame. But that had been naive. She had no control over whether he regretted being with her. For that matter, she wasn't entirely sure he had any control over it. As far as she could tell, sometimes he wallowed in fits of rectitude the way a dog might roll around in something that smelled interesting but a trifle confusing to its tiny, sadly limited brain. Pembroke's bouts of moral superiority were no better than one of the Fenshawe hounds covered in goose shite.

Wherever he was, therefore, was of no interest to Charity. Sooner or later he'd return and she'd give him a bath. Metaphorically speaking.

Purely out of curiosity, and certainly not out of any pathetic longing, she walked past his house to check for any signs that he had left town. And there it was—the door knocker had been removed and the curtains were drawn. That did nothing to put her mind at ease—even if he had been called away on urgent estate business he could have found time to dash off a note.

When she arrived home she found Gilbert, Louisa, and Aunt Agatha in the drawing room.

"Gilbert, where has your brother run off to?" She kept her voice casual.

"Alistair?" he asked, as if there might be some other brother he had forgotten about. "I couldn't guess."

Charity didn't know whether to feel better or worse that Alistair hadn't even let his own brother know his where-abouts. On the one hand, this wasn't a special excommunication meant particularly for her. On the other hand, she was falling in love with a thoroughgoing bastard.

Because that's what this was. Love, or something near enough to it. It would end in heartbreak, but in Charity's experience it generally did. That knowledge was never enough to stop it from happening, though, and thank God for that. Imagine if people carried their hearts around like fragile birds' eggs, carefully preventing the smallest crack or injury. Everybody would keep a polite distance, safe and protected and utterly alone.

She loved Alistair, arrogant piece of work that he was, and very likely he loved her back. But she knew there was no future between the Marquess of Pembroke and herself. Not that long from now, Robert Selby would disappear.

By the looks of things, that would be soon indeed. Gilbert was plainly smitten with Louisa. Charity hadn't the faint-est notion as to why he hadn't yet made a formal offer, but had to assume it was forthcoming. Instead, the pair of them clammed up whenever she entered the room. Could Louisa imagine that Charity would try to prevent the match? Even if Charity had any authority over Louisa, which they both knew she did not, an offer from the childless Marquess of Pembroke's only brother would be nothing to sneeze at, even though Louisa could doubtless have done better. But if they found an added thrill in thinking their romance a forbidden one, then who was she to ruin their fun?

Even now, they were sitting stiffly on the sofa where a moment ago their heads had been bent together.

"Did he not send you a note?" Gilbert asked Charity.

"No. I suppose he didn't send you one either?"

He looked at her blankly for a moment. "Why would he do a thing like that?"

Charity wondered if Louisa could possibly have fallen for a lackwit. "Perhaps to let you know where he was?" she suggested.

"Yes, yes, I know *people* do that. I would do that, of course. If I were to leave town, naturally I'd send a note to those who might miss me." He darted a quick, candid look at Louisa, and then both of them blushed. "But Alistair would never."

No, he wouldn't, would he? Such a gesture would be too considerate, it would make people wonder if he actually gave a damn about them. Much safer to avoid any indication of friendship entirely. She was being unfair to him and she knew it, but she was in too ill a humor to care.

Gilbert, evidently unable to proceed in his wooing with Charity as an audience, left shortly thereafter.

Charity sat on the side of the sofa vacated by Gilbert. "Lou, has he offered for you?"

She blushed even redder. "Yes."

Why the devil was she only now hearing about it? True, Louisa didn't owe her anything, but they were friends, weren't they? Sisters, of a sort? Louisa was not like Alistair; she did not keep others at a distance for no purpose other than pride. "And did you accept?" She was frustrated by this coolness that had sprung up between them, and she could hear an unintended note of irritation in her voice.

"I know I shouldn't do anything without your consent." Louisa was looking at her hands, neatly folded in her lap. "Technically, you're my guardian."

Charity shook her head impatiently. She was nobody's guardian. Louisa would need her signature—false, forged, and utterly illegal—on the marriage license, but that was the end of Charity's involvement. "Why haven't you spoken to me about this, though?"

"I know you have grander plans for me and I don't want to disappoint you." Louisa never wanted to disappoint anybody and she seldom did. "Besides, it's awkward to speak of these things. I don't know how to even begin. You haven't told me of your plans with Lord Pembroke, have you?"

Charity felt like all the air had been sucked from the room and replaced with smoke. How on earth had Louisa figured out that there was anything between them? Was it that obvious? Was that why Alistair had left—fear of exposure? "I don't precisely have plans with Pembroke." That was God's own truth. Her only thought was to enjoy being with him while she still could.

"But there's something . . . happening, I suppose. And you haven't mentioned it." She took Charity's hand and squeezed it. "I'm not reproaching you, only saying that I know these matters are difficult to speak of."

Charity squeezed her hand in return. "He's not that bad," she said, and then wanted to smack herself for so describing the man she loved. "Most of his airs and graces are put-ons, and the rest are because he outranks practically everybody and doesn't want anyone to forget it." Really, she ought to try her hand at love poetry, she was so good at this. She made another attempt. "I've come to be very fond of him, and I feel certain that you will as well, in time."

Louisa let out a sound that was somewhere between a laugh and a weak little sob. "I have to dress for dinner, and so should you."

As Charity changed her clothes, she tried to puzzle over why Louisa had been on the verge of tears when they were discussing what surely ought to have been a happy topic. Louisa had never been given to fits of emotion. She was practical, industrious, calm. She even seemed unmoved by the whirl of London in the height of the season. Charity, by contrast, had been almost dizzy with delight. Somewhere in the recesses of her memory, Charity recalled being spun around by an adult. Had it been the vicar's housekeeper? Perhaps someone at a village fete? Somebody had taken her by the hands and spun her so fast that her feet lifted off the ground and she flew in the air, rooted only by the strong hands holding her own tiny ones. It had been wonderful and terrifying, and the entire world had collapsed into streaks of color.

That was what the past month had been like: a blur of laughter and fun. Clever people, amusing conversation, music and food and wine and all the best things in life.

She wanted to soak up every minute of it because she knew that soon it would be gone. She would be gone. Alistair had to know that her time was running out, and he wasn't even here to share it with her.

At least Louisa was not at home when Maurice Clifton called. Innocently, she would have somehow given them away in an instant, and the man's likeness to Robbie would only have distressed her. God knew, it certainly distressed Charity. She felt like she was lying to Robbie himself.

"I must say, Cousin, that I was quite surprised when I heard that you had done so well for yourself at Cambridge." He spoke with an accent that Charity assumed was native to Dorset. It made him, for some reason, sound honest and kind, and she hated this deceit even more. "I had never taken you for the scholarly sort."

Robbie had been far from scholarly. He hadn't had the temperament for sitting still and working, and had always been happier mending fences or helping in the stables. "I was a late bloomer," Charity said, not letting her smile falter. After all, she *had* been a late bloomer. It felt less filthy to sprinkle some honesty over the top of the deceit.

"In some ways, perhaps." Clifton was stroking his chin in a thoughtful way.

Charity smiled blankly, not knowing where this was going.

"You aren't as tall as I might have expected. I recall you being something of a brawny lad."

"I lost a good deal of weight after my illness." After Robbie died, after Charity and Louisa buried him secretly beneath the rowan tree at Fenshawe, Keating spread word among the villagers that Mr. Selby's illness had left him sadly thin. Thus, they were prepared for a change in the young squire's appearance if they happened to see him from a distance. Charity felt sick repeating the lie to this man who looked so much like Robbie.

"Hmm." Clifton was regarding her very intently. "You seem hale enough now. Agatha Cavendish is here in London with you, you say?"

"Yes, she's at the milliner's with my sister." Another truth, not that it mattered.

"She must be seventy. How long did you say she lived with you at Fenshawe?"

"She came right before I left for university." She didn't like the direction of his questions. He suspected something.

"I haven't been to Northumberland in years. Perhaps I ought to pay a visit."

Was that a threat? An opportunity to confess? Or simply idle chatter?

Clifton left and Charity began pacing.

It was now doubly important to get Louisa creditably married. Then Charity could be done with this deceit.

How would she do this? Would she pretend to jump off a bridge? Book passage to India and, once there, bribe somebody to send home a death notice?

And then where would she go? She could never see anyone she had known in this life or her fraud would be revealed—not only hers, but Louisa's too, and Keating and Aunt Agatha's complicity. In order to keep Louisa safe, she would never be able to see Louisa again. She felt tears spring to her eyes.

Nor would she ever see Aunt Agatha, Amelia Allenby, or any of the people she had met in London.

She would never again see Alistair. Not that he would want to see her.

Not that he wanted to see her now.

There came the sound of the front door opening and closing, muffled voices traveling up from the vestibule. She made an effort to compose herself, but must not have achieved a very convincing result, because no sooner had Louisa appeared at the threshold than she rushed over to Charity's side. "What happened?" She knelt on the carpet, rubbing Charity's hands.

"Cousin Clifton visited." Charity wiped her eyes with Louisa's handkerchief. "He looks so much like—" Her next words were muffled by Louisa's hand over her mouth. When Charity looked up, there was Gilbert, standing in the doorway and looking embarrassed.

Well might he look embarrassed, coming into a room where a grown man was weeping like a child. With some effort, she stopped. Taking a deep breath, she forced a smile. "Sorry, Gilbert. I was being maudlin. A cousin visited, and he looks like our late father." That was a neat recovery, she thought.

"Maurice?" This was Aunt Agatha, who had only now come into the drawing room. "He doesn't look a damned thing like Francis." For a moment Charity was terrified that she was about to go on in this imprudent way, regardless of Gilbert's presence. "You should see the bonnet Louisa bought. It looks like something that washed up on the banks of the Thames."

Charity went over to the table where they kept the brandy

and poured herself a glass. She forced herself to drink it all before turning around and facing the room. There really were times when strong drink was medicinal, and she was fairly sure this was one of those times. As she felt the brandy work its way through her veins, a warmth spreading slowly across her body, she tried to steady herself. If Louisa married, nothing else mattered. Even if they were exposed, Louisa could explain to her new husband that she had been forced by Charity to cooperate in the fraud. And if she married a man of influence and wealth, her husband might be able to buy Clifton's silence.

Gilbert de Lacey was not a man of influence and wealth, but his brother was, and that was close enough, if Alistair could be persuaded to dirty his hands.

Louisa was trying on her new bonnet, which did rather look like a sea creature. It was a frightful shade of green, and if one was in a grotesque frame of mind, one could detect a suggestion of seaweed and tentacles in the ribbons and netting. It would be properly hideous on anyone else, but over the last six weeks in London, Louisa had discovered that she could get away with wearing things that other women might not dare.

Robbie had still been alive when Charity first realized that Louisa would be a beauty. Charity and he had been huddled under the blankets in his bed when she asked if he had anything set aside for Louisa's dowry. "No, but she has her face," was his answer. He had not been a terribly responsible brother, but he had been so young, and his guardian—none other than Mr. Clifton—had been so far away. "We have time," he told Charity, pulling her close against him. But they didn't.

There was never time. Now Charity's remaining time with Louisa could be measured in weeks instead of months.

Feeling abjectly sorry for herself, she went in search of the one person who could be counted on to snap her out of it. She found Keating in the tiny butler's pantry, indifferently polishing silver.

"You'll never get the spots off unless you twist the rag up like so," she said, taking the spoon and cloth from him.

"Never said I wanted to be a proper butler," he grumbled. "You lured me with promises of a life of crime."

When Charity met Keating he had been working at Cambridge as a bedder—a servant who tended to students' linens and washing water. She caught him sneaking out of another student's rooms at an odd hour and supposed him to be a common thief, but in fact he was that student's sometime lover. By that point she had been desperate for an accomplice, someone to pretend to shave her and to handle the laundry so she wouldn't have to burn her monthly rags. And if Keating could keep the secret of his relationship with the other student, then surely he could keep her secret as well. She had not been disappointed.

"Lucky you," she said, pushing her sleeves up in order to save them from the silver polish, "we only have another month or so left, and then we'll go back to being penniless miscreants."

"Hmph." He eyed her carefully. "You don't sound too cheerful about the prospect."

"I think it's only fair to warn you that I'm going to be very bad company at first." Try as she might, she could not remember agreeing that Keating would accompany her. But it seemed he had made up his mind.

"I'm sure I'll contrive a way to amuse myself." He took the half-polished spoon back from Charity. "So. Are we to flee by land or by sea?"

"I don't know yet. Clifton was here. He hinted that he might go to Fenshawe and ask questions."

"Bad timing, with the pretty lordling almost on the hook."

There was no point in taking issue with this characterization of Lord Gilbert's courting of Louisa. "Exactly."

"I'll go to Fenshawe and make sure there's no gossip."

God, that would be a relief. "You'll send word if it looks like he's about to make trouble?" That would at least give her time to get away, time to make sure Louisa knew what she had to say.

And then she'd be gone.

She had recovered from losing Robbie and she'd recover from losing Louisa and Alistair and the rest of it. She had started this life with nothing and nobody, and it would be no great loss to start with nothing again. Being alone and nameless was practically her birthright, after all.

CHAPTER TWELVE

Alistair called on her as soon as he returned to London. Well, as soon as he washed off the dust of the road and changed into something suitable. Although what attire was suitable for this errand he couldn't rightly guess. He was doing what was correct, and that would have to sustain him. The entire week at Broughton he had spent turning this issue over in his mind, finally determining that there was only one acceptable course of action.

Checking once more that his cuffs were even and his collar straight, he entered the drawing room. It was crowded with the usual young bucks and whichever female relations they could persuade to accompany them. Miss Allenby was present and, after only an instant's hesitation, he gave her a cordial half bow. Or perhaps not precisely cordial, but at least . . . Well, it was a bow. Robin couldn't accuse him of treating his half sisters like lepers now, could she?

He didn't see Robin anywhere, though. He caught Miss Selby's eye—he made her a bow and in return she delivered her usual approximation of a smile. She didn't like him in the least bit, and for all her pretty manners couldn't quite feign civility to him. Gilbert had likely filled her ear with tales of Alistair's stinginess and cruelty. It might have been more convenient to be on friendly terms with Robin's pretend sister, but Alistair was rather used to a certain chilliness in his dealings with people, so he didn't concern himself overmuch about Miss Selby.

Without even looking, he knew the minute Robin walked into the room. Maybe it was the way so many people smiled toward the door. Maybe it was her scent or some primal connection they had forged during their night together. Whatever the reason, he felt her presence with his entire body.

When he turned and she saw him, she smiled so brightly and started towards him so automatically that for a moment he thought she was going to launch herself into his arms.

The horrible thing was that he would hardly have minded, so lost was he to all sense of decorum and propriety where Robin was concerned. And that was why he had to go through with this.

Some of his unease must have shown on his face because she checked her progress toward him, adopting a more neutral expression, the bland politesse that was utterly proper in London drawing rooms.

He hated it. He wanted to grab her and kiss her until she gave him that smile again.

This was madness.

He schooled his expression into something decent. "Mr. Selby." He spoke loudly and coolly enough for half the room to hear how utterly unmoved he was by seeing her. "Is there a place where we can discuss that matter I referenced at our last meeting?"

She played along. She was practiced at playacting, after all. A veritable expert at deceit, his Robin was. "Of course, Lord Pembroke. Come to my study."

She must have been out riding, because she was wearing riding clothes, and her hair was even more disordered than usual. Now that he had seen the body underneath the clothes, he couldn't walk behind her without his gaze straying to her legs, her hips, the curve of her arse.

They made it all the way there without dropping the facade. It wasn't until Alistair himself had turned the key in the door behind them that they even touched one another.

And then she did actually launch herself at him, and he was glad of it. "You vile bastard," she said, covering his face with kisses. "Where were you?"

"Shropshire." He scooped her up against him and then, realizing he had better things to do with his hands, pushed her against the wall, caging her in with his body and running his hands all over her—the nip of her waist, the small of her back, the slight swell of her breasts. He wanted to be touching all of her at once. Kissing her, possessing her. *Madness.*

"I was beginning to fear you meant to spend the rest of the season in the country."

So had he, for that matter. "I had to think." He kissed her ear, her neck, the tip of her nose. Her freckles seemed to have multiplied in the last week.

She rubbed her face along his jaw, which he supposed meant she wasn't too cross with him. "You couldn't think in London?"

No, he quite plainly could not. He had come here to behave respectably, and now look at him. He was grabbing fistfuls of her shirt, crudely shoving aside waistcoat and riding jacket, all to get to her skin, and this while only a few yards away, a roomful of ladies and gentlemen sipped tea. "There are other things I do in London," he said, before taking her mouth in a kiss.

She tasted like lemons and sugar and he couldn't get enough. He stroked his tongue along her lower lip, her teeth, her tongue. And she kissed him back relentlessly, like they were having a contest to see which of them could do the most kissing. The thought crossed his mind that they were on the road to total dishevelment, and that he had no strategy for retying the cravat she was currently mangling in her hands, but then she wrapped her legs around his back and he found that he lost even that scruple.

He slid his hands under her backside, bringing her closer against him, making her feel how much he wanted her, how thoroughly lost to all standards he was. He needed her to know how being around her made him lose that part of himself, because maybe she would understand why he had to go through with his purpose in coming here. Maybe even he would understand.

But she made a soft and needy sound, and his thoughts scattered like pigeons startled by a cat. There was nothing outside the four walls of this room and maybe there never had been. There was only Robin moaning when he let his hand settle between her legs.

He had never, not even as a young man, not even in his wildest fantasies, allowed himself to conjure up anything so arousing, anything so utterly indecent as this. Breeches and riding coat, unkempt hair and unbound breasts.

"Too many clothes," he managed to say.

"Do you mean to undress? I won't complain."

"I mean to undress you, because I can't figure out how to properly fuck you otherwise." He knew she liked it when he swore. He was truly far gone.

Her eyes darkened and her face assumed a dangerous expression. "Is that a challenge?"

"It's whatever you want it to be as long as I'm inside you in the next thirty seconds."

She turned to face the wall and pushed her breeches below her hips. He could see the curve of her arse below the hem of her coat and his cock throbbed with need. He unfastened the minimum number of buttons necessary to take out his cock, then rubbed it between her legs, sliding it along her wet warmth. His hips settled against the softness of her backside, and she braced her hands on the wall to steady herself against his movement.

She shot him a sly glance over her shoulder. "You said thirty seconds."

He gave her a quick, hard kiss before tugging her hips back and thrusting into her. He groaned at the sensation of tight warmth surrounding him, holding still for a long, grateful moment. This arrangement didn't allow for much movement. Her legs were bound by her breeches and he couldn't quite position his own legs between them. But the way their movement was hampered only heightened his need. She was rocking her hips onto him in rhythm with his thrusts. Inspired, he shoved the coat and shirttails away so he could watch the place where they joined. Every time his cock disappeared into her flesh she gave a small, satisfied moan.

"You like this," he said, pointing out the obvious. She liked the feel of him inside her.

"So much," she said. "So much. I thought about it all week." She took one of her hands from the wall and slid it down to where he entered her, circling his erection and then stroking herself. He brought one of his own hands to join hers, so she could teach him to touch her the way she touched herself. So light, barely any pressure, only the tip of a finger tracing small circles around that one bud of nerves.

When she came, he felt her tighten around him, and that was enough to bring on his climax. He pumped hard into her, and she had to use both arms to brace herself and take his thrusts. He managed to withdraw in time to spill into his handkerchief, but still he didn't step away from her.

"I came back for a reason." His mouth was against her ear. "Marry me, Robin."

She must have misunderstood. "Excuse me?" Her body had gone stiff, the last lingering traces of her climax chased away by his words.

"Marry me. You're familiar with how it works? Church, vows, ring."

And here she had thought him a reasonable, prudent person. "That's mad." She pulled up her breeches and wriggled away from his grasp.

"It's the right thing for us to do." He looked so bloody solemn she wanted to slap him.

She felt her face heat. "Fuck your right thing to do. I don't want any part of your righteousness. I don't want to be your goddamned good deed, either." She balled her fists at her sides. "Marry you, my arse. Go home, Alistair, and sleep it off. You wouldn't be the first man to make hasty offers after a tumble. You'll think more clearly in the morning."

"Robin." His expression was almost comically grim. Surely one day she would see the humor in having been proposed to in such a manner. He reached for her but she stepped away. "I've . . . we've been together twice. I can't not offer for you."

Did he think that would help the matter? He was an idiot, then. She was in love with an absolute fool. "How dare you? How dare you fuck me against the wall and then treat me like a damsel in need of respectability?" She felt her anger gathering speed, like a cart rolling downhill. "Do you think I ought to be grateful that you condescended to offer for me at all? I'm not a lady. I'm not the sort of person who requires marriage after a tupping."

"What rot. Besides, I *am* the type who requires marriage."

"Oh, to hell with you and your requirements." She tried to set her clothing right, tucking in her shirt and straightening her lapels, more to give her something to do with her hands than out of any concern for what she looked like at the moment. "Do you even realize how insulting that is? You don't want to be like your father—who, by the way, doesn't seem to have been half so bad a fellow as you think. But you need to keep your honor intact, so you throw around offers of marriage like you might toss coins to a harlot after having your way with her."

He crossed his arms in front of his chest. "I've never asked anyone to marry me before in my life, I'll have you know." Now he was angry too. Good. It was so unsatisfying to be the only one fixing for a fight.

"Perhaps that's because you generally prefer men." A low blow, but so was a marriage proposal.

"Unfair, Charity. I don't have any preference on that score, and well you know it. And if you're under the impression that I find lying with men to be less problematic than lying with women who are not my wife, then you're even more confused about propriety than I thought."

Excellent. Now they were openly insulting one another and this was a proper fight. "Your offer presumes that you somehow damaged me and that I need marriage to undo the harm. That I'd be better off as your wife than I am on my own."

That must have hit home because his nostrils flared with anger. "I should very well think you'd be a good deal better off as Lady Pembroke than as. . . ." He gestured at her, evidently unable to explain in words who or what she was.

"Have you given this any thought at all?" Oh, he was lost

to all reason, the poor bastard. She tried to hide her mounting anger and frustration behind a facade of calm, and kept her voice steady, as if she were trying to persuade a frightened child to come down from a tree. "If you marry me—if you marry Charity Church, that is—then what happens to Robert Selby?"

"It would have to be carefully managed, of course, but with a little money put into the right hands we could see our way through. I was thinking a boating accident, perhaps."

She felt sick. "You mean for Robert Selby to die." It was no more or less than what she already knew had to happen, but hearing Alistair suggest it in his commanding, lordly manner made it so much worse. She felt that he was suggesting an act of violence, an actual murder or suicide, or as if he were asking her to cut off her own leg.

"I gather that he must, in order to let the estate pass to the rightful heir."

"So Robert Selby dies," she repeated, her mouth dry. "And what happens to me?"

"You leave town for a time, then come back—properly attired, and so forth—as Charity Church. That is your legal name, is it not? Otherwise I'll have my solicitors draw up a list of foundlings born in Northumberland and you can avail yourself of one of those names."

She would be completely erased. It was to be as if she had never been born, as if the last twenty-four years had never happened. She had hoped that even in killing off Robert Selby, she could still be herself, but Alistair wanted to take that from her.

He didn't understand any of that, though. He was rich, and a man, and an arrogant bastard, and he couldn't possibly know what it was like to have nothing but a name, and a false one at that. She took a deep breath and forced her voice steady. "I have spent over five years as Robert Selby. I haven't worn a gown since Robbie died and I *don't want to.* I don't know how to be a woman, let alone a lady, and certainly not a fucking marchioness. And Alistair, I don't want to even try." For Louisa, she would have killed off Robert Selby and suffered the cost of that sacrifice. But not under any circumstance would she live as a woman.

He was silent for a moment. "Men have more freedom. I understand that. But I assure you that as Lady Pembroke you'd have as much freedom as any woman in the nation."

She shook her head. He still didn't understand. "It's not about freedom." She didn't think she could explain the utter impossibility of her living as a woman. She could hardly articulate it to herself. So she tried a different approach. "Besides, you'd be so ashamed of me. I'd be aware of that every day. You ought to have married someone a decade ago, Alistair. Someone perfect and pretty."

"I want to marry you. I want *you.*" He looked perfectly earnest. The insufferable shite didn't hear an insult when it came from his own mouth. She would have laughed if she didn't want to throw a chair at him.

"How long would it take for your first flush of righteous satisfaction to pass? How long before you realized you had contracted a marriage that had made you a laughingstock? And I assure you, you would be. I have no idea how to behave as a lady and no intention of acquiring that knowledge." No matter how much she loved him, there were limits to what she would do for him, and she was only now realizing what they were. "You'd be ashamed. Here me now, Alistair, I do not want anything to do with your shame." Goddammit, she had enough of her own problems without borrowing anyone else's.

He turned away from her to face the room's single window. He smoothed his hair as if he could see his reflection. "I don't want this to end," he said without turning around.

"I don't want it to end either." Certainly not like this, she didn't.

But what they wanted didn't matter.

CHAPTER THIRTEEN

What did other men do after suffering such a setback? What was the received course of action after being dealt such a crushing blow? Alistair was fairly certain most men found their solace at the bottom of a bottle. Ordinarily he sneered at drunkenness, but today he didn't feel equal to questioning the wisdom of the ages.

At White's he set to work at draining an entire bottle of brandy. When the bottle was three quarters empty—he had no idea how many hours had passed, and didn't care in the slightest, because if time could be measured in brandy bottles then so be it—Hugh Furnival lowered himself into a nearby chair.

"Ah, I fear it didn't go as you planned, did it, Pembroke?"

Now, what could Furnival know of the matter? More importantly, why was the man pouring himself a glass of Alistair's brandy? Alistair snatched the bottle away. "No, it most certainly did not." The words were hard to form, his tongue curiously heavy. But his mind, ah, his mind was light.

"It makes no sense, I tell you. When I saw you leave that house, I said, poor Pembroke, pity the blighter. If he can't make it work, who can?" Furnival shook his head sympathetically. "You'd think a girl would be glad to marry a marquess."

Yes! That was precisely it. Why wasn't she glad? Not only to be married to a marquess—which objectively was a fine thing, Alistair was quite certain—but to be married to him in particular. They got along famously, did they not? That alone was more than most marriages had at the beginning. "I will never understand women."

Furnival made a sound that Alistair interpreted as fullthroated agreement. "I dare say Selby is as upset as you are, though."

This was a level of insight Alistair hadn't expected to find in Furnival. "Quite right. Selby's furious with me."

"With you? I dare say you did as best as you could. It's not your fault the girl can't listen to reason."

"Exactly!" Oh, this was something, to have such a kindred soul at his side. Furnival was a treasure. A diamond. A—

"Excuse me, Furnival, but I need to speak to my brother."

Alistair looked up and saw Gilbert looming over him. He looked angry—everybody was so *angry* today.

"You ought to have some brandy, Gilbert." He held out the bottle but quickly reconsidered. "But you'll need to order your own bottle. This one's mine."

The younger man made a frustrated noise and grabbed the bottle from Alistair's hand, thrusting it at Furnival. He then took Alistair's arm and hauled him to his feet. "I'm taking you home."

This was an excellent idea. There was brandy at home, as well as enough wine to keep him going until he didn't care about Robin or anything else. Gilbert was brilliant to have thought of it. "You're a genius," he said, squeezing his brother's arm. "I never had any idea. Always thought you a bit poky."

"You're filthy drunk, Alistair, and need to stop talking until we're in the carriage."

The ride home did a good deal to discompose Alistair's mind as well as his stomach. What had Furnival been talking about? Why were carriages so damned bouncy? So many questions.

"Public drunkenness, on top of whatever it was that happened at the Selbys' house earlier." Gilbert looked out the window, as if it pained him too much to see his brother in such a low state. "I hardly know what to think."

Alistair tried to summon up some dignity. "What happened at the Selbys' house was a marriage proposal." And screwing against the wall, but they had been quiet about that. Hadn't they?

"Right." Gilbert snorted. "A marriage proposal. You didn't even speak to Louisa about it."

"Why the devil should I have said anything to Louisa?"

Gilbert slammed his hand into the seat. "Just listen to yourself. Christ. I literally never want to hear you speak ill of our father again. At least he was honest about who he was and who he loved."

"It would have been more convenient for all of us if he had remembered to love his wife rather than a string of—"

"Mother never gave a damn about Father's affairs. That was their arrangement and none of our business. And she's been dead ten years, so I think you can stop pretending that your hatred of Father had anything to do with her."

Pretending! Hatred! Alistair objected on every conceivable ground, but before he could manage to make his brain formulate a coherent response, the carriage rolled to a stop.

"Go to bed, Alistair," Gilbert said when they reached the doorway. "Don't let him have a drop to drink," he told the butler. "You remember how the late marquess got when he was low."

Hopkins, blast him, had the gall to bow his head and say, "I quite understand, Lord Gilbert."

Alistair fell asleep on top of his bedcovers, still dressed right down to his boots, which meant that he was a dozen different kinds of uncomfortable the first time he woke up that night. And he must have woken a dozen times before the sun rose.

With dawn came a cottony mouth, a throbbing headache, and the realization that what he had offered Robin was a paltry thing compared to what she needed. He had rank and consequence, a reputation of unmarred respectability, and an adequate fortune. But they would only be shackles to Robin. She did not want to be dressed in a gown or kept in a fine house. She wanted freedom, and she couldn't have it as Lady Pembroke.

The recollection that there were surely dozens of other women, all with more to recommend them than a smattering of freckles and a checkered past, who would jump at the chance to become his wife, did nothing to soothe him. By the time he had taken headache powder and rung for a bath, he was beginning to wonder whether he was as shackled by his fortune and position as Robin would have been.

The sun had set hours ago and the house had grown quiet. Charity climbed into her narrow bed more from lack of a better plan than out of any hope that sleep would come.

Surely, Alistair had known she would refuse his proposal. If he had wanted to continue their affair, he could have offered her a post as his secretary. That would establish her in his household, give them access to one another day and night, and not require her to don what now felt like a mortifying costume. She could continue as Robert Selby; she would not need to lose her friends or abandon her pursuits. The only problem was that she would need to continue stealing from Clifton.

But perhaps Alistair could have done something with his rank and fortune to quietly get Fenshawe transferred to Maurice Clifton. Entails could be broken, Clifton's cooperation could be bought. Somehow.

These weren't gifts she would ever have dared ask for, not from Alistair and not from anyone else. But what he had offered her instead—*marriage*, her mind simply reeled with the inanity of it—was so much more costly to him than a few pounds and a secretarial position, that she was astonished he hadn't thought of it himself.

He must have not given this any consideration at all. He ought to be positively ashamed by his failure of imagination, his want of reason. If he had spent five quiet minutes turning the matter over in his stuffy little brain, he would have realized what a terrible marchioness she would make. He set so much store in being a model of rectitude, a pillar of sodding society. Even if, somehow, they managed to overcome the constant threat of her fraud and deceit being exposed, she would forever be making mistakes a real lady wouldn't. She would cause him a lifetime of shame. Did he imagine that a change of costume and name would effect a transformation of her entire personality? Her identity, even?

Evidently he did. That's precisely what he thought. He supposed she put on the character of Robert Selby the way one might wear a new hat, and that she could just as easily dispense with that persona and return to being Charity Church. And he thought Charity Church, who the last anybody had heard had been a foundling and disgraced housemaid, could simply slip into the role of Lady Pembroke.

Charity Church. She felt like she was being asked to resurrect someone long dead. She had been eighteen when she first cut her hair and put on Robbie's clothes. She had experienced over five years of love and loss and fear and hope, but she felt like all those things happened to somebody other than Charity.

There was a scratching at her door. Charity sat up in bed. "Come in." She didn't want to see anyone, but at this point any distraction would be welcome.

It was Aunt Agatha, wearing a voluminous dressing gown, her gray hair in a plait down her back. "I brought you a sleeping draught. I heard you tossing and turning and thought you might need it."

"Thank you," Charity said, reaching for the glass. Aunt Agatha was not a regular visitor to her bedchamber. They didn't even usually converse. Charity had sometimes wondered whether the elderly lady even remembered that Charity wasn't really her nephew. She certainly never acknowledged it. For Charity's part, she had long since stopped thinking of the lady as Miss Cavendish.

The older woman didn't sit, instead standing at the foot of Charity's bed. "Is it true that you're considering a match with the marquess?"

Charity bent her head over the glass to hide her surprise. There was no shilly-shallying around the matter for Agatha Cavendish, was there? "Considering is too strong a word. He made an offer and I declined." And how had Aunt Agatha even guessed that marriage was even on the table?

She took a tentative sip of the sleeping draught. It smelled like orange water but tasted like honey mixed with something much more nefarious. Likely laudanum. Good. Charity couldn't think of any other way she would fall asleep tonight.

"If he keeps asking, will you have the strength to keep refusing? I recall you being highly persuadable where handsome men are concerned."

Of all the things she had to remember, it had to be that? True, Robbie had persuaded her to go to Cambridge, had persuaded her into his bed, had persuaded her to participate in all manner of harebrained schemes. But she had wanted to go to university. She had certainly wanted to go to bed with him. It hadn't taken all that much in the way of persuasion. It was part of their game. By God, they had been so very young.

"Would it be so bad if I did accept?" she asked. "I'm very fond of him."

"Child." She shook her head. "I know you're fond of him. That's the problem."

It was. If only she didn't like him so much. If only she didn't love him. Then she could . . . she didn't rightly know what. Her head was starting to feel like it was stuffed with cotton wool.

"What am I to do?" She spoke aloud, but didn't expect an answer. There was no answer.

"Young Robert did you a disservice when he raised you above your station. I wish I knew what will become of you when this is over, but I can assure you that Lord Pembroke has no part in it. A man like him, if he knew half of what you had been up to, would have you sent to Newgate as soon as look at you."

But he did know. He knew a good deal more than half, in fact. If only her head were clearer, she would calculate the precise percentage of her wrongdoings that he was aware of. And for all that knowledge, he hadn't sent her to Newgate. Instead, he had offered to marry her.

She was about to explain this to Aunt Agatha, but she was so very tired. She was going to fall asleep, and it was such a relief to know that her eyes would close and she could spend a few hours not turning this matter over and over in her mind. She lay back on her pillow and let sleep overtake her.

Chapter Fourteen

Charity didn't even need to lift her head from the pillow to know that something was wrong. The room was too bright. She was used to rising before eight, but now it looked to be nearly midday.

Stranger still, the house was oddly quiet. The walls were cheap and thin and the carpets were worn and not plentiful. Footsteps echoed down corridors and between rooms. But today it sounded like Charity might be alone in the house.

She threw on the clothes she had worn yesterday and made her way downstairs. The drawing room was empty and no fire burned in the grate.

"Louisa?" Nothing. "Aunt Agatha?" Still nothing. She crossed to the dining room. Empty. Perhaps they had a garden party or luncheon that Charity had forgotten about. Perhaps they had gone to the dressmakers or the fabric warehouse.

In the vestibule, Louisa's evening gloves still lay on the table by the door. Why had none of the maids brought them to her bedchamber? Why hadn't Louisa done it herself? She flew down the final flight of stairs to the kitchen. It was quite empty. She rummaged through her brain for any useful information—it was not the servants' usual half day off, nor was it a holiday.

"Mr. Selby, sir?" A small voice. She turned and saw the little maid who lit the fires in the morning. She had on a gray frock a good two inches too short. Maybe it was the lingering effects of the sleeping draught—*the sleeping draught*, goddammit, what had been in it?—but for a moment it seemed only yesterday that Charity had been the child with a soot-smeared face and a too-small dress.

"Janet, where is everybody?"

"Lud, sir, we thought you'd gone off with the others." The child's Cockney accent did something to break the spell. "The old lady gave us the day off. Gave us sixpence apiece too, she did. I only came back early because it looks about to rain."

"Bear with me Janet. I fear that I'm at a total loss. Strong drink, you know. Ruins the mind. Remind me where Miss Selby and Miss Cavendish have gone, will you?"

"They went with Lord Gilbert. I don't rightly know where, but Miss Selby had me help pack her portmanteau. She was crying something terrible. I thought mayhap somebody died, but the lady didn't pack any black clothes."

Surely Louisa would have left a note if she had been called away on an emergency. No, this business smelled of deceit and secrecy and nobody knew that scent better than Charity herself.

Her head still felt slow and filthy and basically useless, like a bad drain. She tried to puzzle out half-remembered fragments of her conversation with Aunt Agatha. The old lady had been worried about Charity marrying Alistair. No, she hadn't said precisely those words, had she? She had been worried that Charity would agree to a match. She smacked her aching forehead. It was not her own marriage, but Louisa's, that Aunt Agatha had been contemplating. Louisa, too, had been worried about Charity's plans. Now Louisa and Gilbert's urgent whispers and sudden silences took on a new and troubling light.

She ran upstairs to where Louisa's gloves still rested on the table in the vestibule. Underneath the gloves was a folded square of paper. With shaking hands, she opened it.

Dear Robbie,

> *By the time you read this, I'll be well on my way to Scotland. Aunt Agatha told me not to risk leaving you a note, lest you try to stop us, but I couldn't let you think that we had been harmed. I hope to see you soon. Wish me happy, dearest!*

> *Your own sister,*
> *Louisa Selby*

She folded the letter and slid it into her coat pocket. An elopement was far from ideal, but she had no doubt that Gilbert would marry Louisa, rather than leave her compromised and abandoned at some dirty inn. More troubling was the idea that Louisa would spend the next days or weeks believing herself to have gone against Charity's wishes, to have broken Alistair's heart, to have destroyed their fortunes and their futures. And the more time passed, the more she'd work herself up and become thoroughly miserable.

There was nothing for it but to ride out and explain matters to her. Over Charity's dead body would Louisa have weeks of unnecessary guilt and sorrow.

She stepped outside and sighed at what she saw. There were black clouds looming in the north, which surely was the direction the pair of young fools had gone. They would have headed for Scotland.

What Charity needed now was a fast horse, and she knew of only one place to get one.

Alistair decided that today was an excellent day to meet with his solicitor. A hangover was bad, and meeting with solicitors was inevitably trying, so combining the two seemed an efficient way to minimize the number of unpleasant hours.

Also it would give him something to do besides rush over to Robin's house and say a dozen things she wouldn't want to hear.

"I have the papers you asked me to draw up, my lord." Nivins slid the papers across Alistair's desk. "This gives Lord Gilbert a life interest in the Kent property. I think you'll find no surprises."

The only surprise was that Alistair was going through with this. The Kent property was profitable and comfortable and Alistair would miss its income. But if his brother wanted to try his hand at agriculture, this would set him up. And even if he didn't, it would give him an income and a place to live.

It was also an apology. He shouldn't have tried to strong-arm Gilbert into taking up an unwanted career. He wasn't even twenty-five. He had decades ahead of him, and might as well live them in a way that brought him some joy.

Alistair scrawled a note to Gilbert and rang for a footman to deliver it.

"While we're waiting for my brother to come and sign these papers, I do have another matter of business. I need you to investigate a foundling named Charity Church. She was born in Northumberland around 1794 and subsequently lived at the Selbys' estate, Fenshawe. I'd also like you to find any records pertaining to Robert Selby, also born around 1794, possibly earlier."

If Nivins was at all surprised, he didn't show it. After all, the man had been Alistair's father's solicitor and had likely handled matters a good deal more risqué than investigating foundlings and country squires.

He and Nivins had tea and discussed the resolution of a border dispute in Shropshire, and then the footman returned.

Gilbert was not with him.

"If you'll pardon me, your lordship, but he wasn't home. And his man, Lord Gilbert's valet, I mean, said that he had gone away for a fortnight. He seemed to be under the impression that Lord Gilbert had headed to Scotland with the utmost urgency, my lord."

"A fortnight?" He had seen his brother only last night. He remembered those mortifying circumstances only too well. Surely Gilbert would have mentioned having plans to leave town for two weeks without his valet? "Scotland?"

Slowly and horribly, the exact nature of their last conversation began to seep into his muddled brain. How had he not seen it at the time? There was nothing like drink and solipsism to blind one to what ought to have been obvious.

The damned fool had run off with Louisa Selby and it was all Alistair's fault for having behaved in such a way as to convince Gilbert that he intended to marry the lady whether she liked it or not.

Damn and hell. He excused himself, trying not to betray any signs of the urgency that he felt. The last thing he needed was servants' gossip. Quietly, he ordered his valet to pack an overnight bag, then walked as nonchalantly as could be across the mews to the stables.

"I'll need the curricle readied immediately," he told the head groom. While waiting for the horses to be put in the rig, he paced up and down the aisles of the stable.

He noticed the empty stall straight away. "Where is Queen Mab?" That was the mare he had let Robin use, what seemed like five years past but was no more than six weeks ago.

"Mr. Selby took her out not two hours ago," the groom answered.

"Mr. Selby? I was under the impression that he no longer rode any of the horses here."

"He hasn't for the past few weeks, but as your lordship hadn't given any other instructions, I saddled up Mab and he rode right off."

"And he hasn't come back yet?"

Both men looked at the sky, which was an ominous sort of gray that signaled more than the usual London showers.

Alistair thought of Gilbert and Louisa, making a thoroughly foolish and unnecessary trip to Scotland. Elopement was always disgraceful, and this particular elopement made everyone involved look ridiculous. Alistair had no intention of being cast as the villain in a farce, the evil marquess from whose lecherous advances the fair maiden had to escape. That was all bad enough.

But then he thought of Robin riding through a storm on a skittish horse, and he felt a swell of fear rise up in him.

With every clap of thunder, the mare seemed to lose a bit of her nerve. Charity had been sweet-talking her for the last several miles and they were now thoroughly irritated with one another, not to mention soaked and hungry.

The roads were getting muddier and the rain was falling heavier. Charity was about to seek shelter in the next barn or cowshed when her attention was arrested by the sight of what looked like an overturned carriage. She spurred the mare through the mud and driving rain.

It was indeed a carriage on its side. The horses had become unhitched and were wandering freely in an adjacent field. But there was no sign of coachman or passengers. She wanted to believe that they had walked away from the accident, but who would leave a pair of matched carriage horses out in the rain? And she knew at a glance that nobody had walked away from this accident. They were either dead or in need of help. As much as Charity would have liked to catch up with Louisa before nightfall, she wasn't leaving injured travelers on the side of the road.

As she approached, she could see the carriage's wheels still spinning. Perhaps it had only just now overturned, then. She dismounted her mare and looped its reins over a fence post. Sounds were coming from inside the carriage, which had to be a good sign, she supposed.

But then she heard what the voice inside the carriage was saying. "Louisa!" The voice was anxious and loud and definitely belonged to Gilbert de Lacey. "Louisa!"

Charity ran the rest of the way. Since the carriage was on its side, she had to climb on top of it to reach a door. "Open the door, Gilbert!" she cried.

"I can't! My God, is that you, Selby? Louisa hit her head, and I can't get to the door without heaving her about. And one of my arms doesn't seem to be quite the thing."

She managed to open the door and peer inside. Louisa, evidently unconscious, had a gash across her forehead. One of Gilbert's arms was at a nauseating angle. "Is she breathing?" she demanded.

"Yes," Gilbert answered immediately.

That basic fact established, she resolved not to think any more about their injuries. What she needed now was strong men to get them out of the carriage. "I'm going for help. Was Aunt Agatha with you?"

"No, she—"

She cut him off. "Did you have a coachman?"

"Yes! Oh my God—"

"I'll be back."

She found the coachman, a boy of no more than twenty, facedown in the ditch that was supposed to provide drainage for the road. He was quite insensible but not bleeding, and she was at least able to drag him out so he didn't drown. Then she grabbed Louisa's valise, climbed back on the mare and rode for the farmhouse she thought she had glimpsed in the distance.

There was one other task she had to complete. Louisa would need careful nursing. Charity wouldn't leave Louisa's fate up to the ministrations of some incompetent stranger. But only a woman could nurse another woman. In the shelter of a woodshed, she struggled into Louisa's soaked gown. Then she ran for the farmhouse and pounded on the door.

By the time they got Louisa out of the carriage and into the farmhouse, the rain had stopped and Louisa was half awake. She kept asking after Gilbert, which was so bloody typical of her that Charity nearly felt reassured.

The farmers must have been put out by the arrival of four strangers, three of whom were badly injured, but they seemed to be making the best of things. Their good-natured acceptance might have been helped along by the fact that Charity loudly and repeatedly referred to Gilbert as "his lordship." Gilbert's habit of shaking coins out of his purse like he was sprinkling salt on a fresh cut of beef probably also went some distance in winning the couple's cooperation.

When she introduced herself to the Trouts as Louisa's relation, Miss Church, Gilbert hadn't batted an eyelash. In the commotion of rescuing Louisa from the carriage and bringing her into the house, she hadn't found a moment to explain her disguise to the young man. How he supposed Louisa to have acquired a relation in the middle of nowhere, and where he supposed Robert Selby to have disappeared to, Charity could not guess. Either he was a consummate actor or as gullible as a newborn baby, and at the moment she didn't much care which.

It was arranged that the coachman was to be kept in the kitchen, where the farmer's wife wrapped him in a blanket and gave him a mug of broth. Gilbert, who insisted that he'd decamp to the nearest inn as soon as he had his bone set, sat in the parlor awaiting his fate. Louisa was to have the spare bedroom with Charity attending her.

Once they had gotten Louisa dry and warm, there was nothing to do but mop the blood off her head. If it had been anyone other than Louisa—hell, if it had been herself—she would have dismissed the quantity of blood as exactly what you'd expect from a head wound. Oceans of blood, but there probably wouldn't even be a scar in a fortnight. But since it was Louisa, Charity could not be so complacent. When she looked at Louisa, pale hair spread out on the pillow, she still saw a young child, fragile and in need of protection.

The farmer's wife brought dry clothes for Charity to change into. Mrs. Trout was short and blousy, which meant that her clothes fit Charity even worse than Louisa's, but they were plain and sturdy and just the thing for getting covered in blood.

"Charity," Louisa whispered once they were alone, "how did you manage to find me so quickly?"

The girl thought she had been stealthy, had she? Lord.

"Call it a good guess," Charity said dryly. "Listen, Louisa, I don't mean to stop you and Gilbert from marrying, if that's what you want to know. I never meant to stop you. I wish the pair of you happy."

"But Lord Pembroke . . ." The fear in her voice was plain even though she spoke in a whisper.

Charity suppressed her irritation. However faulty Louisa's reasoning and melodramatic her behavior, she truly had feared a forced marriage. Charity wasn't sure what she had done to deserve Louisa's mistrust, let alone a doctored sleeping draught from Aunt Agatha, but she'd try to ignore her hurt feelings until Louisa was well again.

"Pembroke has nothing to do with you. He doesn't want to marry you at all." Charity took a clean cloth and pressed it against Louisa's wound. "You don't need to worry about him. Close your eyes and rest."

Once Louisa was asleep, she went downstairs to find Gilbert. "Miss Church," Gilbert said, rising to his feet. His handsome face was creased with strain and fatigue, he held his arm awkwardly, but still he executed a gentlemanly bow.

"About that," she started. After all, if he were to marry Louisa he'd have to be let in on the secret. "You're quite right that I'm Miss Church, but I'm afraid you also know me as Robert Selby."

His hesitation lasted only the barest instant. "Is that so? Well, that explains a good deal, I dare say. A dashed good deal, in fact. Well, any friend of Louisa is a friend of mine."

Perhaps it was his open mind that had drawn Louisa to him. Charity had known there had to be more to the man than a pretty face and a dash of charm. "I hardly need to tell you this is a secret of some importance to both Louisa and myself, do I?"

Tapping the side of his nose, he said, "Quite right. Your secret is safe with me." And then he went back to poking the fire with his good arm.

Well, that had gone better than she could have expected.

The doctor, a gaunt man of about forty, arrived at dusk. He examined Louisa's head, looked at her eyes, and made her tell him what month and year it was.

"She has no fractures, but she needs close care and plenty of rest for the next few weeks," he pronounced, snapping his bag shut. "I don't want her out of this bed." He eyed Charity critically. "She might become feverish. Do you have any experience nursing the ill? If not, there's a woman in the village who's reasonably trustworthy."

Over Charity's dead body would Louisa be entrusted to a yokel whose only recommendation was being reasonably trustworthy. "I nursed Miss Selby and her brother through all the usual illnesses and injuries."

"Suit yourself." He gathered his bag and made for the door. "I'll check on the lady tomorrow. You may bandage her wound now."

Charity did so; that accomplished, she sat in the hard chair by Louisa's bed and made herself as comfortable as she could, given the unaccustomed clothes and the fact that every muscle in her body ached. She was bone-tired but knew she wouldn't sleep. She had to look after Louisa.

She had to look after Louisa. That was why she had been

sent to live with the Selbys in the first place, to take care of a sad, motherless girl. Not that Charity had been anything other than a sad, motherless girl herself, but she had adopted Louisa's welfare as her purpose in life, and old habits were hard to break. She stood, intending to open the windows and let in some fresh air, but got her skirts caught under the chair leg.

How on earth did women get anything done when encumbered by acres of fabric? Stranger still was how all that fabric somehow left her so exposed. The gown had a high neckline—Mrs. Trout was a farmer's wife, not a debutante— but Charity's throat felt oddly naked without a cravat, her legs indecently free under the short chemise. And there were no drawers at all. Perhaps farmers' wives didn't wear drawers in Biggleswade, or wherever they were. But to be naked under the gown when she was used to wearing breeches made her feel even stranger.

She heard a clock chime ten o'clock. It felt like four in the morning, she was so tired.

The door creaked open, and she automatically turned her head.

There, standing in the doorway, was Alistair, soaking wet and wearing an expression of thunderous rage.

CHAPTER FIFTEEN

It had taken an hour to get these rustic loobies to tell him anything useful.

"You'll be meaning the injured gentlefolk," said the innkeeper, in answer to Alistair's inquiry about the overturned carriage.

Alistair pushed a coin towards the man. It was a shilling, which was likely a good deal over the going rate for this sort of thing, but he didn't care. "Where have they been taken?"

One of the other patrons chimed in with a cheerful description of the quantities of blood that had been involved. The consensus among the fine fellows at the Duck and Dragon was that the chief victim in today's entertainments was a lady of uncommon beauty—that wasn't precisely the language the peasants used, but Alistair was able to make the inference. The other victim was a gentleman the barmaid pronounced as handsome as a prince in a fairy story, which was a nauseating way to hear one's brother described. But evidently Gilbert had walked away from the accident, which was promising. There was also a coachman and the lady's companion, who Alistair assumed to be the ancient aunt, and who ought to be thrown into the sea for lending her countenance to an elopement.

He asked whether there had been another gentleman present, but nobody knew anything. Robin had left London ahead of Alistair, so she ought to have caught up with the pair of absconding fools already. The entire journey from London, he had been certain every clap of thunder would be the one that would cause Mab to startle and toss her rider. He had driven with an eye for loose horses and broken bodies.

The sight of Gilbert's overturned carriage had nearly made his heart stop.

"But where have they been taken?" he asked again, pointedly holding out another shilling.

"It depends who's asking, don't it?"

Alistair didn't really see that it did, but in this case his answer ought to be sufficient. "I'm the Marquess of Pembroke."

Five minutes later he was on the innkeeper's own horse—the roads in this corner of hell evidently not being suitable for anything with wheels—and headed in the direction of a place with the inauspicious name of Trout Farm. But when he arrived, it was only to discover that Gilbert was no longer there.

"He went home with the doctor," said the woman who answered the door. "But the young lady is still upstairs."

"She'll do." Alistair didn't wait for an invitation; he climbed the stairs two at a time and entered the room without knocking. Tonight was not a night for civilities. For all he knew, Robin was lying in a ditch someplace. Alistair wasn't going to leave until he discovered whatever that hen-witted Selby girl knew about Robin's whereabouts.

Miss Selby lay on a narrow bed, her eyes shut and her head bandaged. At the bedside sat a woman wearing an ill-fitting dress and a monstrous cap, likely a village woman who had been pressed into service as a nurse.

"I need a few words with Miss Selby." He used his iciest, most commanding tones. "You may wake her and then take yourself off." Rummaging through his pockets, he found another coin and held it out to her.

"Really?" the woman said. "Seriously?"

It took his mind a few moments to catch up with his eyes. "Robin?" He retrieved his spectacles from his pocket and put them on. "Why are you wearing that cap?" That seemed a safer topic than falling to his knees and thanking God she was alive.

"You." She rose to her feet and pointed an accusing finger at him. "You are nothing but an arrogant, overbearing bastard."

All true. All irrelevant. He opened his mouth to say as much, but she cut him off.

"If you had any kind of relationship with your brother, he might have known you didn't have designs on Louisa. And if you weren't such a bloody ogre, the pair of them wouldn't have thought you capable of forcing girls into marriage in the first place."

She sounded to be in fighting form, so that was something to be thankful for. "I gather I'm the villain in this piece."

"As far as I can tell, the pair of idiots thought you meant

to persuade me or blackmail me into forcing her hand. Aunt Agatha drugged me with laudanum—"

"What!" he roared. The idea of Robin being poisoned like a character in one of those dratted novels made his blood positively boil.

"Shh. You'll wake Louisa." She paused and stared at him. "You're wet. Did it start raining again?"

"Only the pleasantest drizzle, just the thing to add some excitement to the business of chasing my loved ones over hill and dale. Robin, my dear, I could point out that in the melodrama you've regaled me with, you play a role as well. But you've had a trying day and I don't want to be tedious."

She had been fiddling with the edge of her cap, and now gave up and tore it off entirely. Alistair nearly sighed with relief to see her looking recognizable, albeit furious.

"If you think I engineered this elopement, you're an even greater fool than I had thought." Her hands were on her hips and her face was flushed with anger.

"That notion hadn't even occurred to me." He saw that she was pulling at her skirt, as if trying to make it behave. "Why are you wearing those clothes, though?"

She narrowed her eyes. "So I can nurse Louisa, obviously."

He hadn't thought of that. "How is she?" He should have asked that immediately, but in the scope of today's events, Louisa's welfare ranked low. It mattered to Robin, though, and presumably to Gilbert as well, so it meant something to him in a roundabout, secondhand sort of way.

"She has a head wound, but she was awake and sensible

when the doctor was here. Frankly, I think she only swooned when she saw your brother's arm, not due to her own injury. Gilbert is fine. After his arm was set, he insisted on spending the night at the doctor's house so Louisa wouldn't be compromised."

"Good God, he might have thought of that before actually eloping with her."

She cracked a tired smile at that. "Are you spending the night at the inn and then returning to London with Gilbert in the morning?"

"Are you certain you didn't suffer a blow to the head as well, Robin? If you imagine that my brother would abandon his wounded lady love and return to London, you have a very unfair notion of Gilbert. He'll haunt this house day and night, bringing posies and generally making a nuisance of himself. And I will stay here as long as he does. That way this adventure can pass as a family holiday, rather than an interrupted elopement."

"You don't need to—"

"You're quite right that I don't. But it's the only way I can salvage this situation without coming out looking like a fool." More importantly, he wasn't leaving Robin here in this mud-soaked backwater to fend for herself.

She narrowed her eyes. "Very intriguing! I recall us having a conversation only yesterday in which you failed to understand that an imprudent marriage might be cause for embarrassment."

"This is sophistry, Robin. Gilbert is not making an imprudent marriage." This was a lie. Marrying the penniless daughter of a minor country squire was emphatically imprudent for a man in Gilbert's position, even when the girl hadn't aided and abetted a felony. But that was hardly a point Alistair could concede, given his recent matrimonial efforts. "It's the elopement, not the match, that I take issue with. Elopements have a way of making objects of ridicule out of the people who are being eloped from, as it were." He looked pointedly at her.

"True." She sniffed.

"What name did you give these people?" He needed to know how to address her when they weren't alone.

She shot him a withering glance. "Charity Church, of course."

There was no *of course* about it. For all he knew, she had a stable filled with alternate names she trotted out as the spirit moved her, but he wasn't going to needle her about that when she looked so exhausted. "Very well." There was plenty of time for him to sort this out, to sift through her secrets and her stories. He stepped forward and took her hands in his. "Try to rest. I know you won't sleep, but at least rest." She looked up at him, her anger gone, nothing but weariness left.

After giving her hands a parting squeeze, he put his wet, ruined hat back on his wet, cold head and began the muddy return trip to the inn.

Strange surroundings, fatigue, the lingering effects of Aunt Agatha's evil-tasting sleeping draught, and the boneless lethargy that comes after fear all combined to give the day an air of unreality. If Charity had suddenly found herself in her bed in London—or even at Fenshawe, or in a workhouse for that matter—she would hardly have been surprised.

Louisa slept most of the day, waking only to tearfully apologize or ask after Gilbert. Charity felt her patience in great danger of slipping. *Bollocks on Gilbert,* she wanted to shout. *Bugger the daft bastard.* If he hadn't broken his arm in the accident she would have broken it for him, for having convinced Louisa that she needed to elope.

She was likely being unfair to the gentleman, but wasn't feeling very just-minded, under the circumstances.

If only she had a book to read aloud to soothe Louisa and amuse herself. The Trouts had a Bible and a cookery book, neither of which suited Charity's current mood. While she was listing things she wanted and wouldn't get, she wouldn't have complained about a hot bath or comfortable clothing. Maybe also one of those sweet buns they sold on the street in London. A glass of wine, a cheroot, any way out of this mess . . .

She woke to the sensation of nearly toppling out of the straight-backed chair. Immediately, she darted a glance at Louisa, but her chest was rising and falling in the usual manner.

Around midday, Mrs. Trout brought a package. Charity tore it open. Well, well. Alistair had been busy. The only message was a note from Gilbert to Louisa, but the other contents were unmistakably Alistair's doing. There was a selection of novels, a packet of lemon drops, and two gowns.

The farmer's wife had been standing right there when

Charity opened the parcel, so Charity had no choice but to change into one of the new gowns and give Mrs. Trout back her own frock. The woman likely didn't have more than two dresses, so it would be unreasonable of Charity to keep wearing this one when she had an alternative, even if she didn't like the idea of wearing a dress Alistair had chosen for her.

To be fair, she didn't like the idea of wearing any dress at all, but Alistair having a hand in the matter sat ill with her.

Both dresses were printed cotton round gowns with high necks, the sort of thing Louisa wore to pick apples and oversee the cheese-making. Nothing fancy or fine, thank God. No trim, no lace. She shook one of the dresses out and inspected it at arm's length, as if she thought a spider might crawl out from between its folds. There was a closure on the side, so she could dress herself without assistance. If she absolutely had to wear a dress, she could hardly do better than this one. The second gown was much the same as the first.

The chemises were a different story. There were five of them, each made of handkerchief-fine linen. What did the man think, she was, a Russian princess? Five chemises, indeed. She took off Mrs. Trout's clothes and slid into a chemise. It was insubstantial, nothing more solid than the film on top of scalded milk, just the thing to give a laundress an apoplexy. Next she wriggled into one of the dresses. It was a shade of dark bluish gray that looked like wet slate.

And it fit. Had Alistair actually gone to a dress shop in—Charity really had no idea where they were, other than Bedfordshire—and described Charity's dimensions? Had he used his hands to sketch out her measurements? "About so wide across the shoulders, with breasts no bigger than duck eggs." If so, he had done a decent job of it. He must have memorized her body the couple of times he had seen it up close.

That wasn't at all the thing to think about right now, though.

The fabric felt smooth against her skin. She had gotten spoiled by her fine London clothes; Mrs. Trout's homespun felt like sandpaper by comparison. The chemise's soft linen was a blessed relief, and the cambric of the gown skimmed over her body in a mostly unobjectionable way.

"You look well in that." It was Louisa. Her eyes were open and she had turned her head slightly on the pillow to gaze at Charity.

"I feel like an idiot." She felt like she was in costume. But maybe she could think of Louisa's convalescence as an extended fancy dress party.

"I hope you feel like a pretty idiot, at least."

Pretty? Of all the nonsense. "It's from Pembroke."

"He knows?" She made an effort to sit up in bed, then fell back against the pillows, wincing in pain. "That you're not a man, I mean."

"The doctor said you're not to try sitting until he's seen you again." Charity turned her attention to the cuffs of the gown. "He's known for weeks." As she fiddled with the gown—it had pockets, she was pleased to discover—she felt Louisa regarding her intently.

"Why ever didn't you tell me?" she finally said.

Why *hadn't* she told Louisa? If she had been frank with Louisa, she might have spared them all this misadventure.

"At first, because I didn't want you to worry about us being discovered. No, wait, before you scold me, because it only gets worse. Later I didn't tell you because I was going to bed with him." No sense in making only a half confession.

Louisa's eyes opened wide. "Charity," she breathed. "Did he force you?"

"No! Nothing like that!" She sat on the edge of the bed and took one of Louisa's hands. "I told you I was fond of him."

Louisa shook her head, which must have caused her pain because she then grimaced. "I knew he was up to no good with you. I knew it! But Gilbert and I thought he was trying to use his influence to persuade you to . . . oh, never mind. I never dreamt that he was coercing you into his bed."

"He didn't. I promise. He and I are friends."

Louisa was silent for several minutes. "I didn't want to do anything that might get you in trouble with a man like him, especially since you've worked so hard and gone to such trouble to give me a chance to marry well. So I thought Gilbert and I could elope, and then it would be done. Nobody could undo it, and it wouldn't be your fault." She squeezed her eyes shut. "But now I feel like a fool."

"So do I. If I hadn't been so wrapped up in my own affairs, maybe I'd have noticed that you were distressed." Charity ought to have guessed that Louisa would have a good reason for acting as she did. She grinned as brightly as she could. "Since we both feel embarrassed, let's just dispense with it altogether. Declare embarrassment bankruptcy, as it were."

Louisa smiled faintly. "You do look pretty in that dress, though. It's the color. It does something to your eyes."

Alistair had said much the same thing about her silver-blue waistcoat, hadn't he? Had he picked this dress out with that in mind? It was an uncomfortable reminder of the price she might have to pay to be with him: fine chemises and pretty gowns, and a lifetime of feeling like an impostor in her own life. Mrs. Trout stuck her head into the room. "Pardon, ma'am, but I don't know what to do with the goose."

"The goose?" Charity and Louisa spoke at the same time.

"The goose as was sent over with the package," the woman explained.

"A goose? At this time of year?" Louisa asked.

"That's what I said to Mr. Trout. But he said the Quality may eat geese twelve months a year, for all we know. And if his lordship means for me to kill it and cook it for your supper . . ."

"No, indeed." It was Louisa who answered, Charity being quite overset by the idea of Alistair acquiring a goose. "I'm quite certain he means it as a present for you and Mr. Trout."

Charity wasn't sure at all. Alistair was far more likely to consider a goose as dinner rather than livestock. But she didn't want to help kill or pluck the goose, so she didn't argue.

"Well," Mrs. Trout said. "That's kind of him, and after he gave me all those coins last night, too. He didn't even count them out, but I did, and it was two pounds, five shillings, and sixpence. It goes to show, I told Mr. Trout, that even though his lordship has a face like he smelled something terrible, you can't judge from appearances. I'm sure the gentleman can't help what he looks like, now, can he?"

Stunned, and in alarming danger of succumbing to fits of laughter, Charity stepped outside for a turn around the barnyard while Louisa and their hostess discussed the care and keeping of poultry.

Really, it was provoking that at such a short distance from London, one could find no traces of civilization. Gilbert might as well have turned his carriage over in the middle of the Pyrenees or on the surface of the moon.

After confirming that Gilbert was as well as could be expected, but had been given a sleeping draught and therefore could not be removed from the doctor's house until the morrow, Alistair retired to an inn that hardly even aspired to mediocrity. There was a large coaching inn a few miles north, and another a few miles south, at either of which Alistair could likely find a bed that he wouldn't need to share with fleas or mice, but if he wanted to be within an easy walk of Charity and Gilbert, he would need to stay at the godforsaken Duck and Dragon.

He woke at dawn and took himself to the market town of Biggleswade, which, after a night in Little Hatley, now took on the appearance of a thriving metropolis. He posted several letters, visited the dressmaker and bookshop, conducted a few errands of his own, and returned to Little Hatley to collect Gilbert from the doctor's house.

Gilbert, climbing into Alistair's curricle, looked like the cat who got the cream. Nobody who had managed to overturn his carriage on such a useless stretch of road ought to look so smug, especially with his arm in a sling.

"What in God's name were you thinking, running off

with that girl?" Alistair offered by way of greeting. "Do you really think me some kind of Bluebeard, luring innocent girls to their doom?"

"I didn't know what to think," Gilbert replied with infuriating calm. "You were behaving in a dashed odd manner, and you always seemed to be deep in conversation with Selby. When I asked you what you were doing at the Selbys' house the other day, you said you had proposed marriage, and that you didn't consider Louisa's opinion of any importance."

"And so I don't. I have no intention of marrying her and never have."

"Well, I know that *now*. You're after Selby. Or Miss Church, rather. Whatever she's calling herself." He paused, his mouth open, his finger poised in the air, as if suddenly realizing something. "Or himself?" He shrugged. "Can't say I understand the half of it, but if it doesn't bother Louisa it's no business of mine."

"Quite right. I did ask Miss Church to marry me, but she feels disinclined, so I'll beg you not to mention it overmuch."

Gilbert patted Alistair's knee in a manner he doubtless thought comforting. "Why are you covered in feathers?"

"That's from the goose." A frightful animal, that goose had been, and it had been the devil's own work to get it into the curricle. "Where is the aunt?" was the only question Alistair allowed himself to ask about the elopement.

"Oh, we left her with an acquaintance in Hampstead."

Astonishing. It was coming to seem that Robin was the most reliably levelheaded member of the family. "She didn't feel that her niece might benefit from a chaperone?"

"She said it didn't matter since we were eloping anyway, and that my carriage bounced too much for her comfort."

"Were you aware that, in order to clear the way for Miss Selby's escape, she dosed Miss Church with laudanum?"

"What? Of course not. And Louisa can't possibly have known, either. She would never have allowed such a thing."

Alistair supposed he'd have to fetch the old witch from Hampstead at the same time he acquired a special license to marry these two young fools; that way the bride would have at least one relation present. It occurred to him that any idea he might have once had of using the Selbys to discourage people looking for favors had gone up in smoke in the most spectacular way. By the time this was through, he'd have spent a small fortune and gone quite thoroughly out of his way to oblige Robin and her family.

"What are you laughing about?" Gilbert asked.

"The best laid plans, little brother."

Chapter Sixteen

From the small window of Louisa's upstairs room, Charity watched an ancient-looking chaise-and-four pull into the dooryard. She ran outside in time to watch an elderly woman, of approximately the same vintage as the carriage that had conveyed her, alight from the vehicle.

"This, I dearly hope, is the Trout residence," the woman said in tones of patient weariness. "I've been this entire day on the road, and such a road it is."

"This is the Trout farm and I'm Charity Church. May I ask—"

"Oh, yes, my dear. You're the one I'm supposed to ask for." She was short and stout, with iron-gray hair and a traveling costume of much the same shade. "His lordship sent for me to look after the young lady. I don't think I've ever been so glad to be set down from a carriage." She looked doubtfully at her surroundings and seemed to rethink her relief. "Do you suppose these people have tea?"

Alistair had hired a nurse? Presumptuous, arrogant bastard. But how was Charity to send this woman away? She was rubbing the small of her back with obvious discomfort and looked to be in no condition to travel another mile. Besides, even now the coach was driving away.

Mrs. Potton—for that was how she introduced herself to a bewildered Mrs. Trout—pulled a crisp apron and a great quantity of knitting from her bag before stationing herself in the hard-backed chair by the bed.

"Take a walk, Miss Church. Get some air while the young lady sleeps. I've tended invalids much worse off than this lady." When Charity did not move, she added, placatingly, "I looked after his lordship and Master Gilbert when they were nothing more than babies, and I've been in sick rooms for more years than you've been alive. I'll do right by the lady."

"My dear ma'am, I don't doubt it. If there's anything I've learned about Lord Pembroke, it's that he doesn't compromise his standards." Alistair, interfering aristocratic shite that he was, required exact correctness from everyone around him. Surely if he had sent his own childhood nurse to care for Louisa, she could be trusted to do precisely that.

Charity slipped down the stairs and into the barnyard. The ground was still muddy from the other night's storm and dotted with foul-looking puddles. She rucked up her skirts to avoid dirtying the dress, and set out along a lane that appeared to wind between the Trouts' fields.

This countryside wasn't so different from nearby Cambridgeshire—mostly flat, shockingly green. Nothing like hard, craggy, windblown Fenshawe. She had spent her years at Cambridge trying to gorge herself on what she couldn't get enough of at home—sun, books, conversation. She had done the same thing these past weeks in London, only maybe more frenetically, because she knew the end was near.

She ought to be glad. The end of this part of her life was drawing to a close, but after that she could go wherever she wanted. She could *be* whoever she wanted. A forged reference—what was a harmless forgery after so many years of deception?—and she could have a post in Italy or India or any other warm and lively place. Surely, that thought ought to buoy her spirits, should it not? Instead she felt something like mourning, but for what she did not know. It was like imagining her own funeral.

A horse was coming down the lane, and she scrambled to the side, gathering her skirts close around her to keep them clear of splashing mud. But the horse came to a stop a few yards away.

"Robin, is that you? Of course it is. No bonnet, shaggy hair. It could hardly be anyone else."

Alistair. She probably looked like a scarecrow, gangly limbs and straw-colored hair, all wrapped up in someone else's clothing. Shading her eyes with her hand, she looked up at him. He had no right to appear even half so decadently perfect. His cravat was a marvel. His boots were shined to a mirror finish. Had he sent for his valet from London? She wouldn't put it past him.

"You're too big to ride Mab."

"Hardly, and if you think I'll ever again ride one of the innkeeper's job horses, you're sadly mistaken." He slid off the horse and came to her side. "Since you're out here and not in the sick room, I take it that Nurse Potton arrived." He didn't wait for an answer. "Give me your arm and I'll walk you back to the house."

He pulled her gloveless hand into the crook of his arm and steered her down the lane. All this talking and bustling her about wasn't like Alistair. She glanced up at his face and saw his jaw set firmly. Beneath his immaculately tied cravat, his throat worked as he swallowed.

He was nervous, or at least ill at ease. Likely he was terrified that she'd take him up on his offer of marriage. Well, she'd be gone soon and he'd have nothing to worry about. She nearly told him as much. *Take heart, we only have to get through the next week or so, and then I'll be as good as dead.* But that would only have embarrassed him.

The fine wool of his coat was out of place on this muddy farmstead, but it was reassuringly familiar after the tumultuous past few days. She checked her impulse to rub her face against it like a cat. But as they walked, she let her fingers drift along his sleeve, down to the cuff where smooth wool met the warm leather of his riding glove. She didn't let her touch linger there, but skimmed her hand back up to the crook of his arm. She wanted to memorize what Alistair felt like—expensive cloth covering lean muscle. Taking a deep breath, she could make out the scent of his customary shaving soap. Oh, he had *definitely* sent for his valet, then.

Suddenly, he seized her hand, checking its progress back down his sleeve. Presumably he didn't appreciate being petted in such a daft manner.

But he kept his firm grip on her hand as they walked

back to the house, intertwining their fingers. "How is Miss Selby?" he asked.

"Sleepy, and her head hurts. But there's been no fever or any other cause for alarm."

"Well, in that case I don't mind telling you that I'd very much like to take her and Gilbert and knock their heads together for all the trouble they've caused. It's just as well that they're both too injured for me to do so."

"They're very young, and I suppose I can't blame them for flights of fancy or rash actions. Louisa is usually so steady, I sometimes forget that she's only eighteen."

They had reached the door, but he still hadn't dropped her hand. Now he raised his eyebrow and shot her a quizzical look. "Gilbert is precisely your own age, Robin. Four-and-twenty."

"Is he? Well, I don't think I was ever that young."

"Ah, Robin." He squeezed her hand.

"I don't think you ever were either." With her free hand she traced the line between his eyebrows.

"No, and thank God for it." They stared stupidly at one another for a moment. Then, to her horror, he lifted her hand to his mouth and kissed it.

"Alistair!" she cried, wiping her hand on her skirts. "Don't you dare behave gallantly to me."

His eyes were sparkling with merriment, damn him. "Forgive me. I couldn't resist."

"Like hell you couldn't. I can't wait to burn these god-forsaken dresses." Belatedly, she realized how ungrateful she must sound.

"Don't even think of it," he retorted, and for a minute she feared he was going to feed her some utter shite about how becoming the gown was. "At least pawn them."

Now she was smiling at him like the besotted idiot she was. God help them.

He swung back onto the horse, which had been following meekly behind them.

"You don't want to see your old nurse?" she asked.

"Of course I do, but I'll save that for tomorrow when she's more settled. Until then—Wait." He put on his spectacles and peered at something at the edge of the barnyard. "Robin, what is that goose still doing alive and uncooked?"

"Louisa told Mrs. Trout you meant it as a present." She opened her eyes wide with feigned innocence. "They both thought it very gracious of you."

He looked so outraged at the idea of being considered gracious that she couldn't hold back her laughter.

"I wrestled that creature into my curricle—"

"Alistair, you did not."

"I certainly did. I'm not practiced in goose wrangling and I hope never to have the time to acquire that skill. But if it's not to be cooked, I'll have the innkeeper send over pie. Although the food at the inn is very indifferent, and you'll wish you had cooked the goose."

"You don't need to do any of this."

"Quite true. But I will anyway."

"The dresses, the books, Mrs. Potton." She shook her head, the scope of his generosity too great to put into words. "Thank you."

He waved his hand dismissively. "It's my pleasure, Robin. And before I forget, I have another trifle for you." He produced a parcel from the saddlebag and handed it to her before cantering away.

She tore open the package in the Trouts' deserted sitting room. It contained a bottle-green coat, two shirts, several cravats, a waistcoat, and breeches.

There was also a note that read, "R—Just in case. Yours etc., A."

While there was still enough light to see by, Alistair walked from the Duck and Dragon back to the farm, partly because he was bored at that terrible, terrible inn with only lovelorn Gilbert as his companion, but also because he wanted to see Robin again.

Mrs. Trout opened the door and regarded him with wide-eyed panic before dropping a curtsy and stammering something that sounded like his title. The woman was plainly at a loss as to how to deal with someone of his background. He felt faintly embarrassed in her presence, unaccountably guilty, as if he were imposing on her by being a marquess instead of a blacksmith or a ship's mate.

Come to think, he *was* imposing on her.

"Thank you for the girl and the chickens, your lordship," she said, dropping a series of curtsies as she backed away toward the kitchen.

Alistair took her statement to mean that the maid had arrived. He knew that housing three additional women and the recuperating coachman would cause the Trouts a good deal of extra work. So he found a village girl in need of employment, gave her a few coins, and sent her to wait on Mrs. Trout.

He had also sent chickens, because barnyard fowl seemed to be an acceptable gift in Little Hatley. *When in Rome*, he told himself.

Climbing the stairs, he heard Robin's voice. She was reading aloud from one of the books he sent over yesterday. He paused at the threshold, taking in the scene before anyone spotted him.

Miss Selby was propped up on several pillows, and apart from a bandage around her forehead she looked quite normal, which is to say she looked like a Dutch doll. He could see what had attracted Gilbert, if one's tastes ran to extravagant prettiness instead of, say, unruly hair and winsome smiles.

Mrs. Potton, who had seemed quite sufficiently old when Alistair was a child and now appeared to be at least eighty, was bent over her knitting.

But Robin, though. Her dress warped his understanding of the body within. He had taken some pleasure in rifling through the dress shop in Biggleswade for the gowns she would find least objectionable, but hadn't given much thought to what his own reaction might be to seeing her so attired. This morning he had been bewildered, alienated. When she wore her ordinary clothes—which was to say, men's attire—he never paid any attention to the perfection of her collar bones or thought about how very much he wanted to kiss her neck.

She noticed him standing on the threshold and stopped reading, abruptly rising to her feet and letting the book fall to the floor.

He bowed, presented Miss Selby with a letter from his brother, and submitted to Mrs. Potton's remarks about his appearance.

"You look more like his late lordship than I ever might have thought," the elderly lady said. Alistair let himself take this as a compliment since she had rocked his father's cradle and witnessed his first steps and was perhaps ignorant of his later exploits. And also because he heard the fondness in the nurse's voice.

The nurse stepped out, announcing that she would return before midnight to relieve Robin. And so the three of them were left together. An awkward business. He couldn't speak freely with Robin in front of Miss Selby; he doubted Miss Selby and Robin could speak in front of him; and he was damned if he could think of a single thing to say to Miss Selby under any circumstances.

Alistair bent and retrieved the book Robin had dropped. "I'll read, if you'll allow me."

Sitting in the chair the nurse had vacated, and angling himself so the book caught the last rays of the setting sun, he read three chapters. He scarcely paused even when the sun set and Robin lit a candle. Occasionally he felt her eyes on him from across the bed, but when he looked up she hastily glanced away. Was she remembering what had happened the last time he had read out loud? He certainly was.

"Louisa's asleep," she whispered.

He closed the book. Miss Selby was indeed fast asleep, and now he and Robin could have some privacy. "We'll have to let them marry, you know." He kept his voice low. "They'll need to marry by special license or there will be no end to the gossip." He had already sent to London to arrange for it.

"Oh, indeed. The de Lacey reputation must be protected." She rose and turned to face the dark window.

"I was thinking more of Miss Selby's reputation." He stood as well, the ingrained habit of rising when a lady stood. "Besides, they love one another."

"I wouldn't have thought you cared much about that sort of thing."

"Did you not?" He was at her shoulder now, close enough so that if she turned he could take her in his arms.

She remained silent, her arms crossed and braced on the sill of the room's one, high window.

"I wonder what I've done to give you that impression," he murmured. Had he been as cold as that, so wrapped up in his own pride and sense of duty that she thought him incapable of anything else? He brushed the fine curls off the nape of her neck, then ran his fingers just along the inside of her dress. She made a soft sound that seemed to Alistair's ears equal parts pleasure and dismay.

"Don't look at me like that."

"How can you tell how I'm looking at you?" he said into her ear. "You're not even facing me." He smoothed his hands down the sides of her bodice, tracing the outline of her silhouette.

"I can feel it. You're looking at me all gawking-like." She

rounded on him, and he took the opportunity to draw her against his chest. "I feel like a ninny, all trussed up like this," she said into his lapels. "I can't wait to get this off of me."

"I can't say I object." She smelled different. Likely she had borrowed Miss Selby's soap, but he missed her usual scent.

"Oh, to hell with you." But he knew she was smiling. "It's such a hoax."

"A hoax?" he repeated.

"The dress. It's . . . not me."

After years spent dressed as a boy and impersonating a dead man, she felt that it was this dress that constituted the hoax? He took a moment to recalibrate his notions of fraudulence so they might be more in line with her own. "Well, I can see that," he said, although the sentiment was more aspirational than actual. "But regardless of what you're wearing, you look like my Robin." And it was true. She could wear animal skins, she could wear a black robe and a barrister's wig. It didn't matter to him. But it mattered to her. "Only a few more weeks and you'll be back to your usual self," he offered.

She took a sharp breath and abruptly pulled away from him. In the scant light he could see tears in her eyes. "What a mess, Alistair."

"Nothing that can't be fixed." He willed himself to believe that he spoke the truth.

"You don't know the half."

"Then tell me." He'd fix it. Whatever it was, he'd move heaven and earth to make things right for her. Here he was sending her sweets and haberdashery, servants and barnyard fowl. Did she not understand that he would do more, if she would let him?

"There's hardly any moon tonight." Her voice strained with the effort of not crying, her hands in fists at her sides. "You ought to go back before it gets any darker. You're probably not any good at traipsing about the countryside in the dark."

He ignored this. She had to be quite overwrought if that was the best insult she could come up with. "I love you, Robin."

"Stop," she sobbed. On the bed, Miss Selby stirred. "Go," Robin said. "Go."

He kissed her once on her forehead and left.

When he arrived back at the Duck and Dragon, covered in what had to be half the mud in Bedfordshire, he found his solicitor waiting for him in the inn's parlor.

"Good God, Nivins. What possessed you to come all this distance?"

"I . . . oh dear, what a very troublesome business, always to be the bearer of ill tidings." The solicitor let out a panicked sort of laugh, and then adjusted his spectacles. "I have the information you requested. When I heard from your staff where you had gone, and in what company, I knew I had to tell you immediately." He brought himself up to his full height, as if needing to draw on an inner store of fortitude.

It took Alistair a moment to remember what he had asked Nivins to do for him. He put on his own spectacles and took the sheaf of papers Nivins had placed on the table.

"I gather that you did not know the gentleman to be married, and especially not to a lady who seems to have vanished off the face of the earth shortly after the ceremony."

"If only it were that simple," Alistair managed, half stunned by what he was reading. "I saw the lady in question this very day."

"In Bedfordshire, my lord?"

"Correct." Alistair stared at the documents, hardly believing what he read.

"I had, if you'll pardon me for saying so, some indication of why you required information about the gentleman," the solicitor ventured.

"You did?" Now Alistair was fully stunned, if Nivins had any inclination of his relationship with the person known as Robert Selby.

"I had called on Mrs. Allenby several days ago to settle the details about a trust she's setting up for her daughters, and Mr. Selby was there, tête-à-tête with the eldest Allenby girl. I took the liberty of inquiring into the gentleman's background. It would be a tolerable match for both of them, even though it certainly isn't my business to say so. But *bigamy*, my lord. That's quite another story."

"Indeed it is, Nivins. Indeed it is." Alistair balled up the paper Nivins had given him and threw it angrily into the fire.

Chapter Seventeen

As soon as Mrs. Potton woke from her nap, refreshed and ready to sit with Louisa, Charity stealthily dressed herself in the clothes Alistair had brought her that morning, borrowed one of Mr. Trout's caps, and slipped out of the farmhouse unobserved.

She didn't need a lantern; years of rising before dawn to fetch water from the well, or even to sneak back into her rooms at Cambridge after the gates were locked, had taught her how to get by with little light. The lane was muddy but it was straight enough and she arrived at the Duck and Dragon without any mishap.

There was no sign of Alistair in the taproom, of course. It would take any self-respecting innkeeper only a single glance to know that Alistair needed to be put in the private parlor.

"I have a message for Lord Pembroke," she told the barmaid, guessing that he had messengers and parcels coming and going at all hours.

The girl looked up too quickly, an avaricious gleam in her eyes. "If you give me the letter I'll bring it to him myself."

Charity bet she would. According to the maid Alistair

sent to the Trouts, Alistair was giving out shillings like they were farthing pieces. "I have instructions to only give it into his hands."

The barmaid shrugged. "Have it your way, then. He's still in the parlor." She pointed to a door on the other side of the room.

She found him sprawled in a wing-backed chair near the fire. The parlor was otherwise empty, it being late and the Duck and Dragon not being so lofty an establishment as to have more than one patron who merited the private parlor. He turned to face her at the sound of the door snicking shut.

"Robin," he said, and his voice sounded so much wearier than it had only a few hours earlier.

"I wanted to see you." She moved to sit in the chair opposite his, but then thought better of it and sat on the footstool before him. "What's the trouble?"

He brushed a lock of hair off her forehead. "Why did you do it, Charity?"

She knew from the seriousness of his expression—not anger, only a sad sort of gravity—that he wasn't asking why she came tonight. "It depends on what you mean. I've done a lot of things." And wasn't that God's own truth?

"Why did you conceal Robert Selby's death?"

She had a sick sense of foreboding. "I've already explained. The estate was entailed. Louisa would have had nothing. It was the best idea I could think of."

He reached for her hand and held it on his knee. "I have a copy of Selby's will."

She shook her head quickly. Robbie's will ought to have

been locked up at the solicitor's office in Alnwick, the only other copy in the study at Fenshawe. But she supposed marquesses could get whatever they wanted. "Then you'll know he left her nothing." Her voice sounded high and tense.

"In the event that he was married at the time of his death, his widow was to have a thousand pounds." He pressed her hand and looked into her eyes with an expression she could not read. "Why did you give it up?"

She moved to pull her hand away but he held it fast, stroking the underside of her wrist with his thumb. Now he knew the most serious of her deceptions. There were no secrets left; he knew the entirety of her, and still he held her close. "Because there was nothing for Louisa," she repeated. How could she have taken that money and left Louisa—a child of sixteen—homeless and penniless, with scarcely a relation in the world or a friend to her name? Few knew better than Charity what that fate was like. Robbie had done badly by his sister, and Charity knew she had to make it right. "It was my duty." Duty not only to Louisa as her only relation, but also to Robbie, and also to herself. She didn't know how to put those ideas into words Alistair would understand.

He was looking at her with something like perplexed wonder.

"Besides," she continued, thinking to appeal to his practical side, "what would a thousand pounds do for her? That would give her forty pounds a year, not nearly enough to keep a girl who had been brought up to be a lady."

The silence stretched out, the only sound the fire crackling in the hearth. "It would have been more than enough for you."

As if that had ever been an option. "Maybe if I had a few more weeks to think about it, I could have come up with a better idea, but it all happened so fast. He died suddenly, and Louisa was still sick, and I didn't know what to do."

"And you were grieving, I think?" He said it so gently. It would have been so much better if he had thrown this in her face, if he had been angry or even disappointed at her deceit and her secrecy.

"I was," she whispered. She hadn't felt entitled to grieve. Who was she but a servant who had the bad sense to land in her master's bed? The fact that Robbie insisted on marrying her surely said more about his sense of honor than it did about her fitness to be his wife.

And so she had taken all that grief and turned it into action. She turned off any servants who couldn't be trusted to keep a secret. She did what needed to be done to save as much as she could from Fenshawe's income. All to keep Louisa safe.

"How did you guess?" Only when she spoke did she realize she was crying.

"Come here." He hauled her onto his lap, despite her protests. "I don't care if anyone comes in." His voice was fierce. *Now* he was angry? "Do you understand that? It doesn't matter."

Like hell it didn't, but she had her face buried in his neck and he was stroking her back, and it all felt too good to be sensible about.

"To answer your question," he said, "I didn't guess. I had my solicitor look for any evidence of a marriage between you and Selby. You had mentioned being near Scotland, where it wouldn't have mattered if you were underage."

"I was eighteen and he was nineteen." Young and rash, but of course they hadn't thought so at the time. "We had been in and out of one another's beds for years by that point, you know." She said that just in case he thought she had ever been a respectable miss. "But he took the notion into his head that if I were his wife, there would be no dishonesty in my going to Cambridge in his stead. No, I know it's bollocks, but that was his condition. So we rode into Scotland, were married over the anvil, and returned to Fenshawe in time for me to roast a joint for supper." She found that she was braced for his disapproval, but it never came. "We didn't tell anyone," she continued, "because I was to leave Fenshawe on the pretense of going to York as a lady's maid, but of course I was really going to Cambridge."

She had condensed so many misdeeds into a few sentences, but his hand never faltered in the steady rhythm he stroked on her back.

"Is that why you won't marry me? Because you had already been married once and didn't want to settle for anything less than—"

"No!" She couldn't let him think that. "I did love Robbie." She leaned back so they could see one another's faces. "But he's been dead over two years." She didn't want to talk about this, didn't want to put her thoughts into words, to make them any more real than they were. But he had been honest about his feelings and she wanted to give him the same. "I love you." His eyes flared with satisfaction, which only meant that he hadn't yet understood. "I wish like hell that I didn't, though."

"Marry me."

She was going to have to spell it out for him. "You see, if Robbie had lived, it would have been awkward enough for me to be mistress of Fenshawe. Imagine how much more awkward it would be for me to be Lady Pembroke."

"You sell yourself short. You also have an appalling notion of what I require in a wife. Do you think I intend to force you to wait on the queen or preside over tea parties?"

She ignored this, because of course he'd want a wife to do all those things and more. "And there's the small matter of my not having a death certificate for my husband. Charity Selby is a married woman, as far as the law is concerned."

"Charity Selby," he repeated, and it sounded strange to her ears as well. He was silent for too long, his hands still on her hips. She knew that he finally understood. "There has to be a way to have Selby declared dead."

"Not without exposing Louisa's participation in a fraud. And I won't have that."

"You've already given up your name and a thousand pounds for Louisa's comfort. Have you asked her whether she wants you to continue sacrificing for her? It's not clear to me that you owe her a damned thing at this point."

She almost pitied him. "It's not about owing her anything. She's eighteen. I've known her since she was two. We're family to one another." She refrained from pointing out his own treatment of his flesh-and-blood family, but let the implication hang in the air.

He was silent for several moments, long enough that she thought he'd let the subject drop. "That's right, she *is* your sister," he said musingly. "That much was true."

"Sister-in-law."

He cradled her face in his hands. "Imagine if everyone did by their siblings as well as you've done for yours."

She wasn't expecting that, and the kindness and admiration in his voice undid her. Her throat went tight. "Now you think I'm some sort of martyr."

"I think nothing of the sort. I think you're one of the finest people I've ever met."

That set her off into a fresh round of tears, while Alistair stroked her hair and whispered nonsense to her about how everything would come out all right. Charity wished she could believe it.

Alistair drove his curricle with painstaking care lest he jostle Gilbert's healing arm. His brother had only that morning received permission from the doctor to venture forth from the inn, and had promptly and predictably requested to be conveyed to Louisa's bedside.

"Your betrothed has taken a great deal of interest in poultry, Miss Church has told me," Alistair said, trying to casually indicate his acceptance of the marriage.

"That's Louisa!" Gilbert said happily, as if interest in barnyard fowl was precisely the thing to be proud of in a future wife. And why shouldn't it be? Alistair had found stranger things to admire in the woman he wished to marry.

"I had Nivins draw up some papers to give you the use of the Kent property." He didn't turn his head to look at his brother, in case Gilbert thought this an outrageous gift, embarrassingly grand. But with Robin as his example, how could Alistair not be generous? He wanted things to be right between them. He wanted to pledge his support for however Gilbert chose to live his life.

The next thing he knew, Gilbert was hugging him enthusiastically with his unbroken arm. "Thank you! This is wonderful!"

"Careful, or we'll overturn this carriage too." But he couldn't help but smile at his brother's happiness.

"Louisa says the soil in Kent is perfect for . . ."

Alistair let Gilbert prattle on. He was not interested in Miss Selby's thoughts on Kentish agriculture, but was pleased to notice that Gilbert was. For how many months had Alistair been troubled by his brother's lack of direction, worried about his aimlessness? Perhaps Miss Selby was the influence he needed.

While Gilbert and Louisa were fussing over one another's bruises and bandages, Alistair caught Robin's eye. "Perhaps you'll take some air with me, Miss Church," he suggested, offering his arm. He didn't know what else to call her even though Gilbert and Miss Selby were perfectly aware that Alistair had met her as Robert Selby, and Charity Church hadn't been her name for some years.

No sooner had they stepped outside than they were besieged by chickens. "What the devil do they mean by this?" Alistair asked while fending off a winged attacker.

She shot him a look that was pure mischief. "They're paying you a compliment. I've been feeding them, so they likely think anyone I keep company with can be relied on." From the pocket of her gown, she produced a handful of seeds and scattered them on the ground before her.

"You've been feeding chickens. Deplorable." That would explain the new profusion of freckles on her cheeks, if she had been hatless in the barnyard this past week.

"Well, you keep sending more of them. Mrs. Trout has her hands full. And if you're thinking of sending her any more tokens of your esteem, consider a sack of chicken feed."

"I'll send her twenty guineas worth of chicken feed, if only you'll leave menial labor to the domestics."

Now she looked at him with a curious expression. "What am I if not a domestic, my lord?"

"You're a thorn in my side and a great many other things besides, but I wish you'd chiefly think of yourself as the future Lady Pembroke."

She snorted, tossing another handful of seeds. "I thought we had been through this already. There's no way for me to marry you or anyone else without Louisa's name being dragged through the mud."

"I've thought of a way." He had turned the matter over in his mind for days now and kept arriving at only one solution. "A way that won't harm Miss Selby. We go sailing. Gilbert, Miss Selby, you, and me. You'd be dressed as Robert Selby at the outset of the trip. But when we come back, you'd be dressed as Charity Church. We would explain that there was an accident and Robert Selby fell overboard, and in due course we could have him proclaimed dead even without a body."

She was silent for a moment, tracing an arc in the dirt with the toe of her boot. "I'm to fake my own death, then."

"I know it's not ideal, but I can think of no better way for you to end the role."

"The role," she repeated. "Right." She turned back to the chickens, and this time threw seeds so hard that the birds scattered nervously and let out a chorus of squawks. "And we're simply to hope that nobody ever picks up on the resemblance between the late Robert Selby and Charity Church—pardon me, I mean the Marchioness of Pembroke." Her voice was dripping with sarcasm.

"We would have to live a retired life in the country, only coming to town when strictly necessary. Besides, I don't think you realize how different you look in a gown. Even I didn't recognize you at first."

She narrowed her eyes and he saw that her fists were clenched at her sides. "You don't think I realize the difference attire makes? As far as living in the country, you would hate that. You dine out and attend dances and balls and plays six nights out of seven. I can't imagine you cooped up in the country."

"You have it all wrong." He had no need for those entertainments. He had thrown himself into that social whirlwind only to see more of her. And—*oh.* Understanding hit him like a brick in the head. He might not miss London life, but she would. He had seen with his own eyes how happy she was to be gadding about town; with clever company and entertainment she had flourished. He couldn't give her that. It was humbling, knowing that there was something he could not give her. "Perhaps we could travel," he offered, knowing it to be a paltry substitute.

"We could," she said with a smile that was so false it was terrifying. "With the result that it would only take longer for anyone to notice the resemblance. Besides, how long would it take for *you* to notice the jeers and jests at our expense? I'm not a lady. You can put me in a gown far finer than this one and I still won't be a lady. And I don't want to be. I'm much happier in breeches and boots anyway."

Part of him wanted to protest that surely she could make the one small sacrifice that would allow them to be together? She could wear breeches under her gowns, perhaps, if she was so fond of them. She was wearing a dress today to allow her to be with Miss Selby; could she not do so for him?

But he knew it wasn't fair to ask; there was a difference between the span of two weeks versus the rest of her life.

Could he, the Marquess of Pembroke, have a wife who dressed—nay, *lived*—as a man? Not if he wanted to be respectable, he couldn't. He would be quite cast out from decent society. The gossip would last the rest of his life, and likely longer. With this one choice, he'd bring himself lower than his father ever had been.

Robin was avoiding his gaze, instead resolutely focusing her attention on a chicken who was getting caught in her skirts. He bent and picked up the animal. With his other hand he tipped her face up to his own, and pressed a kiss onto her cheek. The chicken squawked anxiously and hopped to the ground. "Quite right," he said. "I'll never ask you to wear a gown." It felt like a small concession, really, if it allowed him to have her by his side.

"I have my own suggestion," she said. The sun glinted off her hair, turning it to ribbons of gold and bronze. She had done something with combs and pins to disguise the shorter length, but a strand had come loose. He reached out to tuck it behind her ear, but she stepped back. "We go on as we did in London," she said. "I carry on as Robert Selby, we spend as much time together as we please. You hire me on as your secretary if—"

"I don't want a secretary," he protested, taking one of her hands and pulling her to him. "I want a wife. And what of Clifton? Is he to continue to be deprived of his property?"

"I don't give a damn about him or his property. He can rot. Fenshawe can rot."

"I don't think you mean that, Robin. It would weigh on you. Anything we had would be tainted by the wrong we had done."

She let out a sob. "I know that. I do. But what else is there? All I want is you, Alistair."

He ought to agree. He *wanted* to agree, to simply say that he felt the same way. He could take her in his arms and kiss her and everything would be right. "I won't make you my mistress."

"Mistress! Ha!" She tugged her hand out of his grasp. "Is that what you consider me presently? Your mistress? *Mistress* makes it sound like there's something sordid about it."

He had been so reasonable, so very calm, during this conversation. But he felt his control slipping out of his grasp and being replaced by a seething, simmering rage. "There would be plenty sordid about it, believe me. My father—"

"He *loved* Mrs. Allenby."

He gritted his teeth. "Hear me now, Charity." He didn't know why he resorted to her proper name, but it felt stiff and dishonest on his tongue. "I will not make a Mrs. Allenby out of you, and I will not follow my father's example."

"So proud, so fastidious," she said mockingly.

"I will not sire any bastards on you."

She sucked in a breath. "Watch yourself, Alistair. I'm likely a bastard."

"Which is precisely why I should have thought you'd know better than to let your own child suffer that fate. Any child of mine will be born with my name and protection, and that's final."

"That didn't bother you when we were fucking in your bedchamber or against the wall of my study, did it now?"

"I was careful," he ground out. "But do you think we'd always be so lucky? Children would be inevitable." A thought occurred to him. He stepped towards her, reaching out. "Are you saying that you think you might be—"

"God, no. Don't you think I would have told you at the outset?" She seemed appalled, offended. Then, more gently, "No, there's no question of that."

The mad twinge of disappointment he experienced was a reminder of why they couldn't continue like this. Eventually he'd be buried deep inside her and the prospect of a child wouldn't seem like such a bad idea. And then there would be another generation of de Lacey bastards.

"Then what, pray tell, would you have us do?" The words sounded as bitter as he felt.

Her chin was raised and her jaw was set but her eyes were watery. "I wish I knew. I don't see a way for us to carry on."

"I won't accept it."

"You can't have everything your own way, Alistair."

"Like hell I can't. What I want—marriage, respectability for ourselves and our children, a fair distribution of your late husband's property—is *right*. What you're suggesting is utterly unreasonable."

"Did it occur to you, even once, that your notions of respectability and justice don't mean a thing to me? Those ideas have never done me any good, so why should I care? Can you even contemplate what it's like to be a person your rules work against, Alistair?"

He opened his mouth to protest but she had already turned away.

CHAPTER EIGHTEEN

She came to him that night. Alistair looked up from the second-rate supper he was sharing with Gilbert in the Duck and Dragon's private parlor, and saw her enter.

She was once again wearing the men's clothing he had given her, along with a wool cap that looked like she had stolen it from someone who could ill afford to lose a cap. She must have sneaked out of the farmhouse on some pretext. As he listened, she told the innkeeper some taradiddle about needing to deliver an urgent message to his lordship in the parlor.

There were so many layers of dishonesty in this performance that it was almost impossible to discern the kernel of truth nestled at its core. Surely he ought to disapprove of such rampant falsehood. Surely the fact that he didn't disapprove was a very bad sign indeed.

Hell, he wasn't even embarrassed that Gilbert was there to witness how eagerly he shot to his feet when he saw Robin at the door.

"Good evening, Miss—ah, I mean Mr. Selby," Gilbert said, and went back to eating his soup.

Alistair wordlessly pulled out an empty chair next to his own.

She didn't sit, though. She only pulled off her ratty wool cap and shook out her hair. "I needed to see you."

And that was the kernel of truth. That was why none of the deceit mattered to him in the least—she had done what was necessary to put herself in the same room as him. And if that need to be together wasn't honest, he didn't know what was.

"Upstairs?" he asked, his mouth going dry.

Gilbert had to know what was going on, but he went on eating his soup, pretending to be deaf and dumb.

She gave him a quick, businesslike nod. He led the way to his bedchamber, trying to maintain a sedate pace while hearing Robin's light step on the bare wood of the stairs behind him.

He stopped just inside the closed door, bracing his hand on the door frame behind Robin's head. "Is this . . ." He needed to know. "Does this mean that you're accepting my proposal?"

She shook her head.

He hadn't thought so, but he had foolishly let himself hope, and now he was angry and disappointed. "Then what *does* it mean? I don't think I'm very interested in a goodbye fuck, Charity."

"Why does it have to mean anything?" Her smile was a tease, an illusion of happiness he couldn't and wouldn't share. "Can't we just be together and pretend that things are all right? One last time?"

He leaned in, crowding her with his body. "That's practically the definition of a goodbye fuck, my dear, and I find that I have no appetite for that sort of thing." He could smell her hair soap and feel the heat of her breath on his jaw.

"I beg to differ," she said, trailing her hand down his abdomen until it reached his hardening cock. "I think you've plenty of appetite for it."

"Unfair, Robin," he growled. Her touch was a mere whisper of a thing, but he had to stop himself from thrusting into her grip. He took hold of her wrist and held it tight. "What is it that you want from me tonight? Do you think that a few moments of pleasure will delude me into thinking that continuing like this is anything other than folly?"

"I know that it won't. I want to push everything to the side and have you while I can."

She had said something like that before. Something about sweeping her worries aside and enjoying herself while she still could. At the time he hadn't understood why she thought she was running out of time, but now he did. "What lies on the other side, Robin? For you, I mean."

She shook her head, then made a sweeping motion with the hand he wasn't holding, indicating that these were all the worries she didn't want to be thinking of tonight.

Fine. If she wanted pleasure, he could give her that. If she wanted to break his heart more comprehensively than might otherwise have been the case, then so be it. His heart was hers to break.

He leaned forward and kissed the corner of her mouth, where her lips turned up in a small, brave smile.

He had her on the bed before he could think better of it, and she pulled him down on top of her, parting her legs so he could settle against her where they both needed it. Bowing his head, he took her mouth in a hard, punishing kiss. She seemed to understand, biting his lip and digging her fingertips into his shoulders. Not only pleasure, but also a little bit of pain.

He pulled off her cravat and opened her shirt and waistcoat. She was beautiful spread out beneath him, her creamy breasts bare beside the white linen of her shirt and the dark silk of her waistcoat. It was more erotic than any sight he had ever allowed himself to imagine. He sat back on his knees to better admire the sight. She was breathing heavily, her small but perfect breasts rising towards him with every inhalation. Reverently, he skimmed his hand down from her shoulder, cupping her breast, thumbing her nipple. A small sigh of satisfaction escaped her lips, and he felt his cock throb in response.

"I want to see you," she said. "Take off your clothes."

And so he did, drinking in her frankly appraising stare. Then he knelt between her legs and gave his cock a few leisurely strokes. "Any other requests?"

She eyed him for another long moment. "Now take off my clothes."

He spent a good deal more time undressing her than he had himself, kissing all the more interesting parts of her as he exposed them. If this was to be their last time together, he wanted to lavish every attention on her. He wanted to memorize every inch of her, every curve and angle, the strong length of her thigh and the delicate bones of her wrist, storing up memories against a bleak and empty tomorrow. But that wasn't how love worked. Love wasn't a sum safely invested in the five percents. One couldn't prevent future sorrow by capitalizing on present bliss. All he could do was have this moment, wring all the joy out of it, and then somehow continue after it was over.

He braced himself over her on one forearm and notched his cock at her entrance. He chased from his mind any thoughts of the future, concentrating instead on the purr of contentment she made as he slid into her inch by inch. She was wet and soft and tight as her body accommodated his. She was lithe and supple beneath him. She was *his*, goddammit, no matter what she thought. Even if they never did this again, she would always be his. Or at least he would be hers.

He rolled them over, so she could ride him and he could watch her. She sighed contentedly as she lowered herself onto him, but then moved her hips only slightly, rocking against him. She was chasing her own pleasure, he realized.

"Touch yourself," he ordered, his voice hoarse. "Show me how you touch yourself when you're alone. And we'll both know that the next time you do it, you'll wish you had my cock inside you." He thrust up hard into her to drive home his point, and she groaned in pleasure.

Her mouth curved up in a conspiratorial smile as one of her hands drifted up her thigh to settle over the pale hair between her legs. Transfixed, he watched as she used one finger to lightly stroke herself, never faltering in her rhythmic riding of his cock.

He propped himself up on his elbows to get a better look, then to take her breast in his mouth.

"Yes," she cried. She was lost to pleasure now, her eyes half-closed, her mouth parted slightly. He settled his hands on her hips, his fingers sinking into the soft skin of her backside, as he felt her work her body onto his.

She was using him, he realized. She was using his body as an instrument of pleasure, and he loved it. He wrapped his fingers around the posts of the headboard and let her have her way with him.

Charity could have spent all night like this, side by side on a lumpy mattress, tracing his long lean muscles, toying with the dark hair that curled on his chest.

But she had to leave. That was the entire point.

"Just think," he murmured, his voice thick with sleep and satisfaction. "I've been trying so hard these last few days not to compromise you."

He had? "Whatever for? That ship sailed a long time ago." She had never had a reputation and it had never bothered her one jot.

"Because I wanted you to know that when I offered to marry you, it wouldn't be to save your reputation."

She nearly laughed, but then realized he was serious. It wasn't that he thought she needed her reputation protected, but that he didn't want her to think that his proposal was a sop to convention. "Thank you," she said.

"Besides, your reputation is unexceptionable. You're a respectable widow as well as the future Lady Pembroke."

"Alistair . . ." she cautioned. He had to be deranged to still believe that was possible.

"Well, you are." He rolled over onto his side and propped himself up on his elbow. "We're going to be married, as soon as I can figure out how."

She shook her head. "I love you," she said, and tried not to make it sound like an apology.

"I've never doubted it. Or, rather, I shouldn't have. From the moment you rushed to see me when I asked for you."

She knew he was talking about the day he summoned her to Pembroke House, only to accuse her of having lied about his father being Louisa's godfather. He had been better off then—safer, less trusting, his heart wrapped up right and tight in layers of pride and dignity. She had ruined that, and he still didn't know it. She winced at the pain he'd feel when she was gone. "I came to you because I thought you were in trouble," she protested. "I thought you needed me."

"I did need you." He drew her against him.

"You needed nothing of the sort," she murmured into his shoulder. "Your life was peaceful before you met me, and now look at you."

"Happy, sated, and warm with the person I love?"

She pulled away and propped herself up on her elbow to look down at him. "Careening headlong into heartbreak. In a shabby inn, just having fornicated with a confidence artist.

About to consent to your brother's marrying a penniless nobody."

He sighed. "I see that I'm going to have to spell this out for you. In order, then." He was using his most aristocratic voice, the one he probably trotted out in the House of Lords. "I'm not concerned with heartbreak, since I take our eventual marriage as a foregone conclusion." When she tried to look away, he took her chin in his hand and tipped her face towards his, planting a soft kiss on her mouth. "This inn is horrible, I'll grant you that. I certainly would never have stayed anyplace half so shabby if not for its proximity to you. That's only one of the many ways you've expanded my horizons." Another kiss, this one more lingering. "As to your being a confidence artist, I think not. You're not deceiving anyone for profit, except the cousin, and we'll figure out a way to make things right for him. Lastly, Gilbert's affairs are his own concern."

She wasn't convinced. She didn't even think he was convinced. He'd wake up tomorrow, and if not tomorrow then one day next month or next year, and realize what a narrow escape he had made. He was quite mad with love, she understood. Someday she'd be able to look back and feel appropriately tender about this, she'd revel in what it meant to have been loved by such a man, such a *good* man. But now she knew she had to think clearly enough for both of them, or they'd be shackled together for a lifetime of resentment.

He rolled on top of her, nudging her legs apart with his knee. "Have you no counterargument, then?" he said into her ear.

"Time is my counterargument," she murmured as he kissed her neck.

"And this," he said hoarsely, fitting himself into her, "is mine."

She slipped out of his room as soon as he fell asleep, dressing as well as she could in the dark and taking care not to wake him. It was too dark to aspire to anything neater than mere decency, so she hoped that she wouldn't attract any attention on her way out of the inn. One look at her disheveled state would give rise to too many questions about what she had been doing in Lord Pembroke's room.

Her borrowed wool cap pulled low over her eyes, she made her way discreetly through the inn's taproom. She had nearly made it to the door when she felt a hand on her arm.

"Mr. Selby, a moment of your time, please."

It was Gilbert, and his expression was so solemn she was momentarily overwhelmed by his resemblance to his older brother.

"Of course," she said. "Outside, perhaps. You can walk me back."

He nodded, too much the gentleman to refuse a lady's request for accompaniment, whatever she might be dressed like. Once there was nobody about to overhear them, he spoke again. "Are you going to marry him?"

"No."

Gilbert didn't bother hiding his groan of dismay. "I had my hopes up, you know. He's always on his damned high horse and I thought that loving a woman who, if you'll excuse my saying so, isn't precisely who one would expect him to marry, would do him a great deal of good. Take him down a notch."

She hid a smile. "Which might make him more accepting of you and Louisa, you mean?"

"Ah, maybe a little bit of that, too. But, you know, I did tell you a while ago that he's a good deal more pleasant when you're around. That was before I realized that the two of you were, ah . . ." He fumbled for words. "Before I realized precisely how things stood between the two of you, as it were."

It was true. When they met, he had been so dour, so coldly respectable. His chief concern had been repairing and maintaining his family legacy and bank accounts. Two months ago he would no sooner have allowed his brother to marry Louisa than he would have let Gilbert go on stage. But tonight, in between lingering kisses, Alistair had simply stated that Gilbert's affairs were his own.

She didn't know if she had single-handedly worked this magic, but she did know that if she stayed around him he wouldn't be happy for long. Even if, improbably, they managed to circumvent all the obstacles that lay in their path, he would soon enough realize that he was saddled with a wife who fell lamentably short of his own exacting standards.

They were approaching the Trout farm now. She touched Gilbert's arm. "After this is all done, you'll take care of him, won't you? You and Louisa will be all he has." Thank God it was dark and he couldn't see the tears in her eyes.

Alistair woke to the sound of paper sliding across the bare wood floor. The sun was beginning to slant through the clouded windows. When he reached out for Robin, he found the bed empty and the covers cool. Of course. She would have left hours ago in order to return unobserved to the farm.

He sat up in bed and retrieved his spectacles from the bedside table, taking his time polishing them and putting them on before padding across the room to where the single sheet of paper lay folded by the door sill. He eyed it suspiciously for a moment, as if it were a half-dead bird brought in by an overzealous dog. There was no possibility that a note slipped under an inn door at daybreak could signify anything pleasant.

With a sigh of resignation, he bent and picked it up. The paper was the cheap, flimsy stuff the inn provided, and the handwriting was Gilbert's messy schoolboy scrawl.

Dear Alistair,

    I know this is dashed havey-cavey for all of us to run off like this but Miss C says it's the only way, and I hope you'll forgive me. I'll send word as soon as Louisa and I are married.

P.S. We'll take Mrs. P home.
P.P.S. Miss C has your horse.

He supposed he ought to be grateful that he had any note at all, even such an afterthought as this one. How long had they been planning to abandon him here? Had Robin known last night that she would disappear on the morrow? Had Gilbert known as they dined that it would be their last meal together? Exactly how thoroughly had he been conspired against?

For God's sake, Gilbert was now in possession of the special license Alistair had sent for. If acquiring the license wasn't enough to prove that he supported this marriage, what else was there? Was Alistair not to be granted the chance to see his brother married? Was he such an ogre, as Robin had called him, that his nearest and dearest didn't trust him to keep his peace at a wedding, and instead ran away to get married in secret?

Evidently so.

An even worse explanation occurred to him: perhaps Robin, whose presence was required at the marriage as Miss Selby's putative guardian, simply never wanted to see him again. Was that the reason for his shunning?

She had told him that last night was their farewell. She had made no secret of it. But it hadn't needed to be like this, fleeing in the dead of night. It hadn't needed to be so immediate.

As he stared at this sorry letter—*shabbily done, Gilbert*—his sense of loss slowly ebbed away, replaced by a tide of much more palatable anger. Good. Anger he could work with. Too bad he knew it for the temporary reprieve it was. It would soon burn off and leave him bereft of even the comfort of his righteous indignation.

But for now he was livid with rage, and he welcomed it.

He rang for his valet to pack his portmanteau and have

the curricle readied, all the while pretending that he had planned all along to leave this godforsaken inn and was merely a few hours behind his companions. He had no idea where he ought to go, but he knew he couldn't stay here, stewing and seething.

He mustn't have done a very good job at pretending, though, because his valet and groom took one look at him and declared as one that they would ride back to London in a hired cart with the baggage.

On the way out of Little Hatley, Alistair stopped at the Trout farm on the chance that Mrs. Trout could give him any indication of where the women had gone. But the farmer's wife only told him what he already knew: the ladies had left at daybreak, Mrs. Potton and Miss Selby riding in the carriage with Gilbert and the now-recovered coachman riding outside, and Miss Church on Alistair's horse.

He had nearly forgotten that detail in Gilbert's letter. Robin was a horse thief now, in addition to her manifold other crimes. And why that ought to make him want to smile instead of curse was a mystery for the ages. He would give her a dozen horses, each finer than the last, if that was what she needed. Even if he never saw her again, even if he never so much as heard her name again, if only he could be assured that she was safe and well.

Thanking Mrs. Trout for all she had done during Miss Selby's convalescence, he counted out enough coins to pay the maid's wages through the end of the quarter. Then he thought better of it, and added a few more sovereigns, enough to pay the girl for the next twelvemonth.

There was something about having lost his heart and having been prepared to lose his respectability that made him free with his spending. He had, even with the constraints imposed by his father's profligacy, more money than he needed. With a few coins that meant little to him, he could grant this woman who had been kind to Charity and her daft sister-in-law the luxury of a maid for a year. He didn't know what precisely that meant for a woman in Mrs. Trout's circumstances—probably nothing more than a set of hands to churn the butter or rock the cradle, which, by the looks of the lady, was to be required this summer. For Alistair, those same coins wouldn't even buy a new waistcoat.

Turning his curricle onto the London road, he recalled that his father had used much the same rationale to justify spending absurd sums of money. If the flowers he sent his favorite opera dancers cost less than a mere tin of hair powder, then how could it be an extravagance? Of course, he had then proceeded to buy the hair powder as well as the bouquets, and a good many other things besides, and that was why Alistair's ledgers had only recently started to add up properly.

Still, it was disconcerting to find that there was any common ground he shared with his father, and it had been happening more and more lately. Ever since he met Robin, he had behaved in a way that a few months ago he would have considered reckless, shameful, wrong. It was more than reckless spending and condoning Gilbert's lack of career and improvident marriage. Christ, if Alistair had gotten his way, the next Marchioness of Pembroke would have been a foundling housemaid turned felonious impostor, a woman who declared she wouldn't give up her breeches and waistcoats.

If another peer behaved in such a way, Alistair would have thought the poor fellow belonged in a lunatic asylum. But even now, angry and betrayed, he felt no regret, not even an inkling of shame. If he saw Charity riding up towards him—on *his* horse, which she had stolen, he reminded himself—he'd marry her in a heartbeat, propriety and respectability be damned.

There were, he reluctantly acknowledged, matters his father hadn't gotten entirely wrong. Love carried a weight that was heavier than honor or prudence or any of the other things he had valued.

A damned uncomfortable realization, but not one he could shy away from.

By the time he reached London, every trace of his anger at having been abandoned, deceived, and robbed had slipped through his fingers, leaving him empty of everything but a dull pain.

Chapter Nineteen

It would take over a week to reach Scotland at this rate, traveling slowly so as not to jostle Louisa's head or Gilbert's arm. Every hour or so Mab would attempt to canter, but Charity reined her in to this tedious pace. It was anybody's guess which of them was more bored. At least she was out of her gown and back into her breeches, so she had that going for her at least.

Before they had traveled fifty miles, Charity was forced to conclude that a third person was decidedly de trop on an elopement, or a marriage trip, or whatever this hellacious journey was. Gilbert and Louisa flirted, they exchanged tender glances, they discussed hopeful plans for the future. They were revoltingly blissful. Even worse, they went out of their way to politely include Charity in all their conversations. She might have been roused to discuss famine or pestilence or any other of life's miseries, but she didn't feel at all equal to happy chatter. So she kept her horse—Alistair's horse—well out of earshot of the carriage.

Hourly, she regretted not having stayed another day or week or month with Alistair. But every moment in his company weakened her resolve; she loved him more with each passing second, and the pain of their eventual parting would only be harder for both of them to endure. So she had persuaded Louisa and Gilbert to leave at once, avoiding painful farewells and recrimination.

What she would have given for Keating's company. She could have relied on him for acerbic commentary and a shared sour mood. But she had received no word from him since he left for Fenshawe, even though the London letters were forwarded to her at Trout farm. She took this to mean that Keating had discovered nothing amiss at Fenshawe and was this moment returning to London. He'd find out soon enough that she was gone.

The happy couple knew of her situation: she was here, and Alistair was not. They knew her heart was broken while their own hearts were full of joy. This disparity made any connection impossible. But still they tried, because they were kind and lovely people, and it wasn't their fault she wanted to scream at the sight of them.

Over supper the first night at the inn, they proposed that Charity come live with them in Kent.

"Kent?" Charity asked.

"My brother is letting us have the use of his estate near Maidstone. I think he means it as a marriage present."

To give Gilbert use of an entire estate was a level of generosity she hadn't expected of Alistair. She knew how carefully he counted his pennies.

They must have mistaken her look of surprise for one of dismay, because Louisa nudged Gilbert and whispered, "I told you not to mention him!"

Charity drained her tankard of ale and excused herself to bed.

Judging by the blushing glances and lingering touches between the lovers the following morning, Charity supposed they had spent the night anticipating their marriage vows. And good for them. She certainly didn't care—they were going to be married in a matter of days, for God's sake. But all that blushing and stammering—Christ, her stomach wasn't strong enough for this. *It's just fucking,* she wanted to scream. *People have been doing it for thousands of years. Mice manage it. So do sheep. It's nothing to fuss yourselves over.*

But it was, though. That last night with Alistair wasn't the kind of thing a person could get over so easily. He had treated her like she was precious to him. She had done her damnedest to return the favor, every moment knowing it would only make their parting more difficult. If Alistair had been here now, they might very well be the ones blushing and making excuses to touch one another.

He wasn't, though, and he never would be again. It was the height of absurdity for Louisa to imagine that Charity could live with her and Gilbert in a house owned by Alistair, where he might show up at any moment.

For that matter, it was already impossible for Charity to live with Louisa, but she hadn't quite told Louisa that yet. When Louisa and Gilbert asked why they still had to be married in Scotland, despite having both a special license and the presence of Louisa's putative guardian, she only explained that she didn't want the validity of Louisa's marriage to depend on a forged signature. In Scotland a minor could marry without a guardian's permission, and Louisa's marriage would be valid without any deception on Charity's part.

The rest of it they would discover later.

The road to Scotland took them straight through Northumberland, right into Alnwick, the town whose market square had given her that first glimpse of a world beyond Fenshawe. It was fitting that this was where that episode of her life would come to an end.

"I'm turning off here," she said while Gilbert and Louisa awaited a fresh set of carriage horses at an inn.

They both looked at her blankly.

"You'll be in Scotland this afternoon," she explained. "You don't need me to be with you. Marry, and then . . ." What? Send word? Write a letter? All impossible. "Take care of one another." She looked pointedly at Gilbert, willing him to remember what she had asked of him. *Take care of Alistair.*

"Where are you going?" Louisa asked.

"Fenshawe is an hour's ride."

"Charity," Louisa protested, sounding panicked. "Please."

She wanted to leap off the horse and hug them both, to tell Louisa she had loved her like a sister, like her own child. But if she got any closer she wouldn't be able to stop herself from weeping, and that would only spoil the happiness of Louisa's day. So she kept her distance.

"Don't be silly," she said, trying to keep her voice light even as she took one last look at Louisa's face. "You don't want me on your honeymoon, and Scottish weddings make me maudlin anyway." There, let Louisa think Charity was remembering her own elopement. Oh God, now she really was going to cry. The tears were already pricking her eyes. She smiled brightly, "Now, be off with you!"

She turned west to Fenshawe.

Alistair went over his ledgers so carefully that his eyes were starting to hurt, but it had to be done. First, because at least this would give him something to do besides pace the floor and worry about Robin. But his other reason was that he wanted to see precisely how much more recklessness this estate could take.

Not recklessness, he decided. Nor extravagance. *Generosity.*

A few weeks at a lamentable inn, wages for the maid, a barnyard's worth of fowl for the farmers, clothes and books for Charity, a gift for Mrs. Potton, the special license, and couriers to and from London. None of it had ruined him. Even discounting the income from the Kent property that would now be Gilbert's, he wasn't stretched quite as thin as he thought he might be.

He had hoped that with a few more years of careful investment and reasonably frugal living, he would know that the estate was safe for future generations. That plan had gone out the window the minute he had met Robin. But a new plan was beginning to take shape in his mind, and it would not come cheap.

This was what money and power were for: not to hoard up in the name of prudence and security, but to spend and use to take care of the people who needed it. The people who needed him, or at least whose lives would be better for a bit of help. Two months of knowing Robin, and his sense of value had twisted around so that he could scarcely recognize it anymore.

How long would it take without her for his sense to return? Best to act now, then.

He ran his finger down the column of figures one final time, confirmed that he had calculated correctly, and called for his carriage.

So this was how people felt when they were about to do something intensely stupid, like diving off a cliff or climbing a snow-covered mountain. Alistair was not a man who was much given to feats of daring. He had always assumed that men who chased danger were half-mad. But here he was, standing at Mrs. Allenby's door, about to pledge a sizable part of his income to his half sisters.

Portia Allenby, who was no doubt used to all manner of shocking creatures showing up on her doorstep, still stared at him in openmouthed astonishment for a few seconds before recovering her aplomb.

"My lord," she said.

"I have a matter to discuss with you."

She nodded wordlessly and led the way to a room at the back of the house. From a chamber off to the side, he could hear laughter and music. This, he realized with a pang, was a happy house. That was why Robin had liked it here. Perhaps that was what had brought his father here too. Alistair would never have this for himself—a house where laughter echoed through the hallways, a place people wanted to be. But it didn't matter. It had never occurred to him to want such a thing, so it shouldn't pain him to know he'd never have it.

"I'd like to make arrangements for the girls," he said, gripping the back of the nearest chair. "Settlements."

"Oh," she said, her eyes wide. "I was not expecting that."

That sounded like she had thought he had come for some other purpose, but he'd deal with that later. "Do they have anything now?" he asked.

"Six thousand to split between the three of them," she replied, sitting in a low gilt chair. "Your father was very generous with us," she said slowly, but with no trace of apology. "However, most of it has gone to school fees and governesses."

He had already gathered as much. He had seen Amelia Allenby often enough by now to know that she had been raised as a lady, and that level of finish cost money. Remembering his own manners, he sat in the chair instead of digging his nails into its upholstery. "I quite understand," he said, and tried to sound like someone who hadn't been in the practice of judging this woman's finances for years.

"To be entirely honest, they don't need any more." She regarded him frankly. "Two thousand pounds apiece isn't a grand sum, not by any means, but it will do."

It was a pathetic sum for the acknowledged daughters of a marquess. "I was thinking of giving them each three thousand pounds." Five thousand pounds was still not a grand dowry—three times that amount would not even be a grand dowry. But in Alistair's scheme, it wasn't only the money, but the family connection, that would serve these girls. By publicly settling money on them, he would be announcing that his sisters were under his protection. "It wouldn't be a dowry, but for them to do with as they please once they come of age. If you consent, that is."

He thought of Robin, without family, without protection. He remembered what lengths she had gone to when her sister-in-law had been left similarly alone. And he imagined what would happen to his half sisters if Mrs. Allenby died. For all he knew, they had friends and relations by the dozen. But he would do his part to let the world know that the Marquess of Pembroke stood by his family.

"Three thousand each," Mrs. Allenby repeated. "I didn't think you had that much at the ready." Her eyes opened wide. "Oh drat, I shouldn't have said that."

"You're quite right. I don't. But I can put a thousand pounds a year away, so that when Amelia comes of age she'll have her three thousand, and then when the other two—" for the life of him he could not recall their names "—come of age, they'll have the same."

"Frances and Eliza," she said.

He nodded. "Frances and Eliza," he repeated.

"I hardly know what to say."

He rose to his feet. "Don't say anything. If my father had lived, he would have done more, and we both know it."

"You're wrong there. If your father had lived, he'd have run the estate into the ground. I loved the man, but he couldn't keep sixpence in his pocket. Now, I think you ought to go into the drawing room."

Alistair didn't think he had it in him to play the part of the elder brother, but he followed the sounds of laughter and conversation to the drawing room door. There, in the same room where he had listened to the cat-carrying astronomer while flirting with Robin, were the three Allenby girls and an elderly woman.

With a start he realized that the other woman was Miss Cavendish, the treacherous Aunt Agatha. What the actual devil was she doing in this house? Or anywhere in London, for that matter? He had driven past the house Robin and Miss Selby had leased for the season and found it closed up, the door knocker removed and no trace of servants within. He had assumed that Miss Cavendish had returned to wherever it was she came from. Northumberland, or perhaps whatever circle of hell was reserved for people who played fast and loose with laudanum. If Robin had been hurt, Alistair would have seen that old witch in a noose.

The two younger girls fell awkwardly silent when they saw Alistair at the threshold. Amelia rose politely to her feet and dropped into a curtsy.

"Oh, it's you," Miss Cavendish said.

Ah, so they were both equally delighted to see one another. It was so much more comfortable when antipathy was mutual.

"Delighted, ma'am," he responded, bowing first to her and then to the girls.

"I've had a letter from Louisa," Miss Cavendish said, looking impossibly smug. "Or, I should say, Lady Gilbert. She and Lord Gilbert are staying at an inn in the Lake District. They traveled directly there from Scotland." If she had stuck her tongue out at him or thumbed her nose, she still wouldn't have looked more smugly satisfied with herself than she did that moment.

"How lovely for them," he responded affably, as if it were not at all insulting that Gilbert had not bothered to write to his own brother but Louisa had found time to inform her sister-in-law's poisoner. Perhaps Gilbert's attention was taken up by his bride. Or perhaps Alistair had thrown away all brotherly confidence by behaving like a controlling bastard for so many years. "And where is Mr. Selby? Did either he or Miss Church accompany them on their wedding trip?" He made this reference to Miss Church with a very pointed look at the old lady.

Miss Cavendish narrowed her eyes, and remained silent for the moment it evidently took her to conclude that Alistair knew about Charity's double role but was not going to reveal it. "Not that I know of," was her only answer.

He forced himself to sit down and drink the tea Mrs. Allenby poured him. He listened to the middle child—Frances, he recalled—play the harp, and admired one of Eliza's drawings. Only Amelia remained reserved, quietly observing him.

Why had they gone to Scotland? He couldn't make sense of it. They had the special license and they had Robin to give consent. There was no need to go all the way to Scotland; with Gilbert's arm in a sling and Louisa still recovering, it would have been a grueling journey. Robin would not have allowed it unless it were absolutely necessary.

He tried to breathe but it felt like his lungs were in a vise. Every shallow breath sent pain through his chest.

There was one obvious reason why Gilbert would have

gotten married in Scotland, and it was that Robin wasn't with them. In which case, where had she gone? Had she decided to stop being Robert Selby and simply vanish? He felt his heart lurch at the notion. He wanted her here with him, not alone and nameless.

He forced some tea down his throat and hoped he didn't look like a man whose mind was reeling. There could be another possibility, he realized. Perhaps she had determined that exposure was imminent, had feared that she would be revealed as an impostor, and hadn't wanted Louisa's marriage invalidated when her signature was revealed to be forged. That was even more alarming, because if she truly feared exposure, she would do anything in her power to prevent Louisa from being implicated. That would mean she would have to disappear, to hide. And he knew his Robin well enough to fear that she would hide too well for him to find her.

He rose to take his leave, blindly going through the motions of wishing them all a good day. When he reached the door, he felt a hand on his elbow. It was Amelia, looking grave and concerned.

"If you hear from Mr. Selby," she said, "will you send me word? It is very strange that he left town without saying goodbye to my mother or to me. We were friends, you see. Or I thought we were."

Some of his pitying comprehension must have shown on his face, because she hurriedly added, "No, not in the way you're thinking. Mr. Selby isn't interested in . . . marriage."

Incredulously, he realized she thought Robin a gentleman who preferred men. Which wasn't far from the truth, in fact. "Quite right."

And now she was giving *him* a pityingly understanding look. "I saw you at your ball," she whispered. "In the garden."

A month ago he would have assumed that she meant to blackmail him, that she was after his money or his honor. But now he understood that she was saying this out of concern for her friend, and she thought her friend's lover would know his whereabouts.

He chose his words carefully. "I saw Mr. Selby a week ago in Bedfordshire, but not since. When I saw him, he was quite well. I give you my word that if I hear of him I will tell you myself."

But even as he spoke, he feared he would hear nothing from Robin.

Charity had taken this road more times than she could count. She ought to know it by heart, she ought to have memorized every sheep-dotted hill and every crumbling wall. But on her previous returns to Fenshawe she was too preoccupied by thoughts of seeing Robbie and Louisa, too busy thinking of the stories she would tell them about what she had seen at the market, at the fair, at Cambridge. She hadn't had any attention to spare for the landscape.

But there would be nobody at Fenshawe today. So now, on her last trip down this road, Charity could properly appreciate every tree and gate and cottage that she would never see again.

She had granted herself leave to be quite disgustingly

maudlin, and didn't even care that she was making a right mess of her cravat by letting tears fall all over it. She would bid goodbye to the only real home she had ever known, and since there was nobody around to see, she could cry as much as she liked.

The lane bent, and now she could see Fenshawe itself, nestled between two hills. She tried to commit the sight to memory: gray stone, gabled roofs, windows and chimneys arranged at a time when symmetry must not have been much in fashion.

Her eyes caught on a detail that was out of place—she could quite plainly see smoke curling dark gray against the clear blue sky. They had closed the place up entirely when they left for London. The couple who looked after the house lived in the old gamekeeper's cottage. Perhaps they had ventured into the house for some reason and lit a fire. Still, she spurred the horse a bit faster.

Once she had Mab fed and watered in the stables, she made her way across the courtyard. This would be the last time she crossed the courtyard, the last time she pushed the kitchen door open. It ought to feel monumentally significant, but instead she felt like she was watching herself from a great distance of space and time.

"I thought it would be you," said a familiar voice.

She gasped and turned to where Keating stood, leaning against the scullery door. "I thought you'd be long gone. How could you possibly guess that I'd come here?"

"You'd never bugger off without throwing some flowers on your fellow's grave. Figured you'd turn up sooner or later."

Of course he was right. She started to cry—really, she hadn't quite stopped since the last round—and found herself pushed by the shoulders into a chair by the fire.

"Like a dog hanging about its dead master's body. Embarrassing, it is. There's nothing for you here, but you keep coming back. Like a ghost, haunting the place."

"Your metaphors are a mess," she managed through her tears.

"Your priorities are a mess." He pulled a flask from his coat and handed it to her.

She sniffed it. Gin. She drank a few swigs anyway. "Louisa's married by now." She heard the scrape of a chair across the stone floor, then the creak of wood as Keating sat.

"That's not why you're crying."

"No, I'm crying because I'll miss her. I'll miss . . ." She tried to make a gesture that would encompass her whole life, without actually saying it.

"Then don't give it up. Stay Robert Selby. Who the hell cares that you aren't? You're as good a Robert Selby as he ever was, and probably better."

She had long suspected Keating of harboring revolutionary tendencies, and now she was sure of it. "I can't. It's stealing."

"You say that like it's a bad thing. It's always been stealing, right from the start, and you never let that stop you."

She took another swig, enjoying the burn down her throat. "I did it for Louisa. She was only a child, and a Selby."

"You were a child when you came here, and you're a Selby now." Keating was leaning forward in his chair, his hands on his knees. He ought to have left weeks ago. She was a losing bet.

"It's not the same." She cringed at the whining note she heard in her own voice.

"So you keep telling me. Here's what you can do. Save every farthing of income from Fenshawe, put it in the bank, and leave it to the cousin when you die."

"He wants to marry me."

"The cousin?"

She would have laughed if the circumstances were any different. "No, Pembroke."

He stared at her for a moment before letting out a long, low whistle. "Well, I don't suppose he can marry you as Robert Selby."

"He can't marry me at all. I'd disgrace him. Besides, I can't put on a gown and be a lady."

"No, I can't imagine you would. Nor would I. So, then. What's it to be? Where are we to go?"

That made her look up sharply. "We?"

"You planning to run off with someone else?"

She almost smiled at that. The gin had taken the edge off and she felt less tragic than she had upon entering the house. "India?"

Before Keating could respond, Charity saw a flicker of movement over his shoulder.

"Well, I hate to interrupt," Maurice Clifton said, emerging from the shadowy passageway that led to the larder. "This conversation has been so entirely illuminating."

CHAPTER TWENTY

"What are you doing here?" Charity managed to say, her voice a mere whisper. Keating was already on his feet, his hand poised over his coat pocket in a way that suggested a pistol might be concealed within.

"I knew something wasn't right when I saw you in London," Clifton said. "I didn't know who you were, but I knew you weren't Robert. You're too clever by half. I came here to Fenshawe to see my cousin and ask him what in damnation is going on. But I find the place shut up, and when I ask any of the villagers they tell me that Robert Selby is in London with his sister, or they slam their doors in my face." He took a step further into the room. "What I want to know is whether you killed him."

"Oh my God." Charity clutched the edges of her chair. "No, he died of influenza two and a half years ago. The same year Louisa had it. He's buried beneath the rowan tree on the south end of the property." Keating had been quite right that she planned to leave some flowers on it before departing.

"I feel that I've walked into a melodrama. You—a woman, I gather—simply decided to hide my cousin's death and assume his identity. I scarcely know what to think." Clifton looked on the verge of swooning.

"Sit down, you," Keating commanded, his voice gruff.

Clifton sat, but otherwise paid Keating no attention. His gaze was fixed on Charity, as if he hoped to find answers written on her face. "You stole Fenshawe out from under my nose."

She knew it would be useless to protest that she had done it for Louisa, that she had meant to give it back. If he had overheard her conversation with Keating, he already knew that, and he didn't care.

She nodded. "Yes."

"Oh bloody hell," Keating protested, but she couldn't imagine what else he expected her to say. There was no use denying it.

"Going to India isn't good enough," Clifton said. "Even if you managed to disappear, it would take years to have my cousin declared dead. What happens to Fenshawe in the meantime? I want a death certificate and I want it immediately."

"I know." She felt like she was hearing this conversation from the bottom of a lake.

Keating slammed his fist on the table, bringing her briefly back to the moment. "For God's sake, Charity!" He never called her that, she dimly thought.

"He doesn't mean my dead body, Keating. It's a woman's body, after all, and wouldn't get him Fenshawe."

"Otherwise you'd throw yourself off the nearest cliff? You don't have to do what this man says, goddammit!"

"No," said Clifton slowly. "But the alternative is that we leave this to the authorities to sort out. In that case, Louisa's complicity in what might very well be considered a murder would become a matter of public note."

The edges of her vision were going dark. "I told you it wasn't murder. I would never have."

"They were married, you sodding bastard." This was the ever-loyal Keating. "And you—" he pointed at Charity "—either act like you have some fight left in you or I'll have to slap you."

"Married? But that's neither here nor there," Clifton replied equably. "Louisa will be dragged into whatever the judge and jury decide to make of this sordid business. So will Lord Pembroke, come to think of it. The two of you have been thick as thieves, by all accounts."

Charity felt her blood run cold. She couldn't even run away—couldn't disappear to India or America. Louisa might stand trial. Alistair would be thrown into a scandal worse than anything he had ever contemplated, worse than anything his father had ever dared commit. He would never live down his shame. She would burden him with a lifetime's worth of humiliation.

"Then what do I do?" she asked.

"I certainly don't know." Clifton shook his head impatiently. "You're the one with expertise in fraud and deceit. Arrange for some way to have Robert Selby declared dead."

"A boating accident," Charity said, remembering what Alistair had suggested. It seemed so preposterous when he suggested it, but now it was the only way to keep him and

Louisa safe. "There would be no body. You could get a death certificate if a witness attested to Selby falling overboard."

"There!" Clifton said with some satisfaction. "I knew you'd come up with something. And that's not so bad after all. You were planning to run off to India anyway. This is a mere errand to perform before you go on your way."

"The merest trifle," Keating spat. "I gather I'm supposed to be the witness. Fucking boats."

Clifton ignored this. "Needless to say, you must also agree never to return to England or have any dealings with anyone you knew during your time as Robert Selby."

Her life would be over. Everyone who mattered to her—everyone to whom she mattered—would be taken away from her. She felt as cold and alone as if she truly were at the bottom of the ocean.

"Fine," she said. She would do this. One last effort to protect Louisa, one last kindness to repay everything Alistair had done for her. "A boating accident."

She really would be as good as dead. She didn't dare write so much as a note to Louisa or Alistair to let them know that she was alive and well—as if wellness were something she could aspire to in this state.

She couldn't even withdraw enough money from the bank to start her new life, whatever that was to be. She couldn't so much as pack a change of clothes. Nothing must draw suspicion.

Nameless, friendless, penniless. That was how she entered the world, but she had made a life for herself. She'd just have to do it again. She glanced over at Keating and he gave her a sharp nod. Not quite friendless, then.

She had made sacrifices before out of love and loyalty. This would only be one more.

"All right, then, Mr. Clifton. We'll do it."

Hopkins handed Alistair the newspaper as soon as he returned from the club, before he had even removed his gloves. "Delivered by messenger," the butler murmured.

Glancing at the front page, he saw it was a Newcastle paper from one week earlier. He flipped through the pages with a rising sense of cold dread.

He found it on the fourth page. A boating accident. "Presumed dead," the notice said. "Robert Selby, Esq., late of Fenshawe, Northumberland," was how the paper referred to his Robin. There was more—something about an inquest and the testimony of a manservant—but the words danced before Alistair's eyes.

Having guessed that Charity would disappear did not lessen his shock at seeing it in print. He would have Nivins look into this. He would send investigators to find out where Charity had gone. He didn't know how to find one woman, presumably dressed as a man, most certainly headed for some absurd and improbable corner of the world, but he would do it anyway. It might take years, but he'd do it.

After all, he had put this blasted stupid idea of a boating accident in her head. But he hadn't meant for her to vanish away from *him*, for God's sake. He had only suggested it as a way for her to start fresh, to put an end to her old identity in order to be with him. That was before he understood that for Charity, starting fresh would mean giving up an essential part of her. And now she had just drowned that part of her in the North Sea.

His heart broke for her.

He gathered up the paper and headed back outside to make good on the promise he had made his sister.

There were carriages lined up outside the Allenbys' house. Alistair cast about in his mind for the date and realized it was the night of Mrs. Allenby's salon. Well, there was nothing for it. Having promised Amelia that he would tell her any news of Robin, he would fulfill that promise without dragging his heels. He found her deep in conversation with a woman wearing a turban. When she saw him approach, her face went pale, but she rose to her feet and silently led him through a passageway into the very room where Robin had teasingly suggested a tryst.

She looked up at him expectantly, her lips pressed together. He had not managed this in a way to minimize her shock, he realized. He was not wearing evening clothes and he was carrying a cumbersome newspaper. And while visitors to the Allenby salon did not as a rule dress or behave with much regard to convention, in the Marquess of Pembroke any deviation from propriety was conspicuous.

"Please tell me," she said, and he realized he had been standing silently for too long.

"I believe he's well. But you'll hear about this sooner or later, and I want you to know I don't believe it to be true." He unfolded the paper and showed her the article.

He watched her squint at the page as she absently patted

her pockets for spectacles that she evidently did not have with her.

"Try mine," he said, handing her his own spectacles. Perhaps they had both inherited poor eyesight from some distant de Lacey ancestor.

She fitted the spectacles to her face, although they were too large and likely too strong for her. He watched her eyes roam across the page of newsprint, widening when she got to the end.

"Presumed dead." Her brows drew together in confusion. "But you said you believe he's well."

"Yes. I'm sorry to say that I don't think either you or I will see Mr. Selby anytime soon, perhaps never again in this world. But I believe he is well."

She gave him a firm nod and handed him back his spectacles. "I see." She was very young, he recalled. Eighteen. Too young to be alone in her sorrow.

"Do you want me to send for your mother?" he offered.

She shook her head, and he impulsively caught her hand and squeezed it before heading back through the crowd and out into the street.

Upon returning to Pembroke House, he told Hopkins that he was not to be disturbed and proceeded directly to the library. Sitting on the sofa, he could have sworn that he still smelled Robin's fresh green scent, like springtime and lemon drops. He remembered the taste of her lips, and if he closed his eyes he could almost feel her fingers stroking his jaw.

This room, he wanted it burned to the ground. Would he ever sit here without recalling the time he had spent here with Robin? For that matter, would he ever do anything without recalling Robin? Would he even want to?

He poured himself a brandy. Before his senses started to dull, he penned a letter to Gilbert, explaining the contents of the newspaper article and his belief that the accident was feigned as part of Miss Church's effort to allow Fenshawe to pass to the cousin. Gilbert would need to tell Louisa.

It was an imprudent letter, one that should not be written. The very fact of it proved Alistair's complicity in criminal undertakings. But Gilbert needed to know. Alistair forbore writing an admonition to burn the letter upon receipt— Gilbert could exercise his own judgment, and Alistair no longer cared. He resolved to get his brother's temporary Lake District address from the infernal Miss Cavendish on the morrow.

His emotions were a welter of confusion, anger tied up with loss and regret. Worst was the certainty that he could have managed things better. Surely there had to have been some way he could have convinced her that she was the only person he wanted to spend his life with, that even if their marriage made him a scandal and an outcast, his life would be immeasurably better simply for having her in it. He was ashamed of himself for not having shown Robin what she meant to him while he had the chance, for having let her believe he cared for his status and good repute more than he cared for her.

From the ground floor he heard the sound of a small commotion, followed by the tread of slippered feet heading upstairs. He scrambled upright, suddenly and irrationally hopeful. He knew it couldn't be Robin. For her to come here, of all places, would be reckless beyond belief, but what if—

The door opened, and Mrs. Allenby walked through. "There you are," she said with obvious relief. "All in one piece." She came closer and peered at him. "Not too badly foxed, I should say. No plans to do anything desperate?"

Hopkins waited at the threshold, plainly mortified at having let an intruder into his master's inner sanctum. Well, it was too late for that, he supposed. He gestured for the butler to leave and shut the door.

"My dear madam," he said, trying and failing to bring his voice to its haughtiest tones. "I have no idea what I have done to deserve the honor of this visit. Do you not at this very moment have a salon to be presiding over?"

"To hell with the salon, Pembroke. Amelia told me about poor Mr. Selby and I came to see if you needed anything. I knew you'd be quite alone. It's not the sort of loss you could openly grieve, I'm sorry to say. But you must see that you cannot be alone, my dear."

"I'm quite at a loss." He summoned up all his reserves of chilliness. "Forgive me for being obtuse, but—"

"Enough." She spoke sharply. "The more you go on this way the more concerned I become. My heart breaks for you."

"You misunderstand. He is not dead."

She put a hand over her bosom and he saw tears spring to her eyes. "You poor child."

Oh, fantastic. She evidently thought him delusional with grief, which he supposed was the only logical explanation for his insistence that Robin was not dead despite a newspaper article saying otherwise, but what was surprising was that she seemed truly distraught for him. Why should she care? And as for *poor child*—he simply could not let that stand.

He gritted his teeth. "I am two years younger than you, madam."

"True, but you've been on ice these last fifteen years. You've done no living at all in that time. You've guarded your heart so closely, and then the one time you let your defenses down, *this* happens." She took one of his hands and chafed it between her own. "Now, I cannot leave you alone. If there's someone else you wish to summon instead, I'll leave. But I won't leave you alone."

There wasn't anyone else. Gilbert was hundreds of miles away, and nobody else could be allowed to know the extent of Alistair's grief. She was wrong. He didn't need company. He didn't need anyone, least of all Portia Allenby, to bear witness to his misery. But as she rubbed his hand—the sort of gesture he might expect from Mrs. Potton, or from his own mother if his mother had been the affectionate sort—he felt his control slip away.

"How did you know?" he finally asked.

"I've seen how Mr. Selby looks at men, or rather how he doesn't look at women. He was spending so much time with you, and one never hears about you with women."

Alistair wanted to interject that one never heard of his liaisons with women because he was discreet, a concept she might not be overly familiar with, but he decided that was rather a moot point by now.

"And then you came to Amelia tonight," she continued,

"plainly overwrought, so of course I knew." She led him back to the sofa. "When was the last time you ate?"

He sat. "I don't recall." He must have had lunch, but couldn't remember.

She went automatically to the bell pull. With a start, Alistair realized that of course Mrs. Allenby would know where to find everything in this house. She must have spent countless evenings here with Alistair's father. No wonder she knew how to get past Hopkins.

"Enough brandy." She collected his decanter and glass and pushed them aside with the firm authority of someone used to tending to half-drunk men. That was something else she must have learned in this house, he supposed. "It'll only make tomorrow worse, and tomorrow will be bad enough. Believe me."

This woman had grieved his father, however much he didn't like to think of it. And she had come here tonight out of loyalty to her lover's child. What had she said about his grief for Robin? Not the sort of loss you could openly grieve. That was how she must have felt about Alistair's father's death.

"You need food, water, and a headache powder," she said. "I'm so sorry to see you grieve, Pembroke, but I don't mind saying that I'm relieved to know that you're capable of it."

Alistair reeled from the force of those words. To be capable of grief. To be capable of having one's heart broken. What astoundingly useless capacities. What a shocking oversight on the part of the creator. Surely, he had been better off when he hadn't let anyone close, when he had used his pride and rank to keep affection at bay.

But then he wouldn't have loved Robin, and he wouldn't have appreciated the gift that was her love. Mrs. Allenby was correct that he had been on ice, frozen and untouchable, for those years before meeting Robin. He had been cold and protected, but not quite alive.

"I would trade everything I have—my rank and position, my fortune, the respect and admiration of my peers. All of it, just to have Robin back." He shut his eyes so he wouldn't have to see the pity on Mrs. Allenby's face.

He only realized the next morning, when he woke up in his own bed with a clear head, how much forbearance it must have required for her to refrain from pointing out that Alistair's father had made precisely that trade. The late marquess had given up money and respect in order to have a life with the woman he loved.

Perhaps this recklessness in the face of love truly was in the de Lacey blood. Maybe those ancestors whose portraits graced the Broughton Abbey gallery had known something after all. And maybe Alistair was a fool for having realized it only when it was too late.

CHAPTER TWENTY-ONE

Every day the post brought letters, but none gave him any news of Robin. Nivins had turned up nothing, nor had any of his investigators. It had been the longest fortnight of Alistair's life.

Gilbert's letter announcing his marriage had been misdirected, and when it finally arrived it was accompanied by three other letters from Gilbert and a very pretty note from Louisa. They were grateful to Alistair for the Kent property, apologetic for having run off the way they did, and utterly confused as to what had become of Charity. As distraught as Alistair was, he was relieved to know that he still had his brother's friendship.

There was the usual stack of letters on estate matters, but none of them brought him that old sense of satisfaction, that small pride of victory over chaos, in seeing his business conducted properly. He had always derived not precisely happiness, but rather relief, from seeing the numbers add up in an orderly fashion, income exceeding expenditures in a way that evidenced the fundamental rightness of his affairs. It felt something like opening a clock and seeing all the gears fitting together sensibly, ticking along predictably and usefully.

It had never brought him joy, though. A few months ago, he hadn't expected these neat columns of numbers to bring him anything so frivolous as happiness, but rather to deliver a reprieve from anxiety. Now that he knew joy and contentment, now that he knew what it meant to have happiness in arm's reach, it seemed that he was ruined for anything less.

Alistair resisted the urge to go to Fenshawe himself, or to climb aboard the ships at Dover and inspect each and every one with his own eyes. Instead he stayed in London in case Robin came back. It was nonsense, but he kept thinking of those tales of hunting dogs straying from the pack and being given up for lost, only to somehow find their way across dozens of miles, arriving home weeks later, filthy and thin but otherwise fine. This comparison was not one he would share with Robin if he ever saw her again, which was seeming increasingly unlikely. But he couldn't let go of the idea that she would somehow find her way to him.

Perhaps this was the sort of delusion that visited grief-stricken minds. He would ask Mrs. Allenby.

During the two weeks that passed since he received the newspaper, various Allenbys found daily excuses to visit. Mrs. Allenby, it would seem, had adopted Alistair and there was no reversing the process. She sent cakes, as if he were an invalid rather than a perfectly healthy grown man. The Allenby girls brought a box of kittens that had been born in their kitchen and abandoned by their scapegrace mother. By all rights, the lot of them ought to be drowned, and it was surely a sign of Mrs. Allenby's poor household management that they hadn't been. The creatures would have to be fed drops of milk, for heaven's sake, and would likely die anyway.

Nobody was more astonished than Alistair when he realized that he had decided to keep one, a very unprepossessing tabby that seemed almost entirely composed of fluff. Alistair was still holding it after his half sisters left.

He did not name it Robin, nor even Charity. He did not name it anything at all. But he fed it by dipping his handkerchief into a saucer of cream and letting the mite suckle away.

One afternoon Lady Pettigrew swept into Alistair's drawing room in high dudgeon, swathed in unseasonable furs. "Tell me that the gossips are mistaken and that Gilbert has not run off with that Selby girl, and that Portia Allenby does not come and go from Pembroke House at all hours. And Pembroke," she said, her voice rising to a fever of indignation, "you have a *rat* on your shoulder."

"It's a kitten, Aunt Pettigrew," he said, removing the animal from where it was trying to burrow into its owner's cravat. "And Gilbert did not elope—both I and Mr. Selby gave our consent to the match." This statement wasn't even fifty percent true, as the couple had eloped not once but twice, and Mr. Selby didn't exist, but Alistair felt he was being precisely as honest as the situation called for.

"As for Mrs. Allenby," he continued, "it occurred to me that she's the mother of my sisters, and that she's done a damned fine job of raising them, given the circumstances. While I may have my own reservations about marital infidelity, I won't stand in judgment of her or my father."

"Won't stand in judgment?" She drew her mantle close around her shoulders, as if an evil wind blew through Pembroke House. "What twaddle is this? It's your job to stand in judgment of those who don't behave themselves. You're one of the highest ranked gentlemen in the land. If you don't uphold standards, who do you think will?"

Not long ago, Alistair had asked the same question. He had thought it his duty to set an example. Hell, he still did. He had only changed his mind about what that example ought to be. "My dear Aunt Pettigrew," he said in his most aristocratic tone. "If you do not find brotherly love and filial respect to be standards worthy of being upheld, then you and I shall simply have to disagree." He drew out that last word, letting it sink in that this was a threat. If Lady Pettigrew wanted to declare war on Lord Pembroke, so be it. But Alistair outranked and outwitted her, and they both knew it.

She begged his pardon in equally chilly tones. Alistair thought that when she got home and took stock of all the favors she wished to have granted by the Marquess of Pembroke, she'd come around. And if she didn't, it was a small loss.

The next morning at breakfast, while Alistair was once again dipping his handkerchief into cream to feed the kitten, a letter arrived from the Broughton housekeeper. This was a highly unusual occurrence—Mrs. Jones had free rein over household matters and required no input from Alistair or anybody else. She hated to disturb his lordship, she wrote, but there had arisen a most awkward matter. A person—always such a damning descriptor, when coming from a servant—had arrived, saying she was instructed by his lordship to make a catalog of the library. Had his lordship commissioned this undertaking? Where was this woman to be housed? And what was to be done with her very strange manservant?

Alistair walked directly to the stables and was in his traveling chaise within a quarter of an hour. By the time he realized he was still holding the kitten it was too late to turn back.

Charity was not even pretending to make a catalog of the library. For one thing, there already was a catalog. For another, she was feeling utterly indolent after the events of the past few weeks. Lounging in the library and reading *Moll Flanders*—predictably, Alistair's father had acquired all the naughtiest novels—was about all she could muster up the energy for.

When Keating had hauled her, cold and dripping and in a very ill temper, onto the deck of the boat, she had only one thought: that she was an utter fool for having whistled down the wind a chance at happiness. Alistair was ready and willing to throw his weight around to help her, and instead of taking him up on his offer like a sensible creature, she had fled from him. If he wanted to make a scandal of himself on her behalf, then so be it.

Now it only remained to be seen whether he still wanted her.

"It takes something from you, coming back from the

dead," she told Keating as she lazed on the sofa in a patch of late afternoon sunshine. "I find I need to restore my strength."

With a clatter, Keating placed a tray of buttered muffins on the table before her. "I wish I knew what your game was. That way I'd know what to tell the magistrate when I get called before him."

"I don't have a game. We wait here for a few more days. If Alistair has come to his senses and realizes he doesn't want anything to do with me, then he'll pretend he doesn't know I'm here. And you and I will go to India, like we told Clifton."

"And if his bloody lordship does turn up?"

"Don't be so boring, Keating," she drawled, languidly stretching her arms over her head. "You can't expect me to spoil all your surprises." In truth, Charity had no idea what would happen if Alistair came. It was quite possible he'd be furious and turn them out into the street. In which case, they'd go off to India as planned and she wouldn't have lost anything by coming here.

"Hmph. Maybe you'll let me in on the secret of why we had to come to this drafty shambles of a house instead of going to London like civilized people."

"I told you. I wanted to see it." Also, she wanted to give Alistair the chance to avoid meeting her or even acknowledging her existence. That would give him a graceful, gentlemanly way to end things.

Keating flounced out. All things considered, he hadn't complained about this interlude at Broughton nearly as much as she had expected. Perhaps he had found some handsome and like-minded fellow to pass the time with.

Charity, for her part, was almost enjoying herself. Never before in her life had she been utterly without occupation. Even during those months in London, which had been the closest to a holiday she had ever experienced, she had been busy; between escorting Louisa and trying to pack a lifetime's worth of amusement into a span of weeks, she had hardly sat still. But here at Broughton Abbey there was nothing to do. She felt wonderfully indolent.

It truly was a terrible house, though. None of the chimneys worked properly, the furniture was almost universally uncomfortable, and there were some very noisy bats in the attic. It was no wonder that previous generations of de Laceys had sought pleasures of the flesh after being reared in such a comfortless place as this.

She read a few more pages of her novel, but was interrupted by the sound of heavy footsteps in the hall, rapidly approaching the library. Realizing that it didn't sound like Keating's step, she only had time enough to scramble up from her reclined position when the double doors to the room were flung open.

And there stood Alistair, the capes of his greatcoat billowing behind him.

"You," he said, relief and exasperation in his voice.

"Me," she agreed affably.

"Why the devil are you wearing that?" He still hadn't moved from the door.

"This?" She touched the bodice of the blue-gray gown. "You bought it for me. And I pawned the other one for Keating's wages." Which he had promptly spent on the stagecoach fare to Shropshire, but that was neither here nor there.

"I damned well know I bought it for you. Why are you wearing it, though?"

"I don't want to tell you when you're acting so abominably." She sniffed. She wanted to fling herself into his arms, kiss that angry line between his eyebrows, then knock him to the ground and kiss him some more.

He was across the room in three strides. "Miss—wait, are you going by Miss Church?"

"I told your housekeeper I was Mrs. Selby."

His voice was a low and sinister rumble. "Mrs. Selby, then. Why are you dressed as a decent and respectable lady when in fact you are a scoundrel who runs off in the middle of the night in order to commit untold felonies and nearly worry me to my grave?"

"The men's clothes you bought me were quite ruined in the boating accident, if you must know, and I was too dispirited to steal another set." She took a deep breath. This was how gamblers felt before rolling the dice. "Besides, I thought I ought to present myself as a marriageable sort of person in the event that anyone wanted to marry me."

He took her hands in his, nearly crushing them. "Hear me now, Robin. I will marry you regardless of what you're wearing. And I *will* marry you. You could be dressed as a goat or as the Archbishop of Canterbury and it's all the same to me."

Perhaps she wasn't made to withstand this degree of happiness, because she thought she was about to burst. "Alistair, do you realize that you have a kitten peeking out of your coat?"

"We'll discuss kittens later. Will you marry me, Robin?"

She couldn't quite bring herself to say yes, afraid that the joy of it might make her faint. But she gave a sharp nod, and was rewarded by the answering flash of triumph in Alistair's eyes. "You'd have to do something about Clifton. He wants a death certificate."

"Then you shall have a death certificate as a wedding present, my dear. But you leave Clifton to me." The look in his eyes made Charity nearly feel very bad for poor Maurice Clifton.

"You do realize you'll be sinking yourself even below your father's bad reputation?" She needed to get all these doubts out of her mind. She wanted to throw them onto the floor before him like birds that needed plucking and dressing before they could be cooked. "You'll be branded an eccentric, possibly a lunatic, for having a wife who goes about in men's clothes. Your heirs—"

"Our heirs," he corrected her, squeezing her hands.

"Our heirs," she amended, her heart giving an extra beat, "will be touched by the scandal."

"It will be my pleasure, my absolute delight to deal with anyone who wants to make trouble for my wife or children. You have no idea how much I'm looking forward to it."

"I'm afraid you haven't yet realized how much trouble this will all be."

"You've been nothing but trouble since I met you. And I've never been happier. I want a lifetime of trouble from you."

She extricated her hands from his and wrapped her arms around his neck, pulling him down for a kiss. This was what it was like, then, to finally know that everything was going to be fine. It was a pair of hands on her lower back, drawing her close.

When they broke the kiss and she laid her head on his shoulder, she could feel his heart pounding.

"Now do I get to hear about the kitten?" The creature was peering around Alistair's neck at Charity. It looked like the head of a dandelion, like if she breathed too hard it might blow away.

"No. Now I take you upstairs to what will be the worst bed you've ever slept in, and I get you out of those clothes."

Alistair leaned against the heavy oak headboard in order to better enjoy the sight of Robin sprawled naked and sated across the monstrous bed. Her presence somehow made sense of the moth-eaten velvet hangings, not to the mention the sheer acreage of the mattress. He planned to use this bed to have her in ways he hadn't even thought of yet.

The kitten was under the decided impression that Robin's foot, concealed by a sheet, was a mouse or some other small creature in need of instant fluffy death. Every time the cat reared up and pounced, Robin let out that champagne pop of laughter.

"I was starting to think you really did mean to leave the country without a word," he said after a few minutes.

"I nearly did," she confessed, rolling over to face him, chin in hand. "I am in a pickle with Clifton, you know. He said either I had to get him Robbie's death certificate, or he would expose Louisa and you as accomplices. But—"

"Me? The bastard dared to name *me*?" Oh, putting this fellow in his place was going to be a pleasure.

"Yes, so I didn't think I had much choice but to go through with that boating accident scheme. Keating entirely disapproved, by the way."

"And rightly so." He was glad that she hadn't been entirely on her own during their time apart.

"Anyway, it wasn't until I had dried off and gotten a hot meal—"

"Wait." His mind was reeling. "You can't mean to tell me that you actually went overboard? Why could you not devise a way to stage a drowning without risking death?"

"I was seeking verisimilitude. Self-preservation wasn't much of a priority at the time. And I thought it was the only way I could make it up to you. Anyway, once my mind cleared, I thought to myself, Charity, you fool, you know a man with power and influence and a bit of ready money. He'll help you."

"You're damned right, I'll help you. That's what I tried to tell you in Little Hatley, but I made a hash of it. Listen, Robin. You jumped off a boat to prevent scandal from touching me or Louisa. Surely you'll allow me to make far lesser sacrifices for you."

She regarded him gravely for a moment. "I'm not used to being on that end of things."

"I know you aren't. But you did let your first husband send you to Cambridge." He watched her face register his phrasing.

"Oh, you're going to be like that, are you? 'Oh, but you let your first husband do such-and-so.'" He gathered that her snooty accent was meant to be an impression of him. "If you recall, my going to Cambridge was the thing that started all this trouble."

"Bollocks. If you hadn't gone to Cambridge dressed as the scamp you are, you would never have found yourself on this lumpy mattress tormenting an innocent cat. Your sister would never have become Lady Gilbert de Lacey. And your pestilential Aunt Agatha would never have become an esteemed bluestocking, which she is, according to Amelia Allenby. And, in a roundabout way, I would never have settled the Kent property on Gilbert or that money on the Allenby girls if I hadn't met you, and surely that counts for something."

Her mouth was hanging open. "You—the Allenbys—money?" He had never seen her so discomposed.

He nodded and then made a dismissive gesture. There was time enough to talk about the Allenbys later. "Robin, I don't think I'll ever have the words to describe what you did for me. I was living a half life until that day you let Louisa's bonnet loose in Hyde Park. Portia says I was on ice, and she has the right of it. I wasn't living. I was only . . . there."

"Well," she said, her eyes wet, "somebody really ought to build a statue of me. I'm amazing."

"Mmm-hmm," he murmured, pulling her close, still hardly able to believe that he had her here, with him. "Never forget it." He had been an appalling fool during his last trip to Broughton, when he hadn't been able to imagine her here. She was the only wife for him, she was the only conceivable mistress for this house. Dreary and derelict, Broughton needed champagne laughter and infinite sunniness. It needed love. He needed love.

A few minutes later Alistair found himself imprisoned in bed. Robin had fallen asleep on one of his shoulders, and the kitten had fallen asleep on his opposite arm. He wouldn't be getting off this lumpy mattress anytime soon. And he was completely fine with that.

"Too unfair, Robin." Alistair looked up from the letter he was writing and tossed his quill aside. "Not sporting at all." He looked at her hungrily, raking his gaze over her body. "Shut that door and come over here so I can look at you properly."

She had spent hours ransacking the attics of Broughton Abbey in search of something suitable to wear, and had turned up some old frock coats and shirts with ruffled cuffs. These garments, along with breeches that must have been Gilbert's at some point, gave her something of a swashbuckling air.

Today was the first time she had dressed like this—she was going to stop thinking of these clothes as men's clothes, because in fact they were hers—because she wanted to wear them, not as part of a necessary disguise. She was soon to be Robin de Lacey, she was dressed vaguely like a pirate, and she was delighted with herself.

She spun in a circle so he could admire her.

He leered wolfishly at her. "You look like a corsair."

"I know!" she said, clapping her hands together in satisfaction. "That's exactly what I thought."

He took her hand and reeled her in so she was standing in between his legs. "I'm going to have you on this desk, you know," he said, his voice low and silky. She felt his hand skim along the curve of her backside.

"Very likely," she said. "But not today." She sank to her knees.

"Oh, hell." He sank back further in his chair, though, giving her access to the fall of his breeches. Twisting his fingers in her hair, he tilted her head so she had to look at him. "This is the first time your hair has made any sense at all. It's pirate hair. Almost long enough for a queue, but not quite."

With his thumb, he traced her lower lip, but she caught it in her mouth and lightly sucked it.

He swore under his breath.

For weeks she had felt lucky to be desired by a man who was open-minded enough to tolerate her strange attire. But it occurred to her now, looking at his darkening eyes and feeling his erection hardening beneath her touch, that it wasn't a question of toleration. He liked this. He liked her, funny clothes and odd hair and the entire in-betweenness of her. She wasn't an ordinary woman, but he wasn't an ordinary man either. They fit together, and it felt right.

Agreeing to marry Alistair had been the biggest gamble she had ever taken, because she wasn't wagering only her own security and happiness but his as well. He was confident that he could find a way to satisfy Clifton's demands; he had assured her that he would be able to weather any scandal that resulted from their union. She wouldn't rest easy, though, until she had seen with her own eyes that she hadn't brought shame and sorrow upon him. It was all well and good for him to say that he wanted to make sacrifices for her, but until he knew what that meant it was only pretty words.

She freed him from his breeches and drew him slowly, inch by inch, into her mouth, savoring his heaviness on her tongue, enjoying every groan and shudder she elicited from him. Even if things went horribly awry, they would have this. They would have one another, they would have the way their bodies connected. She only hoped it wouldn't be spoilt by shame and resentment.

"Robin," he said some time later. "Tell Keating to pack your bag. Let's get back to London where you can make an honest man of me."

CHAPTER TWENTY-TWO

***

Before they left Broughton, Alistair wrote a letter to Maurice Clifton, requesting the honor of his presence at Pembroke House to discuss the matter of the Fenshawe inheritance. The man said he wanted a death certificate, but Alistair was willing to wager that he'd accept something else. Not necessarily something less—for as tempting as it was to punish Clifton for his attempt to blackmail Robin and implicate Alistair himself, the fact remained that under the law Fenshawe ought to be his, and Alistair would do his part to set things right.

He and Robin both wrote to Gilbert and Louisa, begging that they cut short their trip and return to London for the wedding. Because even though Robin had declared that she would sooner die than have a proper wedding at St. George's Hanover Square ("if you think I'm going to deck myself out with orange blossoms and walk down an aisle, you can go sod off," the future marchioness had declared), Alistair wasn't going to get married in a hole-in-corner manner. No, for his plan to succeed he needed this marriage to be properly witnessed and then freely discussed.

He would not have anyone, least of all Robin, think that he had the smallest particle of shame or reservation about this marriage. He was having her and holding her for the rest of his life, rumors and scandal notwithstanding. He was the Marquess of Pembroke, and that had to count for something. People could say what they liked; ladies could whisper behind their fans and men could give him the cut direct. But he was still one of the highest ranked men in the nation. If he held his head high, confident that he was as correct and gentlemanly as he ever had been—no, *more* than he ever had been—then that would put paid to most scandal-mongering.

Not all of it, though. He wasn't that naive. But what did he care if a couple of prigs turned their backs when he walked into White's? They were free to do so, and he'd simply know them for the fools they were. Those dear to him would know better.

That was something else Robin had done for him. A few months ago he hadn't cared much for anyone, and he had been confident that nobody cared at all for him. Now he knew that he had a handful of people who valued him for more than his rank and his fortune.

When they arrived at Pembroke House, he addressed Hopkins in his blandest tone of voice. "This is Mrs. Selby, soon to be Lady Pembroke. You've met her before as Mr. Robert Selby. Youthful pranks, you understand. She'll stay in the green bedchamber until the wedding."

Hopkins, not even raising an eyebrow, merely replied, "Quite right, my lord," and that had been the end of it. Alistair knew the rest of the staff would follow suit, and if they had a problem with the new marchioness, they were free to find other employment.

Robin took this all in stride as well, deploying her customary charm on the befuddled housemaids. Things might be awkward for a while, but he couldn't really envision a world in which people didn't like his Robin, however little she conformed to their expectations.

While Robin settled in, Alistair wrote two letters. The first was to Lady Pettigrew, to whom he announced his forthcoming marriage in much the same terms as he had used to Hopkins. He wrote that her presence at the ceremony was essential to his happiness, by which he knew she would infer that her nephews and grandchildren would not be able to look to the Marquess of Pembroke for favors unless she bent to his will.

The next letter was to Mrs. Allenby, and it contained much the same information, but without the implied threat, because he didn't doubt for the slightest moment that all the Allenbys would celebrate his marriage under any circumstances.

Maurice Clifton arrived the next morning. Judging by his appearance, he had only now arrived in London and come directly to Alistair. Good.

"Mr. Clifton. I won't keep you for too long," Alistair said without rising from his chair. "I'm to marry Mrs. Selby, your cousin's widow." With some satisfaction, he watched the blood drain from Clifton's face. "As you may be aware, the future Lady Pembroke is a high-spirited young lady inclined to merriment and pranks, including masquerading as her husband in order to attend university. My understanding is that this has caused you some difficulties regarding the inheritance of Fenshawe." This was a statement, not a question. Clifton had no information that Alistair required, and he wanted to make that perfectly clear.

Clifton opened his mouth as if to speak, but Alistair held up his hand and continued. "You will acknowledge that Mrs. Selby conducted herself with your awareness and consent. You, Mrs. Selby, and Lady Gilbert de Lacey will all attest that this was always the understanding between the three of you as well as your late cousin. You will have a death certificate within the month, possibly sooner since I cannot marry her without it." Nivins was already obtaining the cooperation of the vicar and magistrate near Fenshawe; likely Alistair would wind up paying for repairs to the church bell tower or some such thing.

Alistair watched as understanding seeped into Clifton's expression. By going along with Alistair's scheme, he would get Fenshawe and render himself an ally to the Marquess of Pembroke. By fighting Alistair, he would have a powerful enemy and spend years litigating his inheritance.

Clifton nodded, but his lips were pressed into a tight line. "I am to say that I knew my cousin sent his wife to Cambridge—the mind simply boggles, if you'll excuse me for saying so—and yet told no one. And that even after he died I did not protest her use of his name?"

"Precisely!" Alistair said encouragingly, as if praising a dog for learning a new trick.

"I don't suppose I have a choice."

Alistair said nothing, only stroked the kitten who had come to sit staunchly on his lap as if to offer reinforcements.

"Well, then. I'll stay in London for the next several weeks to make myself available for whatever you require." He hesitated a moment, then added, "my lord."

"Yes," Alistair said, allowing his mouth to curve into a predatory smile, "you will."

"I don't know if he's a marquess or a magician. Three weeks, and he didn't even have to set foot outside London," Keating said as he adjusted Robin's cravat.

That was how long it had taken to obtain a death certificate. Robin, Keating, Louisa, and Clifton had all written letters reciting the same version of the facts Alistair had proposed. None of them had even needed to go to court. "He has a good deal of influence." An impressive amount, really. It turned out that when the Marquess of Pembroke put his mind to something—whether that be obtaining death certificates or foisting the mysterious and oddly clad Mrs. Selby on the town—very few people dared to get in his way.

"Hmph." Keating stepped back and surveyed her. "Well, I suppose you'll do as a bride or whatever the hell you are." But his eyes were a bit misty.

She gave one last glance at the looking glass. She had on one of the shirts with the ruffled cuffs, desperately out of style, but really, that was the aspect of her appearance least likely to cause trouble. Her coat and pantaloons came from Alistair's own tailor, and her new Hessians had been polished by Hopkins himself. Keating had trimmed her hair, and in her cravat she wore an emerald pin from Alistair.

"You suppose she'll *do?*" Louisa objected from the door. "My dear, you look dashing. Alistair says to hurry up so he can empty this house of poets and vagabonds."

Three weeks, it turned out, was not only how long it took for a marquess to obtain a death certificate, but also the period of time required for London society to come to terms with Lord Pembroke's improbable betrothal. The Allenby set were allies, whereas the high sticklers, including Alistair's Aunt Pettigrew, had refused to have anything to do with the couple. This, Alistair insisted, was a thrill and a relief, as he had spent over three decades dreading that lady's appearance and now he could be done with her entirely.

Hugh Furnival, who had known Robin since Cambridge, seemed only minorly discomfited. "Well, I knew you weren't quite in the ordinary way of things," he said after a mere moment of stunned silence. "I wondered if you might be French."

From Furnival, she knew that Alistair had received the cut direct from a few gentlemen at his club, but when she questioned Alistair about it, he only said that he had been looking for a way to have fewer dull conversations, and that if he had known that making an improper marriage would do the trick he might have tried it a decade ago.

She knew he couldn't truly be so unaffected. He had prided himself for so long on being above reproach. It had to sting for him to be roundly declared the most scandalous de Lacey to date. But she also knew that he was happy, that he laughed and smiled, that he had told her the truth when he said that whatever trouble she brought was better than not having her.

And so she took Louisa's hand and went out to be married.

"You know, I don't think it's a bawdy joke after all." They were in the curricle driving down to see Louisa and Gilbert in Kent.

"What isn't?" Alistair glanced away from the road long enough to see that his wife had a pensive expression.

"Your family motto. *Nil Penna Sed Usus.* You said it means 'Not the pen but its use.' But every dirty-minded schoolboy would translate it to 'Not the cock but its use.' Or, not the cock but rather the fucking. But as far as ribald jokes go, it isn't that funny. I have to believe that if your ancestors meant something naughty, it would have been thoroughly obscene and not merely in bad taste."

"I can't disagree with you there." Not a subtle lot, the de Laceys.

"*Penna* is quill, of course, but it also means feather. I think the motto means 'Not the feather but its use,' or more aptly, 'Not the feather but the flight.'"

"And what does that mean, my learned wife?"

"That feathers are useless unless you fly with them. There's no point to a feather otherwise."

This was not, he realized, the time to mention ostriches. "Go on," he said. He loved when his Robin went on these philosophical tears. As harebrained a notion as it had been to send her to university, he would include Robert Selby in his prayers for the rest of his life for having seen that she needed to go.

"Well, there's no point to having money unless you spend it, and there's no point to having rank and privilege unless you use them."

"My ancestors used all of the above to hold orgies."

"No, they used them to be happy. And for them, I suppose that meant orgies," she conceded, "although one might wish they could also have found happiness in establishing hospitals or endowing artists. And think of how inconvenient it must be to have one's happiness hinge on orgies. I think I pity your ancestors. Consider the logistics."

"Oh, I am," he assured her.

She elbowed him in the side. "Anyway, not to belabor the point, I'm glad you used your money and influence for me."

Oh damn. He should have known she was leading up to something. "You're quite right that there would have been no point otherwise. But it wasn't only for you. I'm quite as selfish as those ancestors of mine, except that I need you, rather than orgies." He felt sorry for the man he had been before knowing Robin. That man had been worried about all the wrong things—money and prestige and respectability, but like she said, those things were only feathers, useless until you fly.

He took the ribbons in one hand and used his free arm to draw her close. She nestled against his side, and they laughed and talked until it was too dark to drive any farther.

Author Note

While at first glance Charity's story may seem improbable, there are historical precedents of people living and passing as members of a gender other than that which they were assigned at birth. Whether any such person was a cis woman, a trans man, or—as in Charity's case—a nonbinary person is a thorny issue; some were perhaps women who adopted male dress as a way to access opportunities that weren't available to women, but others may well have been trans men. Certainly trans, nonbinary, and genderfluid people existed long before those terms and were sometimes accepted in non-Western cultures.

While researching this book, I encountered many examples of people who were assigned female at birth but lived their lives as men, often passing undetected until death or injury. James Barry is probably the most famous instance: born in Ireland in the late 1700s, Barry subsequently enrolled in medical school and served as a surgeon for the British Army. Barry lived as a man in all aspects of life, and only after his death did it become publicly known that he had been assigned female at birth.

There are several women who dressed as men for the purpose of enlisting in the Union Army during the American Civil War. Most apparently went unchallenged as men during their service, and then resumed living as women after the war. Albert Cashier, however, seems to have begun dressing and living as a man before enlisting, and continued to do so long after the war was over, until dying in 1915. Cashier was listed under his male name on payrolls and even the voter registry. What's striking about this case is that we know of at least two doctors who attended Cashier during illnesses and injuries found out that he was assigned female at birth, but did not reveal his secret. Cashier was buried with full military honors and under a tombstone bearing his chosen name.

Shortly before this story takes place, there was several instances in England of AFAB people marrying women. It's hard to say whether they were con artists, trans people, or queer women looking for love. Occasionally they were brought up on charges of fraud (if the wife was not in on the secret, and especially if the wife owned property) but often it wasn't clear what, if anything, the authorities could do. Emma Donoghue's *Passions Between Women* has a chapter devoted to this phenomenon.

A note on pronouns: I considered using they/them pronouns for Charity in the book, but in the end decided against it, not because they/them pronouns would have been historically inaccurate (indeed, the singular they has a centuries-old history) or because those pronouns would have detracted from the story (I don't believe this would be the case) but because I don't think feminine pronouns would have bothered her. That said, when I'm talking or writing about this book, I generally find myself using gender neutral pronouns and referring to Charity as Robin, which is how she comes to think of herself by the end of the book.

Follow Hartley Sedgwick as he finds love in
the next romance in Cat Sebastian's Seducing
the Sedgwicks series,

A GENTLEMAN NEVER KEEPS SCORE

Available July 2018

A LETTER FROM THE EDITOR

Dear Reader,

I hope you liked the latest romance from Avon Impulse! If you're looking for another steamy, fun, emotional read, be sure to check out one of our upcoming titles.

If you like a bit of suspense in your contemporary romance or just love a good *Channing Tatum* movie, then you do not want to miss STRIPPED by Tara Wyatt! The first book in her new Blue HEAT series is a delicious mash up of *21 Jump Street* and *Magic Mike*, as an elite undercover detective must infiltrate a drug ring operating out of a male strip show. What makes this novel extra steamy? His one-night-stand-turned-new-female-partner is in the audience as back up ... and watching the whole thing! One-click away!

You can purchase this title by clicking the link above or by visiting our website, www.AvonRomance.com. Thank you for loving romance as much as we do ... enjoy!

Sincerely,
Nicole Fischer
Editorial Director
Avon Impulse

ABOUT THE AUTHOR

CAT SEBASTIAN lives in a swampy part of the South with her husband, three kids, and two dogs. Before her kids were born, she practiced law and taught high school and college writing. When she isn't reading or writing, she's doing crossword puzzles, bird watching, and wondering where she put her coffee cup.